ASHES OF REVIVAL

ALEX SHOBE

VULPINE
PUBLISHING

First paperback edition May 2019

ISBN 978-1-7330236-0-3 (paperback)

Published by Vulpine Publishing

www.alexshobe.com

"Love the light, for it shows you the way. Endure the darkness, for it shows you the stars."

- Og Mandino

If you enjoy the story, please consider leaving an honest review on Amazon or Goodreads.

Join Alex's mailing list for updates on **DROPS OF HAVOC's** release and to stay informed of all other things to come. Subscribers are also automatically entered to win free copies of her books and merchandise.

Visit Alex at
www.alexshobe.com
Twitter @alexshobe
Instagram @alexshobe

Leona

Chapter 1

A breath is a fickle thing—easy to hold and easier to lose. I exhale as I smooth my hands over the golden lace bodice, hoping to loosen the knots twisting within my stomach. My fingers trail over the silk ties keeping the bodice closed. In the corner of the floor-length mirror, I catch a glimpse of Gracen standing behind me, her forehead creasing with worry.

"Is it too tight, Your Majesty?"

The frail hemline swishes silently over the marble floor as I spin to face her.

"No. It's perfect, thank you." I offer a weak smile and return my view to the mirror. "It's just my nerves."

Gracen takes a step forward, her hands folded neatly in front of her. "If you'd like, I could get you a cup of tea from the kitchen? Jasper has a fresh stock of chamomile.

Or maybe peppermint?"

I lower my eyes to the floor. No amount of herbal tea would be able to ease the gut-wrenching torment within me. If only it were as simple as drinking a tonic to make all my problems go away. After a moment, I lift my head and our eyes meet again. "That won't be necessary."

I cross the room to the vanity with Gracen following behind. She pulls the stool from under the table and absentmindedly sweeps her hand over the cushion. Dust never has a chance to settle around here. Once I'm seated, her hands are in my hair, a brush gliding down the length.

"Earlier," she says, braiding the hair at my temples, "the Lord Commander was determined to see you."

My hands clasp tighter in my lap. "What did you tell him?"

"That you were busy, of course, shoulders-deep in audiences with diplomats." A soft chuckle escapes Gracen's mouth and it vibrates through to her fingertips. "He almost had half a mind to go room to room searching for you anyway."

"He *does* have half a mind. I'm still trying to figure out where he keeps the half that actually works."

At this, Gracen's full laughter carries throughout the room. It's a nice sound to hear. There's not much amusement in the castle anymore. She pins the plaits to the crown of my head, then moves to gather the rest of my hair. I reach up and she pauses when I touch her hand.

"I think I'll wear it down today."

She nods then uses her fingers to fan out my hair along my back. When she's satisfied with its placement, she rests her hands on my shoulders. "I wish I could take this burden from you." Her voice is faint behind me. "Your mother despised attending as well. And she, too, wore her hair like a blanket on these days." She pauses. "I suppose it brought her some comfort."

My eyes sting at the mention of Mother. I press them shut, hoping to will the tears away. It'll only do more harm than good for the Council to see me with puffy, bloodshot eyes. Gracen's hands fall to her sides when I turn around to face her.

I clear my throat, pushing back the emotion from my voice. "That'll be all, Gracen. Thank you."

Gracen drops her head into a bow, her graying hair falling forward in front of her face. It'd been thrown up in a tight chignon at the start of the day, but loose strands have escaped during her morning chores.

She shuffles out of my bedchamber, the thick maple door closing effortlessly as she exits. There aren't many people I like around here, but she's one of them. I hate that I've been keeping her at an arm's length recently, never allowing myself to feel the maternal value she once gave me. Now that my own mother is gone, it feels like a betrayal. Still, she's one of the few people within these castle walls who doesn't smile with kind eyes in my face only to utter their dissatisfaction of my reign behind my back. She's an honest soul, more truthful than those whose allegiance should've been sworn to me. The others follow me only out of necessity, not support.

Six months have passed and this hasn't gotten any easier to stomach. When I claimed the throne, the nobles didn't rejoice at my coronation. They looked on in polite disinterest, muttering words they thought I couldn't hear as I passed. Mother warned me that might happen. I've held onto her hope that I could be the leader the country needs, a queen who could soften the firm edges of a man's world. The country is entombed in its traditions—its games—and the nagging thought pulls at the corners of my mind.

A breeze rushes in through the open balcony doors, carrying with it the spicy scent of the lilac gardens below. There's warmth in the springtime air, yet an icy chill grabs my spine, leaving me paralyzed for a moment. Once the sensation passes, I walk over to the bedchamber doors and hold onto one last deep breath before pulling it open.

The guard posted outside in the corridor stands a whole head taller than me, and still, his body stiffens at attention when my eyes land on him. He peers down at me, eyes wide, as he waits for my instruction.

I give him a curt nod. "I'm ready."

A thunderous crowd grows louder with each step I take toward the arena. They're chanting, not my name— no. The word *fight* echoes like a ricochet around the coliseum.

Everyone's waiting, and when I step into view, the crowd falls silent. I pull my shoulders back as I emerge from the tunnel that leads to the monarch's gallery. A crimson chenille canopy, pulled tight between four stone columns, bucks when the wind catches underneath it.

I march past my Council, six men, whose judgmental glares are lost against the other hundreds of eyes directed toward me.

Everyone's waiting.

My feet carry me to my chair, though they'd much rather had taken me somewhere else—anywhere else but here. I'm numb, my vision focused in front of me, with only the crowd's expectations driving me forward.

I hate this.

I hate the dingy stench of the arena, an odor that comes from hundreds of years of use. I hate looking upon the masses, knowing that they find enjoyment in their lack of humanity.

But none of that matters now, as I am here.

I stand in front of my seat for a moment, letting the noon sun caress my face and the tops of my shoulders. It'd be such a beautiful day, if not for the dread looming over me like a shadow. I lower myself onto the chair and a booming vibration rattles the structure as the crowd cheers.

It's time.

Colton

Chapter 2

I hook my fingers around the iron bars of the cell gate and rest my forehead against the back of my hand. The stone ceiling rumbles and dust falls onto my face as the crowd above me calls for blood and a good show. Very rarely are they left dissatisfied.

Cells line each side of the corridor under the arena. I share mine with nine other men, all of whom are staring at the ground in front of them. None of them blink, as though the ground might disappear if they take their eyes off it.

The other nearby cells are the same way with groups of men filling them. No one's making a sound. Then again, the crowd is making enough noise for all of us.

We've found this is the only means to cope with days like today. Any other time, we'd trade stories, maybe share a laugh or two. But today, we know better, and we are silent.

By nightfall, the number of cellmates will diminish, at least until the guards replenish their losses with a new group of unfortunate men.

My attention shifts down the corridor. A man, with more hair coming out of his ears than the amount of hair on his head, is carrying a parchment paper and speaking in loud tones with a guard. They stop cell by cell and glance down at the paper, then back at the inmates inside.

I wonder, for a second, how the man can even hear anything with all that fuzz. My mouth twitches as a grin struggles to break free. Stop it. Today, I need to be serious.

"Him." The man nods his hairless head toward Kai.

Kai rises to his feet and brushes the dirt from his tattered pants. As he moves from the darkened shadows of his cell to the gate door, the purplish-red streak across his face becomes more prominent in the torch lighting of the corridor. His face is neutral as he eyes the man who selected him.

"All right, open the gate."

A guard dressed in burgundy and black garb steps forward. The keys in his hand jingle while he plucks the right one from the set.

Kai's size towers over the guard's, yet when the gate is completely open and there's nothing standing between the two men, Kai remains still. He's been here long enough to know the consequences of trying to flee at the first opportunity.

The guards are like cockroaches. Where's the one, there's sure to be five more lurking around a corner somewhere. Even though Kai could easily outmaneuver the guard who stands in front of him, he wouldn't get far before a half-dozen more cockroaches caught him and drove their swords through his chest.

The bald man, Kai, and the guard walk down the corridor, the shuffle of their feet being the loudest sound coming from them. The guard drapes his hand on the hilt of his sword, his stance at the ready in case Kai decides to turn around and snap his neck.

If only.

But he won't.

Kai knows better than that.

They travel further down the corridor until they're out of view. I can tell when they've reached the steps leading up to the arena grounds because the crowd erupts into another bout of celebration.

I sigh and find a bare section of wall to sit against. The coldness of the stone wall forces a shiver between my shoulder blades. The ground offers no heat against the draftiness of the dungeon either.

I pull my legs to my chest and rest my arms over my knees. There's nothing left to do now except wait. Wait to die, that is.

A guttural almost animalistic cry travels from the arena down to the cells, causing a different type of chill to course down my spine. I sigh and shake my head. The voice doesn't sound like Kai's. Whomever they selected as his opponent from the other side of the dungeons doesn't seem to be faring so well.

I'm not surprised, though. I'd hate to be the one who goes against him. Yet, it's torture to have to go against any one of us here. My friends. My neighbors. And we're forced to fight one another until one of us dies. As soon as we step before the crowd on the arena grounds, all relationship ties must be severed. It's the only way.

I glance over at Aiden across from me in the cell. He's not much younger than I am, but there's an apparent difference in his body size compared to mine. I've spent my life working on my father's farm, tending to animals and hauling bundles of hay. My body is primed for the physical nature of our situation. His is not. But what he lacks in bulk, he has made up for in his intelligence. Most the time when he speaks, his words are grounded in intellect. He was meant to be a craftsman—yet he's here, awaiting death like the rest of us.

I watch carefully as Aiden twists his fingers into swollen red logs. This is only his second week of being here, and I want to tell him, *Don't worry, it gets easier*, but that would be a lie, so I keep my mouth shut.

Truth is, he'll learn quick once he's out there enough that he'll need to let his humanity fall by the wayside if he expects to live another day. When he's standing before a packed arena, no length of a fancy word will save his ass. The crowd is relentless, and he must match their brutality.

A commotion comes from down the corridor and I snap my head in that direction. Two guards drag Kai back toward his cell while a third guard unlocks and opens the gate. He lands with a thud when the guards release their grip on him.

Kai struggles to roll over to his back, but when he does, his chest rises and falls rapidly as his lungs attempt to fill with air. His face is slick with fresh blood. He drags his arm across it, wiping away the red with his sleeve.

"And him."

I hadn't noticed the hairy-eared man standing in front of my cell. My eyes shoot to his, which are concentrated on mine. Shit. He means me.

I stand, though in no hurry to leave the twisted safety of my cell. The guard opens the gate and steps aside so I can pass. Eyes peek from the other cells as men watch with nonchalance. I don't expect a *goodbye* or a *good luck* from them. Here, those are pointless words that never do any justice in bringing comfort. Even if I win the fight, I still lose.

The guards escort me down the corridor and up the stairs, where another guard is waiting with a sword. My sword, at least for the moment. Semi-dried blood coats the blade, but I take it anyway.

As I walk across the grounds—alone—the gentle heat of spring isn't enough to thaw the ice forming in my chest. The crowd surrounding me is deafening that I can hardly hear myself think. Not that I'd even want to think right now. Thinking leads to feeling and feeling out here is a surefire way to death.

I narrow my eyes and spot my opponent approaching from across the field. It's Henrik. The last time I saw him, we were sitting around a fire pit near the shoreline, sharing a flask while talking about the various women in the village we would never stand a chance with. I taught him how to fish, and in exchange, he helped me to embrace becoming Erenese.

Back then, he was my friend. Now—my enemy.

They did this to us.

I glance upward toward the gallery where the royal and political people sit. It's hard to see around the columns, but as I continue to walk to the center of the arena, the queen comes into view.

Her gray eyes follow me across the field. I remember those eyes, back when we were younger, back when we shared a laugh between us. But things are different now. Long hair falls over her shoulders like a black curtain, and I wonder if it covers the hole where her heart should be. Even from down below, I am certain she doesn't have the same eager expression on her face as do the ones next to her, anxious for the combat to begin. Regardless, she's sitting idly by while Henrik and I fight for our lives. And for that, she's my enemy, too.

Henrik and I stop nearly thirty feet away from one another. I close my eyes and breathe in deeply, savoring the last calm breath I'll have before my adrenaline takes over. There's a switch when I'm out here, as simple as turning on a lantern. I'm no longer myself, but who they've made me to be—a vicious killer.

In the dungeon, I cried for days after my first kill on these sands. It's been a long time since then. Each death has brought less tears, until finally the tears just stopped coming. In its place, nightmares arrived, and then sleep stopped coming as well.

Ding-ding.

At the bell's first sound, Henrik sprints toward me. I follow suit.

The crowd whoops and hollers, but I drown them out, focusing only on the task at hand. Our swords clash together as I block his advance. There's nothing but anger in his eyes, as it should be. One of us will take the other's life today.

He wields his sword. Left, then right. I dodge each move, using my sword to deflect his.

With my free hand, I push him over my outstretched foot. He stumbles, but quickly regains his balance.

He's already huffing, the telltale sign of exertion. Slow down, Henrik. Conserve your energy.

He begins to slash his blade through the air, desperate to make contact. His persistence pays off. My shoulder goes cold when a breeze touches the open wound. I glance down just long enough to assess the damage. Superficial injury. I'll live.

Our swords clash once more until I pin his to the ground. My foot digs deep into the sand as I spin, my elbow colliding with his jaw. His sword flies out of his hand as he reaches out to brace his fall. He spits out a mouthful of blood, the sand in front of him turning a muddy red.

I sidestep around him, stalking him like he's my prey. My eyes dart to his abandoned sword, then back to him.

Come on, Henrik. Get up! He remains on hands and knees, heaving endlessly.

I look up into the crowd, distinguishing face-by-face the people who are shouting *Kill!* from the comfort of their seats. The queen's face hasn't changed since the match began—a mix between disgust and sorrow. She leans over and says something to a smug gentleman. He responds to her words with a careless shrug and scoots to the edge of his seat.

An outcry from behind brings me back to the arena grounds. Henrik charges full-speed, his blade leading the way. I duck and angle my wounded shoulder toward him. The crowd applauds when he flips over my back, landing head first on the ground. Maybe I should've taught him how to fight instead.

As I stand over him, his face no longer displays anger, but despair.

"Do it..." he whispers, tears welling in his pleading eyes. "I don't want to do this anymore."

I kneel to his side and bring my mouth close to his ear. *"Su batale cono tulest. Ghydri fe vali pembrutari fen syntadaros." Your fight is over. Rest in the eternal grace of the gods.* When I stand, his eyes are pressed loosely together, and he nods.

A sad smile creeps upon his mouth. *"Osto vos tynu." Until we meet again.* He speaks the words I taught him long ago.

My body shudders at his acceptance. I center the sword over his chest and drive it in, a blistering pain tearing through my soul as though the sword is piercing my own heart. His final breath comes much too soon.

I pull the sword from his chest and fling it across the ground. The crowd cheers, beside themselves with joy, as they rise from their seats. I spit out in front of me and stomp back toward my cell, leaving the body of my childhood friend as another casualty of this world.

Leona

Chapter 3

I stand up with the other spectators, though not for the same reasons. Smiles stretch far and wide across their faces as men clutch each other in handshakes from well-placed bets. My stomach clenches. I've had enough of this.

The Councilmen smirk as I walk past them to leave the arena. They think I don't notice, but I do. Yet another reason why they have doubts about me being on the throne.

Me.

A woman.

There's never been a female monarch in this kingdom until I came along. I never asked for this, however, it's my birthright—my duty—and I will fulfill it regardless of how they feel.

A guard joins me in the tunnel, flanking my side and staying just a step behind me. I don't too much care for the constant escorts. It'd be nice to take a walk alone sometimes. Lately, they've been a dense shadow of murky air intent on smothering me. Judging me. Watching me. Making sure I don't do anything out of line of what the Council requests.

My muted footfalls get lost in the clumsy pounding of the guard's boots as we descend the stairs and exit into the courtyard. Hurried footsteps come up behind us. I should ignore them. I should pretend the footsteps' owner is as repulsed by the fights as I am. We could be united in putting some distance between us and the bloodshed. I wish I didn't know who's approaching me, but I do. So with a sigh, I pause and turn around.

"Forgive me, love," Aerok says. "I didn't mean to startle you."

I cringe at his use of the pet name *love*. It implies that I should be domesticated, a tame dog that works within the confines of a leash. I dream of the day when I can claw his face off. The slow release of a breath is enough to calm my growing temper. "You didn't." I glance at my guard and hold up a hand, dismissing him from my side for a moment. When I turn to face Aerok again, he's fumbling with the gold commander's pin on his lapel. He always requires it to sit aligned. Anything less than perfect is unacceptable in his eyes. "What is it?"

"I just wanted to make sure you were all right." Aerok runs his fingers through his neatly trimmed hair. "You left the fights early again."

I offer a slight smile, the best I can do for now. "I'm fine. Just a headache." I wish I could feel guilty about lying, but I don't.

Aerok steps forward, closing the already narrow distance between us. The scent of smoke and sandalwood invades my nose.

"Allow me to accompany you—to make sure you're taken care of properly."

I take a step back, my gaze flicking upward toward the sky. "No, that's all right. I'll have my handmaiden."

I turn and begin walking toward my destination when Aerok falls into step with me. I pause again, my limited patience already wearing thin.

"I insist. What kind of suitor would I be if I abandoned you? Besides, it's the first time all week I've been able to catch you alone and there are things I wanted to discuss."

I've done all right avoiding him over the past few days. Meetings with my advisers usually keep me busy, and when those are finished, I seek the solace of my bedchamber. I look into his brown eyes and search for a valid reason to decline his company, but a grin pulls at his lips.

"Very well." Now, my head really is starting to throb.

When he offers his arm, I hook my hand around it, my fingers tucking into the fold of his elbow. The fabric of his sleeve is velvety, the finest material he could find for his garb. His talent for military strategy is surpassed only by his vogue tastes.

The trees sway above us as we walk in unison through the courtyard. The lawn is a healthy carpet of green, made more beautiful by the various gardens speckling the grounds. I do my best to keep them maintained, as my mother did before me.

"Have you settled on a date for our union?" he asks. "I'm sure you would make a stunning summer bride."

I roll my eyes. His gaze is focused ahead so he doesn't notice. "I'm sure I would make a stunning bride regardless of the season." My words are terse despite my attempt to reel in my annoyance.

"Of course," he says, "I only meant that perhaps you'd consider summer as a sound date."

The constant pressure to wed weighs heavily on my shoulders. If Aerok and the Council had it their way, I'd be married tomorrow with an heir, preferably male, conceived the week after.

He's far from my ideal husband. His use of brute force and clever tactics have no place in a marriage, but unfortunately for me, the Council believes our union will be ideal from a political standpoint. Aerok has excelled in maintaining the security of the country. Out of all the possible suitors, the Council urges he is most deserving to fill the place by my side. People like me don't get the privilege of marrying for love.

Love is something that's as rare as an ice storm in mid-summer. Impractical concept, really. It's fleeting. To love someone means one day you can hate them, and hate is a wasteful use of energy. Mother didn't marry for love, although, over the years she came to love her husband. More or less.

Every decision I make is not for myself, but for the betterment of my kingdom. Irony laughs in my face as I sit atop the highest position in my territory, and yet I'm not allowed the simple pleasures of being human.

"I haven't decided on a date, but summer is too soon."

He darts his eyes down to me, his jaw clenched in disapproval of my answer. He catches his slip-up and relaxes his face.

"Perhaps we'll get married here in the courtyard"—I extend my hand toward the nearby wooden gazebo—"at the first sign of autumn. As the leaves change colors, hues of orange and red could be behind us." I force a smile that resembles one of sincerity.

Even when you're upset, Leona, use a smile to hide how you feel.

My father's words play in my head. I wonder if he would've given this advice if I were born a son. If I wore pants instead of pretty dresses. There have been plenty of times over the years where I've had to disregard my displeasure in lieu of a smile. I've mastered the technique.

Aerok nods slightly and smirks. He returns his gaze in front of him as he begins talking about the decorative possibilities that come with an autumn wedding.

My smile fades into a firm line, my eyes narrow. I know getting married will be in the best interest of my reign, but I can't help stalling my current betrothal.

The sounds of Aerok's words blend together into a subtle hum passing over my ears. It's not until we reach the castle door that I realize he's asked me something and awaiting my answer.

"Well?" His mouth is twisted into a devilish grin.

I glance around in search of a context clue as to what he's been talking about. No luck. "Sorry. What did you say?"

"I said, the paymaster predicts the coin made from today's matches will be able to fund future upgrades to the Crownsguard." He flashes a bright smile that would make an ordinary woman's knees go weak.

I'm no ordinary woman.

I tilt my head and arch an eyebrow. "Didn't the Crownsguard just get upgrades last winter?"

"Yes," he says, "but I'm looking to expand the company in the next few months."

I withdraw my hand from his arm, heat welling in my core as my irritation returns. "And, why is that?"

I glimpse over Aerok's shoulder at my escort guard—Regineau, I think his name is. His eyes are focused on a fixed point in front of him and I'm sure he's pretending not to listen. The subtle twitch in his lips suggests otherwise.

Aerok draws his arms behind his back, one hand cradled in the other, and shifts his weight to his heels.

"The ratio of fighters to guards is becoming imbalanced. To ensure the safety of my men, I'd prefer that those odds change." He pauses. "We anticipate an additional ten to fifteen fighters be added by mid-summer."

"The fighters are just criminals, are they not? How is it that anyone can anticipate just how many more criminals will be locked up?"

Regineau's lips twitch once more. I step to the side, removing Aerok from my line of sight of the guard. My mouth opens to speak—

Aerok scoops my hands into his, pulling them close to his chest. A soft beat thumps against my knuckles.

"Leona…"—Aerok drawls out my name longer than necessary—"there have been whispers of minor uprisings in the villages. An increase in crime, and the like."

I remove my hand from his grip. "When were you planning on making me aware of this?"

"I didn't want to bother you with the mundane dealings of the people." Aerok jaw is firm, but his eyes are soft—a deceptive expression that nearly throws me off. "…my love," he quickly adds.

I study his face for a moment. A fib is etched between his brows, though how deep the deception runs still remains to be seen. My lips pull upward into a modest smile. Cue the artificial resolution.

"Very well, Aerok." I force myself to lighten my voice into its non-combative state. "I'm sure they're being dealt with accordingly. Now, forgive me, but I really should lie down for a bit."

His curled lips wrap around his teeth and he drops his head into a bow. "Of course. Rest easy and I'll be by to check on you later."

Before pivoting on his heel, he makes eye contact with the guard, almost as though there are unspoken words between them. Then, there's a bounce in his step as he strides back to the arena.

I push the study's doors shut, separating me from the watchful eyes of the new guard posted in the corridor. Regineau was all too happy to pass on the responsibility. He's a brute of a man, wide shoulders with a thick head on top. When he's my escort, he doesn't talk to me unless I'm giving him an order, and when he does speak, there's an underlying hostility in his tone. Whether it's naivety or apathy on my part, I ignore him. He's one of plenty men in the Crownsguard who are displeased to serve a queen.

The sun's rays pierce through the study's hand-cut tinted windows, an amber glow on everything the light touches. There's history in this room. Dozens of previous monarchs have graced this area with the privilege of using its wealth of information.

Bookcases stretch from floor to high-vaulted ceiling, hundreds of intricately designed tomes stored on the shelves. Leather bound pages, their spines worn from years and years of existence. If I stand close enough, I can smell the almond oil used to condition the leather.

I cross the room to a plush chesterfield near the window. Its velvet fabric and dark wooden legs sit just as it had when I first was allowed entry into the room many years ago. My body sinks into the sofa, and I reach down to loosen the laces of my boots. I kick them off, one after the other, then pull my knees up and against my chest.

The tension in my mind eases when I let my head tilt back against the sofa. My eyes wander around the room, my vision bouncing from the doors to the adornments on the ceiling to the fireplace. The flames crackle, almost rhythmically, as the logs char to the color of night. Even as the heat pours into the room, the coldness on my skin remains undisturbed.

I witnessed two more people die today. That was as much as I could bear this time. They swung swords and behaved as animals for no other reason than they chose to commit a crime and got caught. A theft of a wool cloak shouldn't justify dying in the arena.

In Erenen, being sent to the arena is the punishment for the magistrate's conviction. Once upon a time, the gallows in the plaza were used as the highest level of penance. Now, the outdated structure stands as a place for young children to run around and climb on the beams.

I keep my gaze moving until it catches on a small chest tucked away on a bookcase's lower shelf. I sit up, my feet stinging against the bite of the floor, and walk to it.

The chest is pushed toward the rear. I crouch in front of the bookcase then reach to pull the chest forward, books tumbling over from the sudden lack of stability. The chest, a dark wooden box with metal trim, is one I hadn't seen before. I've had six months in this room, but most of that time had been spent getting out of sight of the guards and Council.

I undo the front buckle of the box and the lid opens with a dampened creak. Parchment papers, some rolled and some flat, fill the brim. I lift one and unroll it, and scoot on the ground toward a stream of light. My eyes scan the document. The precision of the penmanship makes my breath catch in my throat. It's Father's handwriting. He had a peculiar way of writing, always taking the time to make each letter perfect before moving onto the next. I shake my head, pushing past my memories of him and focus on his words.

Line by line, he's listed the countries and what goods they hold. Most of the goods aren't available in Erenen, at least not in as much quantity as the other countries. Intrigued, I drop the paper back into the chest, then carry the box to the desk. My fingers rummage through the papers, a smile playing on my lips as I read all the research my father had done. My father—the man who I thought was devoted to the traditions of Erenen—had a more open mind than he let on. Our country has always prided itself on being self-sufficient, never looking to another nation for prosperity. But here it is, a chest full of evidence that could bring our country to a better future than the one presumed.

I reach the bottom of the box and pull out the last stack of papers. They're different from the others, each formally drafted with the royal letterhead at the tops. I brush my fingers over the embossed foil that bears my family's crest. So much history behind the tiny symbol. So much pain, too. Each page is a letter addressed to the kings and queens of neighboring countries—an invitation, of sorts, to allow open trading amongst us. He wanted to extend a bid for international trade. In the letter, he'd written about how beneficial the policy would be for all countries involved. Both foreign relations and revenue would've stood to improve.

A warmth spreads in my chest, fighting back the chill I've carried most days. I plop in the chair behind the desk, then laugh as I tuck my legs underneath me. The papers stare at me from the desktop, their inked scripts merged together into a sea of black, the gentle waves inviting me to step further from the shore. I smile again and reach for the papers to reread them, this time, committing each of my father's words to memory.

Hours later, I stand in front of the oversized tapestry mounted to a wall above the fireplace. Three times my height, both length and width-wise, the art piece is meant to signify everything I am—everything my forefathers have been. It is made from silks collected from the different towns and villages in my kingdom, offerings from each of the communities I reign over. A mural of golds and turquoises, magentas and indigos, my family's insignia stitched in the middle.

Apparently, this tapestry is more valuable than the silk it was crafted from. It has a wealth that never depreciates, even long after the threads become tattered and worn. I close my eyes, and when I open them again, I'm six years old, standing in this same spot when Mother told me the tapestry's story.

I had tilted my head back, resting it against the center of her belly. My baby brother or sister was inside, and I had pretended that it was listening to Mama talk as well. I'd smiled each time a light thump nudged the back of my head, as though the baby heard my thoughts.

Mama's hands cupped my shoulders, the scent of rosemary on her skin filling my nose. She always smelled so nice. I reached up and slid my fingers around hers, our size difference made more clearly as my tiny digits laid in a crosshatch pattern. I pressed my nose against her knuckles and breathed in deeply.

"Pay attention, my sweet girl." Mama chuckled and kissed the top of my head. "This is important."

I pulled my eyes back upward and scanned the artwork from side to side. It was much too large for me to view in one glance. Golden lace twisted and turned in a flow along the edges, creating a border that retained the mural of images within.

"Each picture represents a territory in our kingdom. There's Durst"—the warmth of her hand left my shoulder when she extended a polished finger towards the wall—"and beside that is Toveen. You'll learn all their names, in time, but what's most important is that you know they are all Erenese."

She spun me around so that I faced her, then dropped to her knees. I could see my reflection glinting in her eyes.

"One day, this will all be yours." She nodded toward the window. The distant mountain peaks were lost among the clouds.

"But why?" My lower lip pouted. "Papa doesn't want it anymore?"

Her smile was all but enough to soothe my confusion. She peered up at me from under her dark eyelashes.

"No, no... Papa loves it, but some day, he'll need to pass it on to you so that you can have a turn at loving it just as much."

"Why?" My voice quaked as I thought about the huge responsibility and stress I saw Papa deal with on a day-to-day basis.

Mama pulled me close, my face nuzzled against her neck. Her long hair tickled my cheek, and I wanted to smile, but I was determined to be upset.

"I know it seems like a lot now, my sweet girl, but hopefully you won't have to worry about any of this until you're much older. And, you know what? You have something that no other King has had, even Papa." She pulled away so that her pale eyes rested on me again. "Do you know what that is?"

I cocked my head to the side, a corner of my mouth lifting as the curiosity overwhelmed me. I shook my head.

"Well," Mama said as she took my hands into her own. "What makes you different from all the other rulers is that you'll be a woman. Do you know what that means?"

I shook my head again.

"Men, like Papa, and women sometimes think in different ways. For any problem that you come across in life, there is always going to be more than one way to handle it. Men tend to choose the more predictable path, less risk. But women,"—she winked—"we like to take the path less traveled. It's usually the more reasonable alternative. Does any of this make sense?"

I wanted to tell her no, but the pride on her face as she spoke made me keep my confusion to myself. I nodded.

"Very good." She pressed her lips to my forehead, pausing a moment before returning to her feet. She draped one hand on my shoulder while the other rested on her belly as she told me the rest of the country's history. She was so much better at this, why couldn't she just take my turn?

"Your Majesty?"

My head snaps behind me at the study's door. Gracen, her body half in the doorway, stands waiting for my answer.

"Yes, Gracen, come in. And please shut the door."

Gracen keeps her eyes down as her hands push the maple into place. She approaches slowly, her eyes focused on the floor in front of her. I know this look. She wore the same one when Father scolded her for letting me miss a session with a tutor.

"It's all right. You haven't done anything wrong."

I can understand why she might think so, though. It's not often I send for her outside of her usual timed routines. I walk back toward the carved desk in the center of the room. The wide desktop is still messy with parchment papers.

"Have you ever seen this?" I hold up one of the letters.

Gracen approaches cautiously, her already narrow eyes slimming even more. She extends her hand as if to take the paper, but pauses when she realizes her misstep.

I nod. "Here, you can see it."

She takes the paper and brings it closer to her face. As her age progresses, so has her difficulty with vision. I watch as her eyes scan one of the letters, top to bottom, until she gives it back to me.

"I remember this. It was written by your father."

I release the parchment from my fingers, and it drifts fluidly back onto the desk. "It's a trade proposal. What do you know about it?"

"I don't know much, only what your mother confided in me." Her voice drops in tone at the comment of Mother. Gracen served as her handmaiden for many years. It's no surprise that Mother would have sought friendship in her in a world of prestige and loneliness. Gracen continues. "Your father had been looking into venturing to other countries for trade agreements but was talked out of it by the Council."

My eyebrow arches. "Do you know why it got dismissed?"

Gracen's eyes look skyward and she fidgets with a loose strand on her apron. She takes a moment as she tries to recall her memories.

"I'm not sure, Your Majesty. But that proposal is dated two days before your parents died in that accident."

I pick the paper up again and look closely at the top. She's right. I hadn't noticed it before, but Father did write this right before he died. I lay a hand on the parchment, drumming my fingers against it. His notes have a broad range of potential. There's no reason why the Council shouldn't have explored the avenues even after Father's death. "Thank you, Gracen. Would you please let the Council know to meet in the dining hall tomorrow morning?"

Gracen drops into a curtsy then hurries to the door. Before exiting, she looks back, opens her mouth, then closes it.

"Yes?"

"Forgive me, Your Majesty. But for what it's worth, I hope you know that your mother would be very proud of the woman you've grown to be."

My face relaxes into a genuine smile. "It's worth a lot." Mother wanted me to take the path less traveled. Now I know just how I'm going to do it.

Leona

Chapter 4

At the head of the dining table, I watch as the Council devours the spread of food. Strawberries overflow in a ceramic bowl, the sweet scent mixing with the aroma of a honey butter glaze on fresh loaves of bread. Platter upon platter of smoked meats and poached eggs line the lengthy table, but most of the dishes have already lost half their contents.

I have a modest amount of food on my plate, yet it all remains untouched. Instead, I silently sip the wine from my chalice. When they've finish with their second helpings of food and begin on their third, I clear my throat. Forks hover in front of their mouths as they snap their head toward me.

"Gentlemen, I've been conducting some research and it appears our neighbors in the south and west have been doing especially well in their economic standings."

The men's eyes shoot daggers down the table, but I continue. Any other time, their glares would be enough reason for me to concede, but I keep Mother's words in my thoughts.

"Lord Mikael, are you aware of these facts as well?"

He draws his napkin from his lap and wipes away the honey in his graying beard. He balls the napkin up and tosses it onto the table. "Yes, Your Majesty. They—"

"Are you also aware that they've revolved the same, if not more, coin as Erenen has with our gladiator fights?" I take another sip, my cup nearly empty.

"Yes...Your Majesty," he grumbles.

"Good. I'm glad you know these things." I smirk, the contents of the wine warming my cheeks. "Erenen has plenty of stock to offer to the other countries. They, in turn, have plenty to offer us. Asharia has a surplus of ivory I'm sure they'd be willing to give us in exchange for our iron ores. The trade could be both lucrative and a smart approach for our welfare." Their eyes glaze over me as though I *am* speaking Asharian. I swirl the last bit of wine around in my cup and then finish it, setting the empty chalice back down with a muted thud. "Killing for sport will no longer be our source of income. Lord Pahlo, establish contact with our neighbors about including us in their trade agr—"

Lord Davrit pushes himself from the table, his chair legs screeching against the marble flooring. As he stands, his round belly bumps into the table, a button on his coat catching on the tablecloth.

"Your Majesty," he says with a sharp tone, "it would be rather risky to do business with other territories when the gladiator fights are a guaranteed win in appeasing the nobles and revolving the kingdom's finances."

Before I have a chance to cower, I rise to my feet as well. "Oh? I didn't realize a War Master's duties now included that of a Pay Master's."

Lord Davrit rolls his eyes and crosses his arms over his chest as he returns to his seat. Aerok looks so much like him, the same angular jaw, same cocoa eyes. The warmth in Lord Davrit's irises don't match the coldness in his demeanor, and it's no wonder why Aerok acts very similar to his father.

I turn my gaze to Lord Mikael. "What are your thoughts on this matter?"

Lord Mikael glances at Lord Davrit, who is both a physical and psychological obstacle between me and the Pay Master. Though I can't see Lord Davrit's face, I can tell by Lord Mikael's that whatever silent facial expression Davrit is doing, it must be somewhat threatening.

After another moment, Lord Mikael looks at me. "I agree with Lord Davrit." Sweat beads along his temples. "And besides, your father understood the dangers of conducting such business."

Heat rises in my chest, but my face remains calm. "My father was against seeking trade agreements?"

The men pause before solemnly nodding.

"I see."

I turn around to Gracen as she holds a copy of the letter nearby. I'd hoped I wouldn't need it, but it turns out, the Councilmen are as dirty as their boots' soles. I nod once and she brings me the parchment.

The six men display the same disgruntled face — furrowed eyebrows, clamped jaw — an apparent look as though they'd gotten a whiff of something foul. Perhaps they've finally caught the stench of misery I've smelled around them for months.

I smile, then turn my eyes to the page.

"To the queen of Gasmana, Her Majesty Gloriette Marsel, I write to inform you of my hope that you'd consider extending a trade port with Erenen." The men stare at me with contempt as I read the letter aloud. "I understand that I declined your invitation years ago. It was a very generous offer from you, and unfortunately, at that time, I did not appreciate it as well as I should have." I lower the letter and set my eyes on the men. "Shall I continue?"

Lord Rodrick grunts and pulls his thin-rimmed glasses from his nose, wiping the lens with a cloth from his jacket pocket. Lord Hensley lifts his fork to his mouth as though I hadn't spoken. It is Lord Leoline who breaks the silence.

"I, whole-heartedly, cannot support your decision," Lord Leoline says, rubbing the back of his neck. "As Magistrate, I'm sure you can agree that I'd know better about what's best for Erenen. I served under your father for many years before his untimely death."

I lay the letter on the table and circle the room to where Lord Leoline sits. The stout, pale man struggles to turn around as I stand behind him.

"That letter was dated two days before his *untimely* death. And as resolved as you all are to dismiss this opportunity, the same opportunity my father was interested in pursuing, leads me to think that maybe his accident wasn't an accident at all."

Lord Hensley drops his fork with a clang against the plate. "Careful," he says, acid in his voice, "for what you speak of is treason." From the other side of the table, his cold eyes hold mine. He leans back in his chair and rests interlocked fingers over his stomach. "We all cared deeply for your father and was disheartened at his passing." His lips twitch slightly at the corners.

Of all the emotions worn on their faces that day, grief was not one of them. They attended the funeral, as was expected of them, but it seemed as though they were eager for my parents' bodies to be consumed by flames on the royal pyre. I brace myself on the back of an empty chair and release a slow breath.

"Be that as it may, I intend to follow through with my father's wishes. My decision still stands." My gaze slides to each man. "Unless you're choosing to defy me, which I'm to understand that you are *not* traitorous men, correct?"

The morning sun continues to pour in through the high windows and prevents shadows from forming. Still, the Council's eyes are dark, made darker by my new reluctance to bend to their will. In these past months, I have allowed them to mold me into a figurehead. I was never supposed to have a voice of my own—only the voice that was beneficial to their cause and their desires. I step around the table and pick up the letter, handing it back to Gracen.

"Lord Pahlo, as I said before, you will need to draft a new proposal for a trade agreement to Gasmana and Obron to start with. Let them know that we have salmon, silks, and iron ores available for trade."

His lips move as though he wants to protest, but he thinks better of it.

"And I'd like to approve the correspondence before it's sent, of course." I keep my chest high and back straight, refusing to show any wavering.

"Yes, Your Majesty," Lord Pahlo says, a small growl trailing after his words.

"Good. Now, there's just one more matter that needs attention. Effective immediately, the gladiator fights will end, and the fighters are to be released."

Lord Davrit, who'd been biting his tongue for the better part of the past few minutes, can't contain his vexation.

"Have you lost…your…mind." He shuffles in his chair, unsure if he wants to stand or remain seated. "Have you any idea what this will do to our kingdom? Our nobles?"

I expected such a reaction from my announcement. I fold my hands in front of me.

"Certainly. And as I stated before, we will seek other alternatives for accruing income for the kingdom. As for the nobles, they will need to find something else to do for entertainment."

Lord Mikael shakes his head. "These fights have been a long-standing tradition, more so, retribution than anything else. Lawbreakers needs to be held accountable for their actions. Do you really think it wise to disband it?"

These men have consistently opposed my judgment ever since sovereignty shifted to me. I heeded their advice because I believed they were acting in the best interest of Erenen. But now that there's a chance for me to do some good in the country, I can't let them sway my decision. I won't.

"We will place our faith into developing the justice system." I shoot a stern glance at Lord Leoline. "And as Magistrate, I'm sure you could figure out alternatives within your scope of intelligence." I keep my voice steady as I mimic the words he'd used with me.

"We've never had a monarch who so carelessly threatens the kingdom's welfare," one of them says.

I shift my eyes from Lord Leoline to find that it is Lord Rodrick who spoke. He's breathing hard, the underlying ire in his veins turning his face maroon.

The six men continue to bicker, each trying to out-yell the next in hopes of proclaiming their opinions on the matters. I let the roaring bunch go on for another few minutes before turning toward Gracen at my side. She drops her eyes to the slight tremor in my fingers, then mouths *You can do this.* I nod and turn to face the men.

Still, the arguing continues. I lift my empty wine cup and slam it against the tabletop, a metallic echo filling the dining hall. In the corner of my eye, Gracen flinches.

Now, they shut up.

"We need to evolve with the times, gentlemen. And, yes, you're right. There's never been a monarch like me.

Never has there been a monarch who is thinking about our long-term prosperity in the face of the rest of the world. One who's willing to look past your blatant disrespect for my rule. And one who's—as I'm sure you're all aware—a woman. With that being said, I expect my wishes to be met."

I stride toward the door with my head held high, my heart pounding in my chest, and their eyes following behind me in disbelief.

Colton

Chapter 5

Water trickles down a crevice of the stone wall, leaving an amber stain in its wake. Sometimes, I daydream about a violent downpour flooding this underground dungeon, drowning us all and putting us out of our misery. But then, I suppose drowning wouldn't be a quick and painless death. We'd probably fare better by finding ourselves at the sharp end of a broadsword.

Negative thoughts prance around my mind as I gaze mindlessly up at the ceiling. With my hand cradling the back of my head, I focus of the steady stream leaking from a crack in the corner of the cell. The rough stones under my back provide little in the way of comfort, but after a while, I've gotten used to their uneasiness.

The scent of rain travels in wafts, the petrichor—a word Aiden called it—riding the breeze like a boat skims the ocean. It's the subtle things in nature that calm me. I used to spend hours outside, long after the sunlight had faded, with my back pressed against the rough bark of a tree. The flame from the lantern at my side danced to the tune of the crickets. Unlikely people, I never had to worry that nature would intentionally do something to harm me. Nature is unbiased—a trait I wish people took the time to learn.

My ears catch the shuffling of feet down the hall. I lift my torso, propping myself up on my elbows. Guards. A lot of them—more than usual. Why are they here? It's hours too early for our daily meal, a corn-based gruel served at the midpoint of the day.

I pull myself completely upright, my back finding the dampness of the wall. My face is stiff as I watch the guards enter further into the dungeon. A couple of guards pause at each of the ten cell gates. A guard pulls out his set of keys and thumbs through it to find the correct one. My heart lurches. We don't come out of the cells except to fight…and our next fight isn't due for another six days.

I gulp, each clink of the keys grating away the solace the rain gave me. The guard opens each gate, ending with mine and pulls it wide open. He stands aside, looking at each of us with utter contempt.

I eye him, waiting for the order that should surely follow. He says nothing.

I glance around at the other men in my cell. They each have just as confused a look as I do. I return my gaze to the guard, who now has progressed from contempt to complete disdain.

I clear my throat, pushing the uncertainty out of my voice. "What's happening?"

The guard snorts and rolls his eyes as though I'd just asked him something foolish. After what seems like a long minute, he finally graces me with an answer. "You're free to go."

Did I just hear him right? I replay the four little words in my head, wondering if I somehow imagined it. Maybe he said *time to go fight* and I only thought that he said that other thing.

"Wait, what?"

The guard shifts his weight between his feet and rolls his eyes again. "Did I stutter? I said, you can go. Queen's orders."

The dungeon buzzes with murmurs as the other inmates hear the guard's repeated words.

I'm the first to stand, my movements slow and cautious, and the others join me. As I walk toward the gate, the guard's eyes burn holes in mine, but I maintain his glare, regardless. If this is a trick, there's no way I won't keep my eyes on my enemy. My body tenses when I pass him, even though our heights are equally matched. Once I'm outside of the cell, I look toward the others, back at the guard, then take a step toward the dungeon's exit. Before my foot completes the first step, the remaining inmates charge out of the cells, desperate to claim the freedom that had been stripped from them for so long.

The guards stand, two by two, posted along the corridor. None of them react as the men sprint past them. Maybe this isn't a trick.

I pass the last cell on the left before the exit. In the shadows, my eye catches the glint of a metal boot buckle. There's someone lying on the ground. I glance back at the guards, but they've gathered in a huddle and speak in hushed voices.

I look back toward the man. He's lying on his side, facing the far wall with his back toward me. I wouldn't be able to identify him if it weren't for the patchwork of cloths that make up his shirt. His wife made it for him the winter after a poor harvest, and he'd worn it every day since, regardless of the next year's profits.

"Phylix." In succession, I flick my fingernail against bar of the gate and hope the dull tinging will get his attention.

No answer.

I step closer and poke my head inside. The faint scent of a rank sweetness lingers in the cell.

"Phylix, wake up. We can go." My voice is a half-whisper, half-shout.

Still no answer.

I drag my feet into the cell, determined to not let Phylix oversleep on his release. The scent grows stronger. I kneel at his side and place a hand on his shoulder. My fingers jerk at the coldness of his body. I pull him over toward me so he's lying on his back. His eyes are half-open, and it doesn't take long to spot the pool of blood left behind from where he was lying. His arm is wrapped around his torso, concealing the large wound to his stomach.

"Damn..." I reach my hand to his face, my fingers forcing his eyelids shut. I whisper the relinquish prayer to his unhearing ears. Then, with a sigh, I pull myself back to my feet. A sinking feeling finds my chest as I walk out of the cell.

Less than twenty-four hours were the difference between his death and his freedom. Now, his wife is left a widow, his four children left fatherless. My foot draws back, and I strike the gate. It rings out, louder than I expected, and remembering the guards, I reach for it to calm the vibrations. I lean out of the cell and glance down the corridor, but the guards are no longer there. The dungeon has an eerie quietness, for at this moment, it's just me and the lifeless body of Phylix who occupy it. There's nothing I can do for him now. I walk toward the exit and pause, taking one last glimpse back before stepping into the fresh air.

Leona

Chapter 6

In the drawing room, a bead of water travels down the windowpane, gaining speed as it collects droplets along the way. I chase it with my fingertip, but the raindrop wiggles away before continuing its descent. A sigh rolls under my breath. I lift my hand to the glass once more and begin pursuit on another drop.

"You could at least pretend to be present in the conversation."

The raindrops on the window become blurry as I focus my vision on the dreary clouds in the distance. "I would hardly call this a conversation, Aerok. This just seems like you are telling me everything I've already heard from the council. Almost verbatim."

He shifts so he's standing at my side, and his arm brushes against mine. "Well, they're not wrong. Those men have served for many years." He tilts his head down, his eyes dull with misdirected sincerity.

"Of course, you would say that. Your father has a seat —" I pause, a bitter taste forming in my mouth. I whirl to face him. "Is that it, then? He sent you to speak to me—to *handle* me?"

He groans then turns his gaze out the window. The skies have gone gray, the clouds casting the grounds into darkness before the wind carries them away and reveals the sun again.

"The fact that he's my father is irrelevant." There's a sharpness to his tone. "The city is spiraling and you're in here watching the rain. Perhaps you could make better use of your time by reconsidering your decision."

I flinch, grateful for the sudden dimness of the skies to obscure my reaction. Aerok's clean-shaven jaw is set and unwavering as he continues to stare out the window. The air around him seems incomplete, like a raindrop without moisture or a flame without heat. I step backward, my feet skimming the floor, before the suffocation claims me whole.

"As you said," I start, my fingernails digging into the palms, "it is *my* decision. How much longer must we hide behind barbaric ways and call them *traditions*? The only thing traditional about the gladiator fights is the turning of the sands to clear the arena grounds of blood, only for more blood to be spilled there the week after." I drop my head, giving a sharp shake before lifting it. "I won't have it anymore. And neither you nor the council is permitted to overturn that decision."

His eyes meet mine, the high collar of his double-breasted coat giving him a much leaner appearance than usual. He stalks toward me, bringing with him his airless air. I release my fists, only to exchange them for jittery fingers. His stature towers over mine, and for the first time, I'm aware of our height difference. His hand reaches forward and tucks a loose strand behind my ear. As the tips of his fingers brush against my skin, my body fills with ice, the coldness maintaining a strong grip on my bones. His mouth twists into an uncomfortable smile.

"Love," he says, crooning the word. His hand lingers near my chin. Then, his fingers hook underneath it to keep my head from turning away. "Reconsider your decision. It will be in the best interest of your reign."

At this, my eyes narrow and I jerk away from his touch. I stumble to the side and bump into a pedestal table, the empty teacup and saucer atop rattling before stilling. My heartbeat quickens, a mix of anger and fear constricting my veins. "Are you threatening me?"

He glances down at his hand and rotates the Barlow family ring until the engraved cobra's head is centered on his middle finger. "Just think of it as a step in the right direction for our union. A wife should lean onto her husband for guidance, yes?" His thin lips pull into a smirk.

The sun breaks through the clouds, a ray piercing into the room and making Aerok's brown eyes resemble gold. As warm as his irises appear, there's frigidity behind them. Heat flushes through my body, my toes flexing in my boots, my face reddening.

"We are not yet married." I turn away from him. There's a slight quiver in my voice but I force it down like a thick gulp in my dry throat. "So, you should leave before this betrothal becomes dismissed as well."

I feel his eyes on my neck and bare shoulders. They glide over my skin, pulling each tiny hair straight with anxiety. The temptation to reach up and release my hair from its chignon crosses my mind, but I keep my hands in front of me, clutching the fabric of my gown instead.

Finally, he clicks his tongue and his footsteps retreat from the room. When the door pushes shut behind him, I gasp and double over. My breaths come in ragged waves. Though he is gone, he's taken all the air from the room with him. I can't breathe. I can't think. My mind replays his words, his underlying threat. Tears sting at the corners of my eyes, but I refuse to allow them to break free. He doesn't deserve my tears. My eyes darken and I set my sights on the teacup, the one he'd been drinking from earlier. I rear my foot back and kick the table. The teacup and saucer fly across the room and smashes against the wall, the ceramic left in shards on the floor.

Colton

Chapter 7

My feet pound against the cobblestone as I sprint through the castle gates. I peer up at the sentry points, but they are abandoned. Each high post watches with an unseeing eye. When I'd arrived a year ago, chained and battered in the back of a splintered wagon, dozens of guards glared down as we crossed into the castle grounds. Now, the wall is deserted.

I enter the heart of the city, the top edges of the stone arena fading from view. I try to use the shadows from the sun to guide me, but this proves difficult when storm clouds fade in and out, blocking the sun's rays. The roll of thunder sounds overhead. Raindrops fall onto my face, breaking on contact and splashing into my eyes. I wipe them with the back of my hand, but each cleared drop is replaced with a new one. Come to think of it, it was raining when I'd arrived, too.

I have no clue how to navigate Demesne. Red-roofed buildings are set in clusters, each apartment picking up where the last one left off. If not for the white shutters flanking the windows and the white doors to match, they'd be seamless slabs of brick. The consecutive housing doesn't allow for the twists and turns of the streets I'm used to in Maburh.

The sun peeks through the clouds, gifting me with a moment of direction. I reach the end of an avenue and turn the corner, but more apartments line the street in an almost identical fashion. Thunder roars again and a streak of lightning courses through the sky. The rainfall increases. I keep moving between the buildings, occasionally catching the glance of residents watching from their windows. I don't know much about Demesne, but I do know that this is where many of the nobles live—the same nobles who fill the arena stands, week after week, demanding blood and gore at the expense of me and my countrymen.

I rake my soaked hair back with my hand. My shirt clings to my skin and rain soaks through my pants and pools into my boots. Up ahead, I hear yelling, but over the steady rumble of thunder, I can't make out the words. It sounds like a great deal of people, different pitches and tones stacked on one another. As I get closer to the commotion, it's clear now why my instinct is to run even though we were released with the Queen's blessing. Those who are screaming aren't declaring celebratory remarks at the top of their lungs.

They're insisting on retribution.

My pace slows at the end of the street and I keep against the wall. My hands grip the building's corner, and I lean out just enough to see what awaits me if I try to cross the intersection. At least ten men, all nobles, stand huddled on a nearby street. Each has the same look of disgust plastered on his face and a sword clutched in his hand. There's only one reason why they'd be gathered like this, and I find it tough to believe that they've assembled to contend with the guards.

I draw back from the corner. My shoulder bumps into an open shutter and it swings shut, knocking loudly against the window. My body tightens and I suck in air through clenched teeth. When I look up at the window, I am met with a woman's eyes. She scans me over, her gaze lingering on my tattered clothes and the dirt on my face that has not yet been washed away by the rain. Her nostrils flare and her wrinkled face stretches into a snarl. She turns away from the glass, the curtains swaying closed behind her.

I let out a breath of relief, but that breath is short-lived when her door opens. The woman steps onto her stoop just far enough to not be drenched by the rain.

Her hands cup around her mouth. "There's one right here. Hurry—get him!" Her voice is shrill and carries over the sounds of the storm.

My knees lock and the only thing I can do is blink at her as she hustles back into her home. I pull my gaze back to the intersection, and the men, whose numbers have doubled, charge toward me.

Fight or flight dashes through my mind. In the arena, its second nature for me to meet a challenger with the same ferocity. However, this is not the arena. And I am not armed.

My breaths become shallow as a glimmer of panic washes over my face. I shake my head, refusing to allow my sanity or rationality to get away from me. I need to think clearly—I don't have time to lose it.

The men are closing in quick with bared teeth. I can't pause. I can't take a moment to figure out where I'm going. All I can do in this moment is run, to go as fast as my feet will allow and hope for the best.

I race back down the street as more people emerge from their homes. Though they don't give chase, they shout encouragements to the men as they follow me. A wave of heat flushes my skin and every raindrop that lands on my forehead feels like a pearl of ice.

Still, I run.

I turn another corner, not knowing what lies ahead. Although the street is clear, further down the stone road, another group of nobles stand over a man, his hands up as he pleads from the ground. The nobles shout at him, then each takes a turn running their sword through the man's body. His screams are deafening. A bitter tang fills my mouth as I make a sharp left into an alleyway, the man's cries dwindling until it ends abruptly.

Discarded barrels line the narrow passageway. I throw a look behind me, the men hot on my trail as they enter the alley as well. Their coordination is awful. They struggle to maneuver, all of them overweight and ambitious as they try to run shoulder-to-shoulder in the small space. This buys me some time, just enough to flee out of the alley, run down the street, and seek safe passage in another alleyway —all while maintaining an eastern direction as best as I can manage.

I continue to rush between the apartments, my lungs on fire and sweat being washed away from the constant downpour of the rain. I find another barrel and hide behind it, doubled over as I struggle to catch my breath. I feel numb. A day that I've dreamt of, but never once thought possible, threatens to be taken from me. It is clear that the nobles, with their fancy clothing and golden spoons, think villagers are less than the dirt beneath their exquisite footwear, but for them to be chasing us through the city? This takes their hatred to an all new level.

How many other villagers lost their short-lived freedom to the blade of a noble? Maybe many of them managed to escape the city before the nobles realized what was going on. I'm sure the highborn were enraged when they saw the same fighters traipsing through their city streets.

I try to regulate my breath, but every inhale is like crushed glass working its way into my lungs. Something pokes my side. I gasp and my body lurches upward, a pins and needles sensation coursing through my veins. My head jerks behind me to find a little boy, probably eight or nine years in age. He's wearing the same gaudy clothes as the men who were chasing me earlier. Clutched in his hand is a wooden sword, carved meticulously with details and its length almost as long as the kid himself. Great.

Even the noble children are assholes.

I put my hands up in front of me and take a step to the side, away from the barrel.

"Hello there, little guy…" I say, my voice as light as I can achieve. "What'cha doin'?" I nod toward his wooden sword.

The little boy, bright blonde hair and deep brown eyes, scowls, his fingers flexing over the smooth hilt. He turns his nose up as though he just smelled something rotten.

"You're not supposed ta be here." His high-pitched voice makes my mouth twitch into a grin. "Come on, I'm taking you back to the jail." He jabs me again with the sword. The rounded edge of the tip produces more of a tickle than pain.

I shake my head, dissolving the humor from my face. "It's okay, buddy. Everything's all right. The Queen let us go." I drop my hands to my sides.

"The Queen'sa idiot." He spits the words and raises his sword so it's pointing at my throat. "Now, let's go."

His voice is getting louder. I put my hands back in front of me, palms down as they pat the air and I shush him. This child's not going to give up.

"Okay, kid. You're the boss." I glance down the alley in the direction I need to go. It's clear. I take a step further from the barrel, widening the distance between me and the young asshole.

He shakes his head. "Uh uh—this way." He jerks his head behind him, back toward the arena, back toward despair.

I nod but take another step toward my destination, my eyes focused on his as though that wooden toy sword he's holding would actually do some damage. I take one more step backward, and he growls, his teeth clenched between chubby cheeks.

"Papa! Come quick! I got one!" he says at the top of his prepubescent lungs. "Papa!"

I turn my back on him, my legs launching myself forward into a sprint unlike no other. My soaked clothes should be slowing me down, but I feel weightless—a new surge of adrenaline overwhelming my body. In seconds, I leave the little boy behind, his top-heavy stature failing him in his quest to catch me.

Another mob, or maybe it is the same one as before, emerges into the alley after me. It's no use, though, I'm too fast and too far ahead.

These nobles have never had to run for anything in their lives. Well, maybe to run after a merchant who's selling the latest in assholery apparel. Most of them are obese, a natural side effect from having too much to eat and plenty of time to eat it in. Nobility will be their downfall.

I run freely for a few more minutes, avoiding the various mobs that have formed around the city. The rain has let up and the sun takes its rightful place in the sky, no longer hindered by the clouds that threaten its presence.

As I near the city's outer edge, the sounds of chaos fade into a low hum. I reach a tall mahogany tree, one of many in the forest that lies ahead. My palms smack its bark, my arms wrapping around it to keep my balance.

The lower half of my body is paralyzed and can't be trusted to support my weight. I press my forehead against the tree. A rumble begins in my stomach then rises through my throat, and a soft chuckle escapes my lips. I'm free. I'm actually free.

Something a short distance from me moves in the corner of my eye. Not again. I drop into a crouch. At my side, the top of a rock juts from the ground between exposed tree roots. I jiggle it loose, my fingers just long enough to wrap around it. If the nobles have found me, I'm going to make them earn my death.

A faint moan gets louder as it approaches me. I grip the stone tighter, then spring out from behind the tree. My body freezes, mid-hurl, and the stone falls into a puddle at my feet.

"Help me, Colt," Aiden says. "He's dying."

Leona

Chapter 8

I've spent most of the day in my bedchamber, still upset with Aerok's words. They loom over me like a shackle to the floor, an invisible wall that no one can see but me. Both my morning and midday meals sit untouched on the table despite Gracen's hope that the bisque would lighten my mood.

I sit at my vanity, its hundreds of tiny gems painstakingly mounted by hand to the decorative wooden trim. This piece of furniture once belonged to Mother and holds a special value to me. Father had it commissioned in Gasmana shortly after she and Father wed. It was the first token he presented her and was meant to bring good luck in their marriage. Although it failed to provide good fortune, she loved it all the same. My fingers graze over the gemstones, and I take comfort knowing in a way, she is still with me.

Evening is drawing to an end and Gracen is late to do my hair. After our lengthy conversation earlier in the day, it concluded with me agreeing to come to the dining hall for dinner, to allow the guards to see that their hushed rumors haven't shaken me.

I grow tired of waiting for her and begin the task myself. From root to tip, I drag the brush through my strands. I'm not especially skilled at doing my own hair, but I manage to braid two sections near my temples and wrap the plaits around to the back of my head, securing them in place. It's not extravagant, not like how Gracen does it, but it'll have to do for now. I reach for my crown and settle it on top of my head. In the mirror of the vanity, the diamonds embedded in the elaborate design of the headgear sparkle as they catch the light of the candles.

I stand and walk over to my balcony doors. They've been closed all day, the result of the intermittent rainfall. Water pelts the balcony in a steady cadence, leaving puddles in the crevices of the stone flooring. The smell of rain is calming, so I crack one of the doors open to catch the scent.

Once the barrier between me and the outside world is broken, I catch more than the rain's fragrance. It sounds far away, but muffled shouting makes its way to me from beyond my grounds, out in the city streets. I pause and close my eyes, giving my ears a better advantage at tuning into the yelling.

It's the nobles—it must be. By the tone of the shouting, they aren't happy, as I knew they wouldn't be. But are they rioting? I hadn't expected that from them. The success of my reign depends partially on the support I have from the nobles—and their success depends largely on the support they have from me.

Are they willing to jeopardize their social standing just because I ended the gladiator fights? I shake my head, upset with their boldness and determined to get to the bottom of it.

I turn to walk toward my bedchamber door. My footsteps are inadvertently strong as my shoes pound the floor with each step.

"Guard," I call out as I approach the door.

There's always a guard posted outside my bedchamber, and it shouldn't take him long to rush to my aid whenever I call.

"Gua—" I start to say again. I pause when I hear equal commotion in the corridor.

My bedchamber door bursts open and it's Gracen. Her face is long, her eyes streaked with fear. She has one hand on the doorknob, the other's on the door frame. Her shoulders rise and fall rapidly as she struggles to find her breath. She opens her mouth to speak. "Run—"

Her voice ceases, the air in her lungs no longer supporting her speech. A sword emerges from her chest, right between her breasts. Blood drips from the tip of the blade, then builds up against her clothing as the sword is retracted.

The light in her eyes fade, her eyes rolling to the back of her head as her body crumples to the floor like a discarded doll.

My body goes numb and my eyes are concentrated on her as I force myself to inhale, to deliver air to my own lungs. Her last word rings in my ears.

I stumble backward and grab onto a nearby table for support. Regineau enters my bedchamber, his leather boots stepping carelessly over Gracen's body. His dark eyes barrel down at me, a hint of mischief in his irises. In his hand, he clutches the blood-soaked sword that ended my handmaiden's life.

He isn't alone. Three more of my sworn guards follow him in. Each hosts the same thirsty grimace on his face, a hunger the can only be satisfied by my blood.

I can't stay here.

I force my legs to move, to maneuver through the room filled with all the things that were meant to bring me comfort.

Davrit enters and stands between the men, two by two posted on either side of him. He puts his hands behind his back and settles into his stance. "Silly girl, you should've left well enough alone."

My eyes flash from his to each of the guards. "Lay down your swords...or you will be executed for treason." My mouth is dry, and each word feels like its grating along my throat.

Davrit chuckles and uses his elbow to nudge the guard to his left. The other guards snicker, joining in Davrit's amusement.

"You no longer hold any power here," Davrit says. His voice is hearty, made louder by the high ceilings of the room.

I shake my head in disbelief, an involuntary response as though the recent events weren't proof enough.

I can't stay here.

I take another step back, one after the other, away from the men who have betrayed me.

"What are you waiting for? Kill her," Davrit says in a cool tone.

The men approach in unison with their swords drawn. I spin around, my turquoise dress nearly tripping me, and glance around the room frantically as I search for a way out of this. My gaze lands on the half-open balcony doors. I snatch the front of my dress up in my hands and run. When my palms smacks against the thick wooden doors, I ignore the pain coursing down my forearms and force the doors open as quickly as I can.

The outdoors greet me with a steady rainfall. Raindrops land on my eyelashes and my vision goes blurry, but I carry myself forward anyway. I hurry to the edge of the balcony, just as the men come out the doors.

My mind drifts away from sanity and hones in on survival mode. I climb and throw my legs over the tall railing, my feet dangling twenty feet above solid ground. The handrail feels like it's made of lightning, hundreds of zaps firing against my palms as I grasp it.

I glance back and gasp. Regineau is the closest to me. Charging toward me, he pulls his sword up over his head, two hands on the hilt as though he's about to chop a log. My head snaps back in front of me and my crown flies off, landing with a heavy clang on the balcony floor. I take a deep breath, lean forward, and release my grip on the rail.

A loud crash resonates as Regineau's sword narrowly misses me and strikes the rail instead.

My hands claw out, reaching for something, anything, as I free fall to the lilac gardens below my balcony. My eyes close right before impact, and I land on my arm. I wince in pain, unsure if my arm is broken or not.

I don't have time to check.

I scramble to my feet, but the waterlogged ground and silky flower petals make it a difficult task.

"After her!"

Rain pools in my eyes, but I look up toward the balcony to find Davrit and the guards glaring down at me.

"I want her dead," Davrit says.

The men quickly leave his side and are out of my line of sight. I reach out and my fingers find the jagged surface of a stone sculpture, a wolf pup in memory of my stillborn brother. I use it to support my weight and get better footing on the slippery ground. A dull throb radiates along the arm I fell on, but it doesn't hurt like it's been broken. I force out a sigh of relief out, wasting seconds that I can't spare. The men are coming, and they have one goal in mind.

I move out of the lilac bushes, ignoring the limp in my gait and moving my feet as quickly as I can manage. My hair sticks to my face as cohesively as my clothing sticks to my body. I used to enjoy the rain, but now I see it as a hindrance.

I hurry through the courtyard, unsure of where I'm going or where I'd even want to go. The whole city of Demesne harbors hostility. I'll be in danger as long as I'm within these city limits.

Over my shoulder, the grunts and groans of the guards travel to my ears as they run to catch up with me. With the sun rapidly setting, I'm appreciative of the incoming cover of night. A hollowness fills my chest with the realization that I wouldn't stand a chance, otherwise.

I approach the castle walls, gaining speed toward the still open gate. Any other day, it would've been closed at dusk. In the dimness, I watch for the silhouette of any guards posted at the wall. There's no one here. Part of me is relieved, but the other part is enraged that they'd leave the castle's perimeter unprotected.

I race toward the city. It's been so long since I've traveled these city streets, but I remember the sharp turns of the roads as though an internal map is ingrained in my mind. It turns out those frequent outings with Mother proved to be helpful, after all. I navigate through the city without being detected by the numerous nobles who have gathered in the streets. Most of them, guards included, are gathered in the plaza, next to the monument that, ironically, displays the honor and respect of my family line. Apparently, that honor ends with me.

Exhaustion settles in my body, and after a few moments to catch my breath, I reach the outskirts of the city. The cobblestone eventually tapers off into dirt roads, now flooded from the day's storm. The lower part of my gown is completely soaked. Water has absorbed through the fabric up to the middle of my thighs. What was once a bright blue-green gown has now taken a more tattered look, dingy and muddy by comparison.

The ground is flooded, and a pool of water separates the city from the forest ahead. I glance around, hoping to find a better way to get around it, but with the sun gone and the moon's light hiding behind more storm clouds, my visibility is reduced to none.

"Is that her?"

"Yeah, that's her!"

My skin jumps off my body, my feet frozen in place. I don't bother looking behind me to see who spoke, or even to see how many of them it is. My brain is still in survival mode, and there's only one thing it wants to do—get away at all costs.

I take a step into the water, my foot submerged at ankle level. My face contorts as my toes flex inside of my shoes, water filling up the entire cavity. The men are still behind me, and I'm sure they can hear the sloshing my feet produces as I wade through the water.

Keep going. Don't stop.

My shoes feel heavy each time I lift them to propel myself forward. I make it to the other side of the flooded area, still unable to see where I'm going and unable to hear the men's voices. I don't hear the inevitable splashing of the water as though the men were following me, but I don't dare take a chance. I need to put as much distance between me and here as possible.

With my arms outstretched in front of me, I maintain a quick pace through the woods while I avoid running directly into trees and other obstacles. I continue like this for what seems like a few more minutes until the moonlight gradually breaks through the clouds.

I can see, not clearly, but it's better than nothing.

I pick up my pace now, the rain tapering off from this territory. With the back of my hand, I wipe the excess water from my eyes. I'm exhausted. My legs are on the verge of giving out, my thighs and calves on fire from running. Maybe I could take a few more moments to rest? I shake my head and dissolve such suggestion from my mind. Keep going.

My feet sprint me forward despite my craving for rest. At the last moment, my eyes catch a downed tree, probably from the storm. I jump over it, land clumsily on the other side, and run into something. No, not something —someone. A man.

We both tumble down a steep slope, our bodies rolling over branches and rocks, until solid ground disappears from underneath us. Air whooshes around me as I fall, my hair lifting from my scalp. We land against the sodden earth of a crevice, and in a daze, I reach out to defend myself. He shifts and uses the weight of his body to pin mine against the ground. I wriggle my arms free and claw out, pushing with depleted strength to get him off me. I try kicking too, but my legs still feel like fresh noodles from the kitchen. A scream wells in my diaphragm, but constricted lungs prevent me from letting it out.

"Get— off—" I say through panted breaths.

He grabs my wrists and straddles my stomach, though no longer bearing his complete weight on me. My body won't let me stop thrashing, but my mind quickly comes to terms with closure.

This is it. This is where I die.

Colton

Chapter 9

A distinct burn stings my forearms from where her fingernails broke the skin and drew blood. My hands wrap around her wrists, pushing them into the ground to keep her from clawing my face off next. I can't tell who she is, only that she's not one of the men who was chasing me earlier.

"Relax..." I say, her body bucking underneath mine.

The rain picks up again. Heavy drops pound against my back and fall in sheets from my clothes. The girl squirms, sinking herself further into the bed of soggy leaves, and bares her teeth. Dark hair streaks across her face in wet ribbons.

"Let— me— go."

"Then, relax," I say again. "If you stop thrashing about like a trapped fox, I'll let go."

She releases another burst of energy despite my compromise. When her actions get her nowhere and her movements subside, I ease my hold on her wrists.

"Are you okay?" I ask, though she should be asking me that. I rub my palm over the minor gouges on my arm.

"Yes," she snaps. "Now, get off of me."

My jaw drops and eyebrows squeeze together, but I comply. My hand smacks against a puddle as I center my balance and rise to my feet. "You're the one who ran into me."

I wipe my muddy palms on the back of my pants and offer her a hand up. The moonlight overhead cuts through the trees and bounces off her eyes. Her face is contorted into disgust, so I withdraw my hand.

"Suit yourself." I step away from her and turn in place within the hole. Both ends of the narrow crevice we fell into taper to a point. I run my hand against the stone wall, searching for any sort of foothold, but there's nothing except ridged rock. I let out a heavy sigh and turn to face her. "Look at what you did."

She shuffles to her feet. "Me? It's not like I put us here on purpose." She flicks wet leaves off her shoulder, then reaches up to wring the water from her hair.

"You should've watched where you were going."

Even in the dimness of the crevice, her glare doesn't go unnoticed. "Well, you shouldn't have been in my way."

I give her a sidelong look and I'm sure she returns the expression. After another moment, I release a sharp exhale and turn back toward the wall. My fingers find just enough of a ledge to grip. I dig the toe of my boot into the rocky wall and lift just barely to test my weight. I pull myself up and search for the next hold. As I'm reaching, the portion of the wall holding up my feet gives way. Chunks of rock and dirt plummet to the ground with me following. The girl throws her hands up in front of her to guard from the puddle splashing outward as my back smacks against it. My fist pounds against the water, and I remain there for a moment, letting the rain beat against my face.

She moves to help me, pauses, then stays where she is. "Are... you all right?"

I swipe my hand over my face to clear away the constant drizzle. "Uh huh," I say through clenched teeth. I groan then pick up both myself and my dignity from the ground.

"Are we going to die down here?" Her voice is quiet. She shifts her weight between her feet, drifting in and out of the stream of moonlight.

The tightness in my face loosens and I shrug. "The walls are impossible to climb even if it wasn't raining — so, probably." A shudder passes through my body. I've survived the arena and an angry mob, yet a hole is going to be what claims my life?

I lean against the wall and watch the girl as she paces the narrow pit. In the darkness, she bumps into me each time she passes, never once bothering to apologize or even acknowledge me. The growl of thunder fills the silence between us as the rain begins to fade.

"Can you lift me out?" she asks, stopping in front of me.

My brow raises. "What?"

She nods toward the top edge of the crevice. "It's not that high. You can probably lift me out."

I push off the wall and look upward. "Maybe. But who's to say that if I do, you won't just run off and leave me here?"

She scoffs, her arms crossing over her chest. "I wouldn't do that."

"I don't know you *or* what you will and won't do."

"I won't." There's a hardened edge to her voice.

Another round of silence passes between us. Droplets of rain pat in a steady cadence against the puddles at our feet. I don't want her help. I don't want her to run back to the city and gossip with her highborn friends about how she helped a lowly village boy out of a hole. There's enough that separates our two social classes without adding charity to the mix. But the fact remains—I can't get out of this hole by myself.

"Fine, but if you do and I die down here, I'm coming back to haunt you."

A soft chuckle rolls from her mouth, one that sounds like she's trying to conceal. I smirk as my fingers interlace and I hold them low so she can step into them. She places her hands on my shoulders. There's a faint scent of jasmine on her skin. It's a sharp contrast to the pungent odor I'd become accustomed to in the dungeon. Once she has a firm grip, I lift her. My forehead presses against the silk fabric covering her stomach as I support her feet. Pebbles drop from above while she works to find a part of the wall to hold. I push her higher, as far as my arms can extend, until the weight of her body eases from my hands.

At the surface, she scrambles to her feet then peers down at me. Her lips shift and I could swear she grins before disappearing. She's going to leave me down here. I knew it. It's clear she's from a noble family, and I'm a fool to believe her word was anything more than self-serving.

Long minutes pass as the hole becomes more cramped from my growing solitude. The sound of shuffling above me pulls me from my renewing hatred of nobility, and I look up. She's there, lowering a thick bough down to me.

"Watch your head." Her hands work, one over the other, and the branch inches closer. My eyes widen and a breath of relief deflates from my chest. I lift on my toes to guide the wood.

"Got it." I wedge it so it lies at a slant. As I step on it, the wood doesn't bend under my weight. I take my time climbing, but the incline is too steep at the top. There's no way I'd be able to continue up the branch without the top-heavy imbalance sending me tumbling back to the floor. She must realize my predicament because she bends down and extends her hand to me.

"Come on," she says.

I reach and close my hand around her wrist. As she pulls with what little strength a noble girl must have, I balance my feet on the branch and climb the rest of the way out of the hole. She lets go of me and leans back so she sits with her arms stretched out behind her. Her chest rises and falls in rapid succession. My heart is pumping as well, though, I'm not sure if it's because I just escaped a slow and tortuous death.

Her breathing slows to an even pace. "Are you all right?"

"Yeah. You?"

She nods and gets to her feet before turning from me and stepping away.

"For a second there, I thought you were going to leave me behind."

She pauses at my words and turns back around. There's a slight smile on her lips. "For a second, I thought so, too."

My mouth falls open and I give her an incredulous stare, though I doubt she can see it in the dark.

"I'm only teasing," she says with a smile. The light of the moon glints off her teeth.

I grin then rake my fingers through my hair to free it from its matted mess. "So, are you going back to the city?"

Her smile fades. "What do you mean?"

I gesture toward her clothes. Even though the gown is ruined, it still is of a higher quality that screams nobility. "You don't dress like you're from the villages."

She wraps her arms around her as though it'd prevent me from seeing her garb. "No," she says simply, "I'm not going back. I haven't figured out where I'm going yet."

"You're more than welcome to come back to the camp with me." I rub the back of my neck when she tilts her head and presses her lips into a line. "I mean, at least for the night until you figure out where you're going."

She stands for a moment in the quiet of the night then drops her arms to her sides and nods. "Just for the night."

We take off toward the camp. Her footsteps follow close behind mine, the squish of the soggy branches flexing under our weight. We zigzag through the trees. Their shadows are casted on the ground like skeletal fingers under the moonlight.

"Down here," I say over my shoulder. We near the edge of a crest before it drops down into a slope. She hesitates at the top, then together, we slide downward, the wet ground making our descent all the easier.

I fight back a smile as her nobility shines through once again, the utter disgust on her face at the mud that accumulates on her legs. She doesn't let it slow her down, and soon we hurry between dense trees toward the cave just ahead.

I slow my pace as we near the entrance of the den. A soft orange glow pours from its mouth. My hand runs along the cave's exterior walls, my fingertips grazing along a combination of textures, rigid rock and spongy moss. She stops at the entrance and wraps her arms around her stomach. Her eyes dart from me to the cave before turning her head to scan the woods.

"This is your camp?" she asks.

I shrug. "Good protection from the rain."

She takes a calculated step inside, her clothes catching on the rocky wall as she moves along it. Damp hair sticks to her face and she brushes it away with delicate fingers. The same fingers that scratched my arms up in a desperate need to survive. The modest fire casts a golden hue on the girl, and for the first time, I see her. I *really* see her—the high cheekbones of her face, the elaborate gown plastered to her body from the rain, the dark hair falling around her shoulders like a cape.

"You leave to find firewood and come back with the queen?" Aiden startles her as he approaches from the far side of the den.

She glares at him, then at me, letting her eyes settle back on him. "Who else is in here?" She cranes her neck to look around Aiden and her gaze finds Kai lying in the darkness.

Aiden looks at me, his head tilted. I drop my eyes to the ground as all my memories of her, the way she sat unaffected in the monarch's gallery, come rushing to my mind. My body tenses under my drenched clothes and heat churns in my core. After a moment, I raise my head and set my eyes on her.

"So, you're the queen." My words come out as more of an accusation.

She steps further into the cave, closer to the fire. Her gray eyes, the same ones I remember from long ago, level with mine. "Not anymore."

Leona

Chapter 10

I sit with my back against the jagged wall, staring at the ground between my knees. The man who helped me, Colton, left to get more firewood. Hopefully he hurries. A shiver runs down the length of my back, but I'm not sure if it's from the dropping temperature or because of the chaos burrowing holes in my mind.

The space between my lungs clenches into a dull ache that drops down to my stomach and ignites. The internal heat warms my veins and smothers the chill from my skin. I loosen my fists—when did they become fists?—and rub my clammy palms over the shredded fabric of my gown. My throat tightens, and I want to scream out. Not because it'll do any good, but because in this moment, it feels like just the release I need to keep the tears from falling. If there's one thing I learned from Father, it's that rulers don't cry—it shows weakness. Then again, I guess I'm not much of a ruler anymore.

The moment when things all went to hell keeps replaying in my mind like a nightmare coated on the walls of the cave. Everything I've held onto for the past nineteen years has come crashing down around me in less than twelve hours.

I was born to rule, born to lead my people to a more prosperous life, or so I'd been told. Maybe Mother had a different outlook on my future than what the universe has planned. She was always the optimistic one, the one who convinced me that I would someday be a great leader. What a load of shit that turned out to be. How dare she fill my head with endless possibilities and the notion that I could be the queen Erenen has been waiting for. She instilled a sense of misguided strength in me and isn't even here to help me navigate these uncharted waters.

I hate her.

My eyes sting and my chest hollows. I didn't mean that. I push out a slow breath to bring myself from the brink of truly spiraling out.

I look over to the man sitting across from me and hope that he didn't witness my near-meltdown. He's leaning forward, his ginger hair falling in a fringe over his forehead. He concentrates his eyes on me.

"Are you all right?" he asks.

I clear my throat. Guess he did get a front-row view of my insanity.

"Yes," I lie.

"Are you sure?"

I sit up straight and roll my shoulders back. "What was your name again?"

"Aiden." Melancholy rolls off his tongue as he speaks his name. "Should I call you Queen… or Your Majesty… or—"

"Leona is fine." There's a tinge of bitterness in my tone. This is my new reality, so I might as well embrace it.

Nothing could have prepared me for today. When I set out to disrupt the stillness of my kingdom, I never thought in a million years it would cost me my crown or a dear friend her life. I never outright considered Gracen a friend, but in hindsight, she may have been the only one I had.

And now, she's gone because of me.

A coldness trails down my spine and my body vibrates uncontrollably, no matter how tightly I wrap my arms around my chest to subdue the shivers.

"Are you sure you're all right?"

Calm down. Breathe. I open my mouth to speak, but nothing comes out. Luckily, Colton's return veers the attention away from me.

"I managed to find a few good pieces of wood," he says, dropping kindling into a pile in the center of the cave.

The den isn't particularly large, not the size and quality of living spaces that I'm familiar with, but it'll do for now. At least until I figure out what my next move is.

Colton kneels beside the pile and Aiden crawls over to join him. Colton passes him a wedge-shaped rock about the size of his hand, and they begin pounding the rocks against chunks of wood.

The hairs on the back on my neck stand up. The noise echoes in the cave, amplifying the sounds ten-fold. My eyes dart to the cave's entrance and then back to them.

"What are you doing? You're being too loud!" I lean forward and shift so I'm sitting on my heels.

Both men pause mid-strike and look at me as though I'm the crazy one.

I nod to the entrance. "The guards are going to get lured here if they hear you."

Colton shakes his head. "No, it's clear out there. I checked—twice. Those men are probably home tucked in their warm beds by now."

I tilt my head and raise my hands in front of me, palms up. "All right… Still, what are you doing?"

The men shoot each other a glance. Colton mutters something under his breath, to which Aiden responds by snickering.

How disrespectful.

I clear my throat. "Excuse me?"

Colton sighs and sets the rock down so that it leans against the wood he was working on. His gaze meets mine. "I said, yeah, you must be a noble girl."

My face flushes with heat and I stare with wide eyes. "What's that supposed to mean?"

"It means—" he hesitates and turns away from me. "Nothing. Nevermind."

The tension in this cave thickens in a short amount of time. Ever since he realized my position, he's been acting like a child. He has something he wants to say, so he might as well say it. I fix my lips to pursue the conversation, but

Aiden beats me to the silence.

"So, what we're doing is preparing the wood for the fire." His voice is calm and steady, nonthreatening. "Here." He tosses me a piece of wood. It bounces once on the ground before rolling to a stop at my knees.

"Feel how the outside is soaked from the rain?" he continues.

I turn the wood over in my hands a couple of times, my fingertips grazing over the cold, damp bark. "Yes…" I roll it back to him.

"Well, a fire won't start with wet kindling, and the moisture shouldn't have gotten to the inside of the wood yet. We need to break the logs open to get to the dry section."

I nod, and the men resume their task. As Colton works, our eyes meet for a lengthy second before he snatches his gaze away to something else. It doesn't take long before they build the fire back up. Hues of orange flames flick the air as wind tunnels into the cave and breathes life into the fire. Warmth kisses my skin and delivers a speck of comfort. My fingers comb through the length of my hair, detangling the strands the best I can, and removing as many dried mud clots as possible.

I look at the flames dancing violently above the kindling. The crackling sound it produces soothes away the bundled nerves I had earlier. I've never really taken the time to notice how relaxing a fire is.

My eyes focus beyond the blaze at Colton. He's sitting across from me, staring, and this time, he's not averting his gaze when I catch him. I toss my hair back over my shoulders and rub my hands together to get rid of the dirt.

"What's your problem?" I say, breaking up the relaxing atmosphere.

His eyebrows raise but his body remains stiff.

"Well? Spit it out."

"You have a lot of blood on your hands." He props his elbows on his knees and rests his chin on interlaced knuckles.

I flinch as though his words slap me in the face. "And, how is that?"

He gestures toward the man moaning softly from pain. "Kai probably won't survive the night, all thanks to the entitlement of your nobles and their belief that we're inferior to them." Kai's brawny stature is reduced to fragility as his chest rises and falls with constricted breaths. He lies on his back, sweat trickling from his forehead, an ugly scar tacked onto his face. "A lot of innocent men—and boys—have died under your and your family's rule."

"You're talking about the gladiator fights?" My voice tries to rise in pitch, but I push it back down.

He nods once, never taking his eyes off mine.

"I disbanded it, didn't I? How are you angry at me for that?"

So, that's where I remember him from. His face looked so familiar to me, but I couldn't pin-point where I'd seen him before.

"Your coronation was six months ago, yeah?" His question is rhetorical, and he doesn't give me a chance to answer. "You've had plenty of times to end the fights before now. But instead, you sat casually by while injustice ran rampant in the kingdom. You're no better than the men who chased you out of Demesne."

My jaw drops. Usually, I'm used to dealing with the accusations and lectures from my Council, but this feels different. This feels personal. My heartbeat accelerates and I clasp my hands together to discourage the trembling.

I take a deep breath. "Yes, I could've stopped the fights months ago, but if it wasn't for me, you'd still be locked up under the arena." That last part came out harsher than I meant. "And what are you talking about injustice in the kingdom?"

Colton looks toward Aiden, shakes his head, then returns his glare on me.

"You're really going to sit there and pretend you don't know what I'm talking about?" The flames jump when he tosses a sliver of wood into the fire.

My eyes shift from Aiden to Colton and then back again. I search Aiden's face for a hint as to what Colton is accusing me of. Aiden presses his lips together in a tight line, drops his head down, and fidgets with a loose pebble on the ground.

I inhale a sharp breath. With everything else going on in my life right now, my head aches from trying to figure out what he's talking about. "I don't know what you mean, so just say what you're trying to say. I'm done with the backhanded comments." My heart pounds against my arms as they lay crossed over my chest.

Colton places his hands on his knees and sits up tall. His skin has an amber glow about it, subtle shadows in the hollows of his face.

"For the past year, more and more of us have been taken prisoner for crimes we didn't commit. Boys as young as twelve have been stripped from their mothers' arms, accused of stealing from shops they hadn't set foot in. No trials. No nothing. Just thrown in the dungeons."

I blink. Blink again. My mind recalls the last six months of fights I've had to sit through—my attendance now more mandatory than optional. Though I've done my best to suppress the images from my memory, I do remember seeing more juvenile males than normal, most of whom died their first time in the arena.

He continues. "Do you have any idea how it feels to be forced to kill a friend? To know that if you don't kill in the arena, the guards will be back to murder your entire family? You don't, do you? How many times have you had to watch the life drain out of someone's eyes and know that it was because you've just drove a sword through their heart?"

I loosen the tension in my shoulders and drop my hands to my lap. His words swirl around my mind, my brain struggling to make sense of what he is telling me. I want to ask if he's joking, but the grim look on his face suggests he's beyond serious and asking would only insult him.

"I didn't know," I say, my voice lacking strength.

"Wow." Colton laughs. "What kind of queen doesn't realize what's going on right under her nose?"

"Colt…" Aiden says, noticing the anguish building up within me.

The heat under my skin is nothing compared to the fire separating me from Colton. My whole body is on the verge of combustion—all I need is a spark. Apparently, he'll do anything, say anything, to meet this request. My fingernails dig into my palms as I ball my hands into fists. My palms throb, but I squeeze a little harder.

"All right. You made your point." My throat is dry, the words grinding against my tongue. "Obviously, I didn't know what was going on—that much has been made evident from me being ran out of my own castle." My tone is rising, and I can't stop it. "So, I'm sorry, all right?—I'm sorry that all of this happened. It's not like I told the guards to say and do all the things that they did. If I'd known, I would've stopped it the moment I found out, but chances are, my assassination attempt would've only been moved up six months." My pulse pounds in my ears and I can hardly hear my own words. "You don't like me? That's fine. You and everyone else in Demesne have that in common. I have enough shit going on without adding yours to the pot."

I stand up and stomp out of the cave, leaving scorch marks behind in my wake.

Colton

Chapter 11

"Was all that really necessary?" Aiden flicks the pebble aside.

My face shrinks into a scowl. "She needed to know."

"Maybe. But you could've cut her some slack. She did just get ousted."

I shift my gaze from the fire to him. "Why should she have it easy? We're the ones who've suffered. She did nothing but watch."

"Her own guards just tried to kill her."

"It wouldn't be the first time they've tried to kill in cold blood. I'm sure it won't be the last."

Aiden runs his fingers through his shaggy auburn hair and sighs. "She did have a point though. After generations of upholding the fights, it was her who decided to put an end to them. She risked her life for us. And by giving us back our freedom, she lost her throne."

I release a long exhale and pinch the bridge of my nose. I hadn't thought about it that way. I have thirteen months of rage built up. Night after night, mental anguish bred into a hatred for all things noble.

"So, maybe I was too harsh?"

He nods, the corner of his mouth pulling up into a grin.

"Fine. I'll go find her." I roll my eyes. "She'll probably get lost out there."

"Most likely," Aiden says with humor. He adds more wood to the fire and the flames devour the fresh fuel with no problem. Most of the remaining kindling has dried and we should have enough to last the night.

Kai starts in a fit of coughing, a ragged wheeze punctuating each whoop. Weakly, he rolls over to his side and coughs out a spurt of blood.

Aiden and I exchange a glance. It's not looking good for Kai. Although we bandaged him up as well as we could, he's bleeding from somewhere inside of his body. I shift to crawl toward him, to offer him something, anything, to ease his pain, but Aiden places his hand on my shoulder.

"I've got him," he says, his voice grim. "You go find Leona."

I stand and dust the dirt from the back of my thighs. At the cave entrance, I wait a second and glance around. She couldn't have gotten far, but as upset as she is, it's no telling how far her feet would take her in the heat of the moment. I look at the moonlit path in front of me and suspect that for a noble girl, she'd likely take the most obvious route. I start on the trail, stopping every few meters to check for any activity, but I don't see her.

I continue on the path and take measured steps with my eyes closed so I can block out the nature tones—especially an insatiable owl hooting above—and focus on any out-of-place sounds that could lead me to her. I pause and listen. To my right, somewhere in the darkness of the trees, I hear a subtle noise, almost like, sniffling? As I get closer, there's no doubt that what I'm hearing is someone crying. And not just anyone—Leona. Her shoulder peeks out from behind a tree.

"Leona?" I approach carefully and she snaps her head up when she sees me.

"What do you want?" She turns away into the shadows.

"I, um, wanted to apologize."

"For what? You were right, weren't you?"

The sound of her soft sobs chips away at my stubborn exterior, gradually wearing down the pent up anger that I've held onto for far too long. At this point, I'm not even sure if it's her whom I'm upset with. But she's here—an easy target—and the only one available to direct the brunt of my wrath. My eyebrows relax from their firm hold. I jam my hands into my pockets and let my fingers twirl around the frayed edges of the fabric.

"I'm sorry." The words come out as a whisper between my lips. "I shouldn't have taken things out on you."

She quiets for a moment and then steps from behind the tree into the moonlight. Her cheeks glisten as the light catches the tears trailing over her face. She looks up into my eyes, as though she's contemplating the sincerity of my words.

Her chin trembles but she stiffens it. "I swear I didn't know."

"I understand that now."

She wipes her eyes with the back of her hands. In an attempt to get rid of the pain in her voice, she clears her throat and moves her mouth upward into a weak smile. "It's been awhile since I last cried. It feels weird."

A laugh comes from me before I can stop it. "I don't think crying is supposed to feel weird. Maybe you're doing it wrong."

Her smile widens and she drops her gaze to the ground. She nods but doesn't say anything. Only the sound of the owl continues the conversation.

"Are you okay?" I ask, still maintaining a gentle tone. Not that it's particularly difficult now. Seeing her like this, her guard let down so low that it's nonexistent, makes me remember that she's still human—like me. "I was an ass. You didn't deserve me tearing you down like that."

She holds up her hand. "No, I did deserve it. I was so out of touch with what was really going on in my court. I knew the odds were going to be against me, but I—"

"What do you mean?" I step closer and lean against the tree she'd been hiding behind.

"Well, it can't come as much of a surprise to you that no one was happy when I took the throne."

"Why not? Did you try to claw their faces off too?" I smirk and glance down at my scratched-up arms.

She leans in close, narrows her eyes on the red welts on my arms, and gasps. "I did that to you?" Her hand rises to cover her mouth, and when she drops it, an uneasy smile is revealed.

My lips pull into a smile of its own, amused at her concern for such a minor injury. Nothing but flesh wounds. I've survived much more serious incidents than this.

"It's okay." I laugh. "Though, it's good to know that your fingernails can be used as a deadly weapon if it comes down to it."

Her smile fades into a frown. I recoil and push off the tree. Did I say something else to offend her?

"What was it like"—she twists her face up and softens her voice—"in the arena?"

I pull a hand out of my pocket and hook it around the back of my neck. There's a brief silence between us as I take a moment to organize my answer. It'd be easy to just write off the experience by saying it was no big deal, but the fights were anything but. I've already given her a taste of what happened, and I'm surprised she wants to know more.

My chest clenches as I try to take a deep breath. "Think of your worst nightmare and then imagine living it daily while you're set on fire. And imagine that the smoke around you is so thick that every breath you take is suffocating you just enough to leave you clinging for life, but not enough to put you out of your misery."

She drops her head down into a bow. Her arm swoops around her head as she collects her hair and pulls it to one side. She coils the ends of her stands around a finger, lets it go, then coils it again. I can only imagine the thoughts rolling around in her mind as she tries to grasp the extent of the hell she'd freed us from.

"You said that they forced you all to fight, yes? Threatened to kill your families if you didn't?" She lifts her head.

I nod once, my eyes locked on hers.

"Did they ever follow through?"

I shrug again and let my eyes roam to the spots of light coming from the city. "At the beginning, yeah. A few men's families died in a *tragic house fire*, but we knew better. It didn't take us long to fall into line after that."

"Is your family"—she hesitates another beat—"all right?" Her eyes drift from mine and land on my chest.

"As far as I know, yes. I did everything those piece of shit guards demanded of me."

Leona flinches and she brings her arms up to wrap around her chest. Her hands rub over tiny bumps on her arms raised from the chill in the air. A current of wind grabs the branches in the treetops, and they sway in unison, collectively saying goodbye to the storm as it charges through to another territory.

"Come on." I nod toward the cave. "Let's get back to the fire."

She takes a step toward me and pauses, her eyes glued on the ground before us. "Look," she whispers. "What is that?"

I sense her caution and mirror it. My head turns slowly until my eyes meet what has caught her attention. My lips turn up into a grin. "That's dinner."

With very little turbulence, I crouch down and wrap my fingers around a rock about the size of an apple. My eyes zero in on the rabbit as it nibbles mindlessly on the foliage a few yards away.

Leona stands motionless next to me, watching with intensity as her eyes dart between me and the rabbit. I clutch the rock in my hands, feeling the rough shape for the best grip. Lifting it above my shoulder, my weight shifts onto my back leg, causing a dull crunch under my foot.

The rabbit halts its eating and points its ears in our direction. I hold my breath, the rock hovering over my right shoulder. Before the rabbit has a chance to launch into a sprint, I hurl the rock toward it. Its sharp cry cuts through the forest, outperforming the owl above that takes off in flight.

I stoop over the rabbit as it convulses and struggles to find its footing. My fingers slip around the plush fur of its neck, twisting once to silence its screams and subdue its wrestling.

Behind me, Leona draws in a sharp breath.

I look over my shoulder at her, then stand up. "What? You've never had rabbit before?" I hold it out to her, the animal's limp body hanging in my hand. She steps backward with wide eyes and raised eyebrows.

"Yes… but I've never seen one killed."

"Must be rich girl problems."

She rolls her eyes and steps past me, her arm brushing against mine. "Let's go back."

I chuckle to myself and follow her back toward the cave.

"Everything all good now?" Aiden asks when we return.

"More than good." I hold the rabbit up for him to see. "Leona found us dinner." I glance at her and grin.

Aiden stares at her with an open mouth that shrinks into a smile. "Really?"

She creases her brows. "Well, I only spotted it. He's the one who caught it."

"All the same. Nice work, you two." Aiden holds his hands up and I toss him the rabbit.

I catch a glimpse of hidden delight on Leona's face as she sits near the fire. Her eyes crinkle when they meet mine and she forces the beginnings of a smile away. Her gaze diverts to the flames, but I've already seen what she's tried to hide. Peace of mind—and I have a feeling it's not something she's used to.

It's not long before Aiden has the rabbit skinned and ready for cooking. With a few spare pieces of wood, he fashions a way to hold the rabbit over the flames until it is completely cooked.

"Thank you," Leona says as I hand her a section of the meat.

The thought crosses my mind to tease her about the lack of gourmet food she's probably accustomed to, but I quickly dismiss the notion. Instead, I offer a simple, "You're welcome," and take my seat around the fire.

The moon drifts across the night sky in the last few hours before sunrise. I'm so exhausted, but I can't sleep. Insomnia—a side effect of my time in the dungeons. I keep my mind busy and tend to the fire, adding more kindling when the flames begin to die down.

Aiden lies stretched out on his back, one arm resting over his stomach while the other's pulled up under his head. His chest rises and falls in a steady tempo, and a soft whistle sneaks past his mouth on each exhale.

In a way, I'm envious of him. His mind hasn't yet been forever warped by the memories our twisted reality. The guards stole his freedom only two weeks ago when he was brought in during the last round of phony arrests. *'He attacked a guard,'* they said. Lies. In the short time I've known him, I know being combative isn't one of his attributes.

I lay the last piece of wood into the fire and pull myself to my feet. Loaded thoughts cloud my mind. They roam free and wield a weapon far worse than the finest Erenese sword. Their constant threat to drag me into a dark place looms overhead. Mentally, my legs never stop running from it. But someday, those legs might collapse.

I step with caution past the sleeping bodies on the ground. Leona lies on her side toward the fire, her face nuzzled into the crook of her elbow. She didn't say much after dinner, though, I guess that's to be expected. It's been a long day for all of us.

At the cave opening, I lean a shoulder against the wall and look out into the forest. The night is quiet except for the occasional croak of a frog. At least I'm not the only one around here who can't sleep.

This all feels surreal. Part of me keeps waiting to blink and find myself back in the dungeons, back with a blood-crusted sword in my hand as I stand over a friend's body. I'd long accepted that I would never see another sunrise. I'd grown used to the idea that I'd never lay eyes on my parents again—that I'd never hear another of my mother's endless words of wisdom or help my father with the chores when the pain of his arthritis is too great. And now, my future has changed.

I look up through the treetops at the twinkling lights in the sky. There's not as many out here than as when I'm at home. Must have something to do with all the lamps in the city. Back in Maburh, we don't have the luxury of running more than a handful of street lamps all night. I guess that's what separates the villages from Demesne and the other cities. The differences are black and white, or more accurately, dark and light.

It never made much sense to me why the eight villages were depended on to produce the goods and shell out labor, and yet the nobles in the cities reaped the benefits. Those in Demesne live an easier life only because of their family name. The wealthy stay wealthy—and free.

I press my hands against my eyes. So tired. It'll be nice to be back home. Maybe I'll find much needed rest in my own bed. Maybe all I need to take back control of my sanity is to look upon my parents' faces and bask in the comfort of returning home to them. We may not share the same blood, but they've been my family for long enough.

I close my eyes and try to picture our cramped home with the leaking roof that never stays fixed. *'That'll hold it,'* Pa would say, only for the roof to prove him wrong during the next storm. I wonder how well it fared today. How many pails did my mother have to empty to keep the kitchen from flooding? The inner corners of my eyes begin to burn, and I blink back the impending tears. I slip my hand inside my collar and feel for my pendant, but I'm met with bare skin. A sinking feeling seizes my body and I scan the ground in a fit of wildness.

I can't lose it. Of all the things I own, I *can't* lose my pendant. It's the only thing that reminds me of my previous life.

With my eyes still fixed to the ground, I step back inside the cave and give a quick glance around before returning outside. My chest tightens. I check my neck again as though I'd somehow missed it the first time. Sweat beads along my brows and I hurry through the woods, backtracking to the areas where my feet touched. I had my pendant right before Leona sent us into the crevice, and I offer a silent prayer that it's not back in the hole.

As I weave through the trees, my eyes, already strained from fatigue, try to catch any hope of my pendant. I approach the crevice cautiously. The ground is still soggy and slick from the rain. I peer into the hole, but there's nothing but darkness at the bottom. A brief thought crosses my mind. It'd be worth it to jump back into the hole to check for it. Whether or not I'll be able to get back out, that's a whole other thought entirely.

I fall to my knees at the edge of the crevice, then shift so my legs dangle inside. My boots bump into the thick branch still set in place. I close my eyes and take a deep breath. When I open them, my gaze falls on the slope at the other side of the crevice—where Leona and I collided. A small piece of metal gleams in the moonlight. A sharp inhale cools the heat under my skin. That has to be it. I clamber to my feet, nearly slipping into the hole in the process.

When I reach the other side, there it is, tucked into the mud, the turquoise gem hazy from grime. I pluck it out and wipe it clean with my shirt. The chain is cold as I slip it over my head, but the pendant offers a surge of warmth as it settles against my chest.

A soft chuckle eases the tension in my shoulders as I bring the gem to my lips. I whisper Daolic words to it, a language I refuse to let anyone else in this country hear. *You are forever with me, Mama.*

Leona

Chapter 12

My feet hammer against the tile floor, each footfall propelling me forward with more agility than I've ever thought possible. I look over my shoulder and catch a glimpse of the dark shadow following close behind. The air in my lungs turns cold and I turn my attention back in front of me. The identical stark red doors lining the corridor turn into a crimson streak as I sprint past them. The doors are unfamiliar to me. I've lived in this castle my whole life, yet I can't remember coming across this corridor. And, when did we get red doors?

A low rumble travels down the passage, vibrating from the floor and up the walls, rattling the gold framed portraits with enough oscillation that they fall to the ground with thunderous clunks. One after another, the portraits cascade to the ground as I pass them. I don't let it distract me, though. I need to get away. I'm running—running as fast as I can manage without losing my balance on the increasingly unsteady flooring. As my feet touch each tile, the ceramic falls through the floor into the deep trenches of whatever is down there. I'd look, but I can't stop running. I won't stop.

The shadow is getting closer—I can feel it. The hairs on the back of my neck stand up straight and ice spreads across my shoulder blades. The scent of ashes fills my nose and glazes my tongue. The air around me becomes denser, as though its weight is pushing me to the ground and slowing my speed.

I stumble further down the corridor and pause at the upcoming red door. It's open wide but reveals a wall of darkness inside. A burst of icy air pours from the room, blowing my hair like a flag behind me. I step toward it, my hands flying to my face to shield from the blast. The door slams shut when I reach the threshold. My shaking fingers grasp the doorknob, but it doesn't budge.

I dash to the door across the hall, and it's tightly sealed shut as well. I pound my palms on the door in a desperate plea for it to open. When I withdraw my hands, my palms are covered in red paint.

No… not paint. The texture is thinner and murkier—this is blood.

Blood pours from my fingers and pools at my feet like an unattended faucet. My eyes dart from one hand to the other and I take a step backward, leaving behind a bloody footprint. A solid mass behind me stops me in my tracks. When I pivot, my eyes settle on the familiar face of Aerok, though something is not right. Black fills his glossy eyes and they no longer offer the same deceptive warmth as before. He peers down at me and strength drains from my body, like somehow my energy—my life—is seeping out of my pores and collecting into nothingness. Instinct tells me to move, but he holds my gaze with nothing but my icy breath between us.

Aerok opens his mouth and reveals rows of stacked needle-like teeth. His jaw drops until his chin is level with the base of his neck. I open my own mouth to scream, but nothing comes out. There's tension on my vocal cords, but my ears are deaf to the sound that should've followed. The distance between my life and death slims when his head lowers to mine. He smells of misery and demise, and the odor burns my nostrils and waters my eyes.

My body tenses, or at least I think it does. I'm paralyzed in place and the only movement I can manage is my eyes widening as this ghoul of a man comes closer. Venom drips from his teeth and sears my forehead on contact. The pain should probably be unbearable, but my body is numb, and my strength has been stolen.

I squeeze my eyes shut as his acid breath roasts my face and shakes my body.

"Leona."

My eyes snap open. Aiden is kneeling beside me with his hand cupped on my shoulder. His eyebrows pull up in confusion.

"Are you all right?" He drops his cool fingertips from my overheated skin.

I sit up, my balance unsteady, my stomach and head churning with nausea. I wipe sweat and damp hair from my forehead with the back of my hand. My heart is pounding, and I take a second to calm my racing nerves.

I nod, but that just makes the nausea swirl faster. "Bad dream, I guess."

His lips stretch up into a wistful smile. "Yeah, sounded like it. You were screaming."

I reach for my throat. "Sorry..."

"It's all right. It happens." He looks over his shoulder toward the cave's opening. "Morning time."

I glance around the cave as he helps me to my feet. The pile of wood from last night's fire is reduced to nothing more than a smoldering heap of ashes. Colton is nowhere to be seen. My eyes fall on Kai's still body, his chest no longer expanding from breaths.

My hand flies up to my mouth. "Is he...?"

Aiden rakes his hands through his hair and lets out a long exhale. "He didn't make it."

"What do we do?" A prickling sensation starts in my feet and travels up to my fingertips. "Does he get taken back to his family?"

Aiden doesn't answer. Instead, he walks the short distance to where Kai lies motionless and crouches near him. His back faces me, and for a long moment, he's silent. I step closer and drop to my knees beside him. Up close, the bulkiness of Kai's body is intimidating. Half of his face is covered with the shadow of the cave. The half that is illuminated is plagued in fine scars, some of which hadn't healed properly.

"He doesn't have one," Aiden says. "Not anymore. His wife and three sons died in a house fire."

A bolt of cold and heat channels through my veins and I reach out to touch Aiden's arm. He turns his gaze slowly from Kai's sallowed face to mine.

"The guards?" I ask, my voice barely audible. The answer is obvious, based from what Colton told me last night, and a flush of heat singes my cheeks from embarrassment.

Aiden gives a sharp nod, his eyes remaining locked on mine. Then, he turns his head away from me. "It happened much earlier than when I'd arrived, but Colton had said their deaths destroyed Kai. His was the first family to be collateral damage for disobedience."

A teardrop splashes on the back of my hand. I tilt my head back and look up at the moss-covered ceiling, my eyes rimmed with tears begging to be released. A pain burrows within me, a pain that feels so familiar although I didn't know Kai or his family.

"We should have a proper burial for him—to honor him."

Aiden smiles, the freckles on his cheeks contrasting against his pale complexion. "I'm sure he'd like that."

I return the smile and pat Aiden's arm before rising to my feet. "Where's Colton?"

He juts his thumb over his shoulder. I walk out of the cave into the brightness of the new day. Colton stands nearby with his back to me, his head on a swivel as he checks the activity of the forest.

"We're lucky the guards aren't patrolling yet, with all that screaming you were doing," he says as he turns to face me.

As soon as our eyes meet, a memory from many years ago rushes through my mind. I hadn't noticed in the dim lighting of the night, but now, I can see him clearly. Same curly brown hair. Same pale green eyes with a patch of red on one of the irises. This isn't the first time we've met.

When I was eleven years old, my parents took me on my first tour of the kingdom. Father thought it was time I got to know my subjects and learn the lands I'd one day rule over. While he and Mother drew a crowd in the town square, I wandered off to explore the lands on my own. I'd never been out of Demesne before, and the rustic smell of this village invited me to learn more.

I wriggled through the crowd and away from my parents, away from our guards, leaving the chatter behind me. Without hesitation, my feet carried me to a narrow dirt path near a house. I followed it until I ended at a barn with a boy standing outside. He looked to be my age, maybe older. His hands clutched the reins of the brown-spotted horse he was trying desperately to calm. He wasn't doing a good job at it and didn't hear when I approached.

"You're making him more nervous." I interlocked my fingers behind my back and glanced from the horse to the boy.

The boy darted his eyes to me, scowled, then returned his gaze to the horse. "Shh... shh... it's okay, boy." The horse thrashed and the boy responded by yanking harder on the reins. "Shh."

"Don't do that," I said. "He'll never calm down that way."

"Go away," the boy said over his shoulder. His voice had a slight accent to it.

I pulled my lips to the side and took a step forward. With an open palm, I rubbed the area between the horse's eyes, applying just enough pressure to soothe him. It calmed its hooves and relaxed its body. The boy scoffed and glared at me.

"I could've done that."

"Didn't look like it. When they get like that, you have to show them there's nothing to be afraid of."

The boy dropped his grimace and peered at the horse, as though he were considering my words. He nodded then looked back at me. "I could've figured that out by myself."

I grinned, but then something caught my attention. I squinted to get a better look at the boy. "What happened to your eye?"

His eyes were light green but one of them had red, too. I'd never seen someone with a half-red eye.

He turned his head back toward the horse and rubbed its snout. "I don't know… I've always had it."

I sidestepped to renew my inspection and fixed my lips to ask another question, but paused mid-breath when my father's voice boomed from in front of the house. The boy looked toward the direction of the voice, then at me and smiled. My father called for me again.

"Leona? That's your name?" the boy asked.

I flashed a smile, then took off into a sprint, leaving the green and red-eyed boy behind.

"I remember you," I say as I approach Colton.

He looks at me and tilts his head. "Huh?"

"When we were kids," I start, "I helped you with your horse."

He raises his eyebrows. "*Helped* is a bit of an overstatement."

"You're lucky the horse didn't kick you in the face." I pop my hip to the side and place a hand on my waist. "Why didn't you say anything?"

Colton's face turns a shade of red. "Didn't think you'd remember."

"I do." I bite my bottom lip. "That was the last time I was ever able to wander off."

"For what it's worth," Colton says, his mouth shifting into a half-smile, "I didn't know you were the princess, but I should've guessed. Even then, you had fancy clothes."

The morning breeze whips warm air through the forest, picking up the shredded ends of my gown as though to illustrate his point. The sun peeks through the openings of the tree canopies, spotting the ground in flashes of light.

Aiden emerges from the cave, the tax of Kai's death still worn on his face. His eyes bounce from tree to tree until he settles on a massive oak and points at it. "I was thinking we could bury Kai in front of that one."

Colton and I follow him to the tree, its trunk extending up so far that our chins point skyward to see the top.

"This one's perfect," I say, "broad and strong, just like he was."

Colton smiles, then steps away to pick up a couple of fallen boughs, handing one to Aiden. Aiden starts tapping out the grave's shape with the pointed end of his branch.

"I can help."

Colton raises a brow and studies my face. "Are you sure? It's not the cleanest task in the world."

Of course he'd be skeptical. Queens don't usually get their hands dirty, or perform manual labor, for that matter. Even when Mother tended to her gardens, a dainty pair of gloves always protected her hands. But I don't want to be the stereotypical highborn people perceive me to be.

I nod and hold out my hand for his branch. "I want to help."

He smirks and passes it to me, then retrieves another one from the ground. I turn it over in my palms. Clumps of green moss speckle the bark, the textures contradicting one another. I kneel close to the outline Aiden made in the dirt, and mirror both men's posture. They ram the edged end of the branches into the ground, loosen the wet dirt, and shovel it aside.

After watching their repetitive motions, I try it myself. My hand cups the blunt end and I strike the soil, but the tapered end gets stuck and snatches out of my grasp. I wince and suck in air through my teeth. An intense stinging throbs in my palm from a sliver of wood burrowing under my skin. Aiden and Colton stop and look at me.

"Are you all right?" Aiden asks, holding out his hand for mine.

I lay my hand in his and with a light touch, he pulls the splinter from my palm. A bead of red rises and sits on the surface.

Colton pulls at his ear, and then scratches just behind it. "You really don't have to be bothered with this if you don't want."

I shake my head. "I'll try again."

He pulls my branch from the ground and hands it back to me. "You're holding it right, but you'll want to drive it in at an angle." He simulates the motion at a slow speed with his own branch.

I nod and grip the bark, my blood soaking into the moss. I hit the ground once more, and this time, the branch loosens the dirt without getting stuck. Colton grins with bright eyes, and both he and Aiden continue to work on their sections.

After hours of breaking up the mud and scooping it out with our hands, the sun shifts its position in the sky and glides to its midpoint. My shoulders are sore, and my hands are filthy, but once Kai's grave is complete, all of my discomfort pales in comparison.

In the cave, I untie the sash from my torso and slip it around Kai's head, securing it in place over his eyes. Erenese funeral customs require a veil soaked in holy water to cover the eyes of the deceased. It allows the person's soul to be cloaked as it purges from the body and begins its passage to the afterlife. We don't have a veil or holy water, so the lacy cincture of my gown will have to do.

I fold Kai's hands over his stomach. There is no trace of warmth on his skin. His knuckles are scarred, and I shudder at the life he must've had to endure. I don't know what he did that caused him to be sent to the arena, and at this point, I don't care. He died much sooner than the expectancy of his life. His hair has only begun to lose its dark color and fade to gray. He should've grown old with his wife. He should've been able to watch his sons get married and start families of their own. But he's dead, and I can't help feeling that it's my fault.

My eyes sting and I tear them away from Kai's face. I nod and Colton and Aiden each take an end of his body. Together, they lift him, the sash's tails swinging just under his head. I stand just outside of the cave as they carry the fallen gladiator to his final resting place.

Countless birds, their feathers burning bright with red, line the branches of Kai's oak tree. A chorus of their trills beckons more birds to them, until there's more red than the green of the leaves. The timbre of their song lowers in volume as the men lower Kai into the hole.

We stand at one side of the grave in silence. The birds show their respect as well, the only sound coming from the rustling of the treetops. After a long moment, I reach down and pick up a handful of dirt. I tighten my grip to keep it from slipping through my fingers.

"Though your body is dead, your soul will live on. Safe passage to your eternal destination." I toss the dirt into the grave. It lands on Kai's stomach, covering his marred hands.

At my side, Aiden grabs his dirt and says the funeral rites, then tosses it so it builds on mine. His shoulders slump, as though by letting go of the dirt, he also let go some of his strength.

Colton's fingers tremble as he takes a mound of dirt into his hand. He holds it, his eyes locked on Kai's expressionless face. A deep crease forms above his brows. He shakes his head, his lip pulling to the side as he bares his teeth. My chest hollows out as I watch him. There's pain in his eyes—but also anger.

"Though your body is dead, your soul will live on." His voice is seething with unsaid words. He grips the dirt tighter, some trickling to his feet, and throws it into the grave. "Safe passage…to your eternal destination." A tear rolls down his cheek. He swipes it away, leaving a smear of dirt across his skin.

Aiden extends his arm to comfort Colton, but he crouches out of Aiden's reach. He shoves dirt back into the hole as though the soil may disappear if it doesn't return to its origin. Dirt cascades over the edge and surrounds Kai's feet first, then his legs. Aiden and I exchange a look. Neither one of us are sure how to respond, so we kneel and help Colton bury his friend.

Aiden takes a jagged rock and scratches Kai's name into the base of the tree trunk. *Malakai Russo*. Apparently, he was the last Russo. There's no one else to carry on his family name. He'd already lost his older brother to illness years earlier. Aiden finishes and tosses the rock aside, then joins Colton and I. Together, we stare past the freshly packed grave at the carved letters.

"They can't keep getting away with this." Aiden swats at the air and disrupts the silence among us.

Colton presses the heel of his hand against his eye. "They've been getting away with it for well over a year. Why would they stop now?"

I drop my head and focus on the dried mud on my boots. He's right. Even when I sat on the throne, attended weekly council meetings, and met with diplomats, the Council and guards were the ones controlling the country. I wonder, for a moment, whether the guards threatened the diplomats to withhold their true concerns from me.

"Regardless of how long it's been going on," Aiden says, "it doesn't mean it should continue. There has to be something that can be done."

I tap my knuckles against my lips, the taste of earth finding its way to my tongue. I'm sure Aiden means well, but there's nothing left to be done. Aerok and his father have everything they need to govern the country as they see fit. They have a four-hundred-man guard under their control as well as the support of the nobles. If I would've kept my mouth shut and married, I would've only been a puppet while they pulled the strings. "Erenen's sovereignty is in their hands. But if they did what you say —"

"If?" Colton whirls to face me with an arched brow. "They tried to kill you last night, and you're doubting whether or not they'd be so bold as to claim false crimes?"

My brows pinch together, my mouth pulling into a frown. I pick at the beginnings of a hole in my dress as though it is the source of my discomfort. "I'm not doubting it. I'm only saying that maybe they can be reasoned with if attention is brought to their deception."

"That's a bit naive, yeah?" He laughs with an edge to the tone. His eyes narrow, a blaze rising behind them. "You want to march back up there and tell them to cut it out? Tell them that what they're doing is wrong and they should behave? Remind me again—how'd that work out for you last time?"

My pulse quickens. A surge of heat radiates under my skin and flushes my cheeks. I stomp toward him, our glares mixing into a maelstrom of fury. He stiffens his jaw. I open my mouth to engage in his discord, but my prudence snaps it shut. I'm not used to this level of insolence. There's no point in arguing with him. I'm probably not even good at it. Even when the Council challenged me, they always surrendered to my wishes, albeit at their own undisclosed terms.

The fire in Colton's eyes burns brighter than the red in his iris. I hold his gaze and wait for his concession, but he doesn't budge. Such a brute. It's not too late for me to claw his face off. He's close enough. Each exhale he makes brushes my cheeks, warming the already strained air between us. Before I turn thought into action, I storm away, my shoulder knocking against his as though he isn't there. My eyes flash to Aiden. He sways in place, his hands resting on top of his head. How he's able to tolerate Colton's audacity must be an acquired skill.

I set my sights to the north, the trees offering no clear destination. The forest ahead is a wall of browns and greens, only pausing when the elevation changes.

"Where are you going?" The insult in Colton's voice is still present like a thorn in my side.

I ignore him, my feet pounding harder against the damp dirt. The squish each step makes is oddly satisfying. I need to get away from Demesne—away from Colton's unbridled arrogance.

Braer. That's where I'm going. It's only an eight-day trip on the water. There's nothing left for me here. No throne. No legacy. No family. At least in Braer, I could start over—maybe cut my hair and lose all the fine clothing. I could do that. I could live a normal life. I could be happy.

"No wonder the kingdom is in shambles," Colton calls behind me. "I didn't think a queen would bow down so easily."

I freeze, my body tensing with nerves I didn't know I had. His words cut deeper than I expect, and I pivot. Colton stands with his chin up, his arms crossed over his chest. Aiden gawks at him, the taunt a surprise for him, too.

My heartbeat hammers in my ears. Why is he so aggravating? A streak of adrenaline courses through my veins, severing all ties of caution. A few short moments and angry steps later, I'm back in front of him. "You've made it quite clear that I'm useless here, both on *and* off the throne. So, since you apparently have all the answers, what do you propose I do? What do you *want* from me?"

"Fight back." His voice is a hush, a stark contrast from the volume only seconds earlier. "You feel that rage building within you? Instead of running from it, channel it and fight back."

I groan and throw my arms up. "Fight back, how? I'm only one person."

"You don't have to be." The flames in his eyes dim to reveal their harmless shade of green. The pale color stands out from the rest of his tanned skin. He lowers his arms and relaxes them at his sides.

I stare at him with a blank look. My fingers reach up to ease the tension welling between my brows. "You're not making any sense."

His lips twist into a slight grin, and he looks to Aiden.

Aiden nods, a dimple settling into one of his cheeks as he smiles. "*My brother is my shield, and I am his armor.*"

"*That* makes even less sense."

"It's a saying we use in the villages," Colton says, leaning in. "It means that we will protect one another, no matter what, no matter which village we're from. We couldn't count on the crown for that safety, so we secured it ourselves." He lowers his eyes from mine, focusing his gaze on Kai's grave.

His words circle in my head and a pain forms in the back of my throat. I never realized the villages were so unified. That sense of alliance doesn't exist among the nobles. Most highborns' loyalty extends as far as what they deem your value is. ...And the arena! I gasp and let my face fall into my hands. My eyes burn behind their lids. No... I can only imagine the torture the villagers had to endure by being forced to kill the same people they swore to defend.

"Use us." Aiden touches my elbow. I lift my head to meet his eyes. "You just released over a hundred men.

Maybe they'd be willing to fight on your behalf."

I shake my head, my vision lagging, and pull away from his contact. "I can't ask that of them. They just got their freedom back. They wouldn't want to risk it again."

"I would."

"So would I." Colton lifts his shoulder in a half-shrug.

The ache moves from my throat and travels down to my chest. I turn away from the men. Although the warm air wraps me in its embrace, there's a biting chill on my skin.

In the distance, the Erenese banner hangs from the highest tower of the castle. The burgundy and white flag billows, its edges snapping against the wind. *Hope*. That's what Mother told me the flag meant. She'd said it was strung there so anyone within Demesne's outer limits could see it and be reminded that hope will never be lost. Well, I hope you were right, Mother.

I hook my fingers behind my neck and keep my country's flag in my view. "Do you really think they'll go for it?"

Aiden nudges my arm. "Only one way to find out."

Colton

Chapter 13

"Watch your step." I point down at the blended snake hole in the forest leaves and lost branches. As the sun begins its slow descent, most of the land is dry for an easier travel. Some obstacles can't be avoided though.

Leona nods and steps lightly over the earth, as though the snakes could snap at any moment. I let her pass me and smile, careful not to let her see my amusement. I don't know her very well but seeing how she reacts to life outdoors firmly establishes my opinion of noble folk. They wouldn't know how to survive on their own even if game smacked them in the face.

"So, Aiden," Leona says, "are you from Maburh as well?"

Aiden slows his pace to step in line with her. His pale freckled skin is distinct from her tan complexion.

"Nope. Durst."

Leona smiles. "Ah. It's been awhile since I've visited, but I remember that it looks so beautiful there in the autumn."

"When *was* the last time you stepped foot out of Demesne?" I ask, swatting a hornet in front of my face.

"Ever since—" She looks back and twists her face up in confusion as she watches me slap the air. The hornet takes off in an angry buzz, so I'll probably regret that in a second. "Are you all right back there?" Her mouth shifts into a grin.

Aiden glances back as well with a failed attempt at stifling a laugh.

My eyes drift continuously, taking in my full scope of vision, on the lookout for an insect with a vengeance. "Yep, I'm good."

She shakes her head and turns her focus back in front of her. "After my parents' accident, I haven't been in a rush to go outside of the city." The silence of the forest amplifies the tone of her words.

"Did they ever find out what really happened?" Aiden asks.

Her voice lowers in volume. "The Magistrate has stood by his initial conclusion—that the horses got spooked by the storm and tried to run through a fast-moving river."

"You sound like you don't believe that." I pick up my pace so we're walking side by side.

She looks up at me, her gray eyes appearing bluer in the sunlight. "They always took the same path when they went on tours. They shouldn't have been anywhere near that river."

"Is it possible that they could've taken a detour that one time?" Aiden presses his lips together.

"I doubt it. My father was all about traditions. He would've never opted to go that route, especially knowing how dangerous the storm was making the journey home." Her voice trails off and she stops in her tracks. Aiden and I both stop with her. "I don't believe their drowning was an accident." Aiden and I exchange a glance, but she continues. "I found a trade proposal that was drafted by my father two days before his death."

I narrow my eyes and totter my foot over a tree root. "What's wrong with a trade proposal?"

She sets her jaw, a flash of anger in her eyes. "The Council was against it." There's venom on her tongue as she refers to them. In the arena, I could always spot them in the crowd. The golden badges shined on the thick sashes they wore across their bodies. They always sat close to the monarch's gallery, but never inside it.

A breath hitches in my throat. "So, you're thinking they killed them?"

"It seems like motive enough," Aiden says.

"Seeing as how the Council was behind the attempt on my life, it's not too hard to believe they were behind my parents' deaths as well."

"Damn." I shake my head. "They'll really kill to get their way?"

Leona sighs and continues walking. "Guess so."

A speck of leftover guilt dries my throat as my harsh words from last night replay in my mind. I was an ass. She was only trying to do her best with the crap odds that life dealt her. When you have a whole group hellbent on using you like a puppet, it's insane how easily they'll clip your strings when you stop cooperating.

The sun peeks through the tree canopy and warms the back of my neck. I half-close my eyes, open enough to watch where I'm stepping but still take in the moment of peace at the same time. The sound of trickling to my right catches my attention. I stop and turn my head in that direction.

"Hold on," I say to the others, and they pause and backtrack toward me.

I walk past some brush and scan the ground. A stream. Fresh water glides over the rocks, separating and merging past larger stones. My throat aches, as though the sight of the water reminds it that it's thirsty.

"Good job." Aiden shakes my shoulder as he moves past me to a spot along the stream.

I kneel and cup my hands together. The water rushes in, filling my makeshift cup until it overflows. I lean down and quickly drink the water from my hands, going back two more times to satisfy my thirst.

When I look up, Leona is ahead of me, sipping with care. Water runs down her arms, wetting the tattered edges of her dress. Her thighs, smooth and appealing, are exposed from the worn fabric. My eyes linger on them, then on the roundness of her butt, the arch in her back, until my eyes meet hers. I flinch. My mouth goes dry. She doesn't say anything, only returns my gaze and offers a kindhearted smile. My cheeks turn ablaze, but I return the gesture. If she's offended by my staring, she isn't showing it. She looks away, splashes water on her face, and stands upright. With her back turned, I steal another glance in her direction. Heat buzzes my skin from either shame or arousal — at this point, I'm not sure which.

I can't ignore the way her dress hugs at her hips. It's been so long since I've laid eyes on a female, my body can't hide its response to her. Her skin looks so soft. I remember the scent on her skin as I lifted her from the hole. I wonder — Stop it. She's a queen.

I splash my face with the cool water, an attempt to wash away the thoughts conjuring in my mind. With a quick shake of my head, the excess water gets casted off and I rise to my feet.

After a while, we continue in silence and leave the dense part of the forest. With no trees to filter the afternoon sun, it beams down in its full force. Sweat rolls between my shoulder blades, and I tug at my shirt to let my skin breathe. We step onto a dirt path, leveled from the repeated use of travelers. Sparse grass and weeds line the trail.

"How much longer to Maburh?" Aiden asks.

"Maybe another hour, hour and a half. We should get there by dusk," I answer. "You sure you don't want to go home first?"

"Home?" He breathes a laugh. "Don't have much of that left."

Leona tilts her head, her eyes easy with curiosity. "Don't you have a family back in Durst?"

"Family can be overrated." Aiden lightly kicks a stone away with the side of his foot. "I have a father there, but he isn't much of a father."

There's a pause, then Leona asks, "Why's that?"

I glance at her. She examines Aiden with such concern. Her eyebrows are furrowed, her head still tilted. She's probably used to asking questions regardless of their privacy factor.

Aiden takes a moment before responding. Leona looks on, waiting for her answer.

"Let's just say he blames me for something I had no control over."

Leona nods and keeps quiet. It's hard to miss the reluctance—and pain—in his voice. In the weeks I've known Aiden, I've never heard him talk about family. Then again, there wasn't much talking about the things that mattered. Only jokes and lighthearted conversations shared between cells to ease our minds and maintain our sanity.

"Psst," Aiden says under his breath.

My eyes dart to him, then I follow his line of sight. Two guards walking toward us.

"Should we run?" Leona whispers.

"It's too late—we've already been spotted," I say to her. "Get behind us."

Her eyes widen as she follows my direction. She hovers close behind me. I feel the heat of her skin and the tremble of her nerves through my shirt.

We move to the side of the road, opposite the guards, and keep our heads down as we walk. In my peripheral view, the guards' eyes are concentrated on us. Their dark cloaks flap in the wind at their backs. The metal buckles on their boots clink in time with their steps. Their coats are a deep shade of blood, probably colored with the lives of all the innocent people they've taken.

My eyes shift from the ground to their waists, taking in the weapons they possess. Each walks with a hand resting on the hilt of his sword, fingers flexing in anticipation. There's at least two, maybe three, knives between both of them.

"Aye, stop right there," one of the men says.

I hold my breath and watch the guards come closer. I scan them over like I do—did—every time before a match. I look for weaknesses I can exploit, strengths I could tarnish, anything that could help us in the here and now. There's only one way this confrontation will end, and I'll be ready for it.

Leona clutches my arm and drops her head down, resting it against my spine. I'm sure she can feel the tension building in my back.

"What're you doing out here?" the other guard asks. He digs the toe of his boot into the ground. His feet move into a wide stance to make himself appear larger than he is.

Aiden and I look at one another. He tenses his jaw, then relaxes it. His head drops into a subtle nod.

"We're on our way to visit a friend," he says. His voice is calm, and he maintains eye contact with the guardsmen.

The guards regard us with a fake smile. Their eyes scan us, taking in our battered clothing and the film of dirt still in our hair.

"Visiting a friend, huh? Well, ain't that nice..."

The odor of stale ale and dung invade my nose when the shorter of the two guards takes a step closer to me. Sunlight glints off the steel clasp on his cloak, the symbol of Erenen engraved on its face. "Who's that you got behind you?"

Leona grips my arm tighter.

My eyes narrow on the man. "It's just my sister, sir. She's very timid around strangers." I bite the inside of my cheek. "We don't want any trouble. We'll just be on our way, if you don't mind."

The short man licks his lips and puts his hands on his belt. "I don't suppose your sister's for sale, huh? Just for an hour, or so." He lifts on his toes to peek over my shoulder. "What's she worth? Ten, fifteen coin? Let me get a look at her."

Heat shoots up through my feet into a chaos of flames in my chest. I run the pads of my middle fingers over my thumbs on both hands, searching for a way to keep my cool in this toxic situation. I focus on my breath. "Sir," I say again, carefully. "We don't want any trouble."

This is the last warning I'm allowing them. Aiden and I share a quiet glance. I've never seen him fight before but I hope he can hold his own.

"It's not up to you whether you get trouble or not, boy." He tries to shove me out of the way, but I don't budge. He gruffs then tries again. I square my shoulders and my feet remain planted firmly in place.

The short guard draws his sword, and his partner follows suit. I drop into a defensive stance, revealing Leona to the men.

"Aye!" the tall guard says. "It's that queen bitch!"

I whip my head behind me. "Get somewhere safe."

My arm goes cold where she breaks contact. She runs toward the nearest treeline and takes cover. The short guard grunts as he swings his sword. A cool breeze rushes past my face as the metal slices the air. He grunts again with each jab in my direction. My agility allows me to dodge his attacks. Left, right, left again. He's a horrible fighter, giving away all his movements with his sour breath.

I glimpse at Aiden. He's bleeding from his arm. I can't tell how badly he's injured, but he continues to fight the other guard with a relentlessness I've never seen on him.

I duck under the guard's sword and land a punch to his side. He stumbles backward, nearly losing his hold of his weapon. As I advance on him, I keep the tip of the blade in my sights. The guard finds his footing, grasps the hilt with both hands, growls, then raises it above his head. I strike, my fist connecting with his jaw before he has a chance to swing the sword. The impact causes him to fall to the side with a furious groan. The sword lands with a thud on the ground a couple of feet from him. My eyes dart from the blade to him. He claws at the ground and manages to roll over onto his hands and knees. I hurry over to the sword and scoop it into my hand, the texture of the hilt caressing my palm. I stalk toward him. The bottom of my boot finds his balding head, and he collapses onto the ground, his yelling muffled by a mouthful of dirt.

I've thought about this moment before. I've fantasized about what it'd be like to silence a guard's life. A slow smile crawls on my lips. I touch the tip of the sword to the middle of his back, poking gently along his spine until I find a soft spot. I settle on the area where his heart would be—if he had one—and drive it in. I'm swift and the blade is sharp. There's no tension as the metal passes through his thick leather uniform and the ruggedness of his skin. He writhes, clinging to whatever life he has left in these few seconds. I put my foot on his back and wait for his body to still.

There. Silence.

I withdraw the sword and look up as Aiden approaches, breathless, leaving another dead guard behind him. He nods. I roll the man over and pull back his cloak, granting me access to the two knives he has holstered to his belt. Each blade is inscribed with a delicate scroll pattern. Beautiful weaponry for a deadly cause. I slide the knives into my own belt and use the man's cloak to clean his blood from the sword.

"You okay?" I ask Aiden, eyeing the wound on his shoulder.

"Yeah. Looks worse than it is." He looks over to where Leona is standing. "It's safe now."

She has one hand pressed against the tree and the other wrapped around her stomach. She treads slowly from the cover of the trees to the trail. Her face pales as she looks in horror at the two dead bodies lying in the middle of the road.

She swallows, hard. "We can't just leave them there."

She's right. Dead guards lead to questions, questions we're still working out the answers to. I look around for a good spot to hide them and find a pile of thick brush several meters off the road. Options are limited. It'll have to do.

"Come on." I nod toward the brush and Aiden helps me conceal the bodies.

"We need to get going before any more come through." Aiden looks back and forth along the road.

"Yeah, we're almost there. But first—" I slide one of the knives from my belt and hold it out to Leona. She raises an eyebrow and reluctantly takes the dagger. "You need it," I say, casting off her uncertainty. "Have you ever used one before?"

She blinks and I take that as a no.

"It's really easy. Just put the sharp pointy end into their body and twist."

She rolls her eyes and scoffs. "Oh, is that all?" Her eyes are concentrated on mine as she tucks the blade under the thin gold chain around her waist. "I'll keep that in mind, *brother*."

I fight back the urge to smile, but a grin gets the better of me. Her stern eyes soften, and she brushes between Aiden and I, taking long steps toward our destination.

A panicked breath chills my lungs. I'm almost home. An ache throbs my head and I suck in air through my teeth. I rub my eyes with the back of the hand, easing the tension in my skull, but it doesn't do much for the heaviness in my chest. I'm not the same person I was when

I was taken away in the night. I'm a little more older. More wiser. More darker.

Colton

Chapter 14

The familiar scent of sweet honey and smoke welcome me home as we pass the weather-worn sign leading to Maburh. Arching branches of young leaves with open buds line the road. The owls above hoot softly, their eyes tracking our every move. A chipmunk dashes in front of us, desperate to make it to safety before becoming a late-night snack.

We enter the village and walk down the winding path between the houses. I feel like a stranger, a tourist seeing the unique homes for the first time. The wooden columns on the porches are inscribed with fancy scroll work. Between the designs are sentimental phrases the residents etched in as recognition of values. Each house whispers the personality of the family that lives inside.

"It's quiet here," Leona says as she looks around. The moonlight bounces off her skin, giving her a cool-toned glow.

"Most people retire once the sun sets." I lead them through the village square. Only four street lamps illuminate the area, casting long shadows from the stone well in the center. By morning, the square will be bustling with people as they socialize and trade their wares.

We pass the postal tower, set adjoined to the meeting hall. A falcon dives in through the port at the top of the spire, where a waiting keeper will untie the correspondence from the bird's leg and deliver it to its recipient in the morning.

As we continue away from the square and toward more houses, a door bursts open and a woman runs out. I turn my head and recognize her as Culima. Visually, she hasn't changed much in the past year. She meets us in the middle of the path.

"Colt? Is that you?" Culima asks. "Oh, my goodness!"

Her voice is as shrill as I remember it. I offer a weak smile as she wraps her arms around me. The pale moon casts shadows onto her face, deepening the fine lines around her eyes and mouth. She releases me from the embrace and keeps her hands on my shoulders, looking down the path we just traveled.

"Is Geoffrey with you?" she asks, her eyes round with desperation. "He hasn't made it back yet."

My gaze lowers from hers. Heat flushes my cheeks, and I'm grateful for the lighting of the night. How do I tell her that her son isn't coming home? That a boy of only twelve years not only died in the arena, but that it was by my hand that his life was ended? My throat goes dry, and I scramble for words.

"No, sorry," I say, "I haven't seen him either." Her hopeful smile drops from my disappointing words. "I'm sure he'll be home soon, though." I shouldn't lie but the grief on her face pulls at the strings of my heart—one good yank and it'll collapse.

She smiles and touches a hand to my cheek. "Thank you. You're a good man. Now, you should get home. Your parents'll be thrilled to see you."

We walk away, leaving Culima standing on the path, looking downwind in anticipation for her little boy who won't be coming.

My heart thrashes against constricted lungs. That was much harder than I could have imagined it to be. I should've told her the truth. A shiver overwhelms my skin and stops my feet from moving. I double over, my lungs burning with the need to breathe, my nails digging into my kneecaps. A tender hand touches my shoulder.

"Are you all right?" Leona asks. She keeps her hold on my shoulder until I pull myself upright.

I look toward Culima then back to Leona. "I lied. Her son's not coming home."

"Well, he could, right?" Leona says softly. "I mean, it took us some time to get here. Maybe he's on his way—"

"He was killed in the fights." Aiden regards me with a look of comprehension.

I look at him and nod. "By me."

I don't wait for another response from her. She wouldn't understand. The threat of darkness looms over my head, and the quicker I make it home, the safer everyone will be. I take off down the path.

Leona and Aiden's footsteps are in sync behind me. A murmur of conversation passes between them, but I keep my focus ahead of me. Around the bend, the familiar sight of my mother's tiger lilies on the porch slows my pace. I stop in front of my house, take a breath, and climb the short flight of steps. My hand runs over the splintered wood of the door frame, the aftermath of when the guards made forced entry. Pa probably would've needed my help to fix it. I drop my head down and sigh, recalling the memories of that night.

The loud boom shook me awake, and my eyes were barely adjusted before I was dragged out of the house. The screams of my mother pierced my ears, the sound of torture lacing her voice as she cried for my innocence. That night, I was arrested for the rape of a woman whom I'd never laid eyes on. *'She was the wife of a duke,'* they said. When I'd asked the name of the woman whom I allegedly assaulted, the only answer I received was the swift blow of a guard's fist against my head.

I knock on the door and turn around as I wait. Aiden shoves his hand into his pockets and Leona looks on with uncertainty.

The door creaks open. I keep my face turned away, afraid to see who answers. Is it Ma? With her deep chestnut hair streaked with gray, a new strand for each new stress. Or could it be Pa? A man of very few words, but plenty of heart.

"My boy!" Ma says.

I stiffen as I turn toward her, but when my eyes find hers, I fall into her embrace. She smells of primrose just as I remember. My eyes burn and I blink back tears before they have a chance to fall.

"Roland!" she calls into the house. "Come quick!" She takes my face in her hands, examining me from side to side, as though I may be an illusion. Then, she lifts on her toes and kisses my forehead. The moon's light reveals thick tears as they roll down her cheeks.

"My goodness..."

The deep voice of my father croons in my ears. Ma releases me and I step toward him. I stand still for a moment, face to face with the man who taught me how to be. The man who took a chance on me when Ma brought me home as a lost child.

His cane falls to the floor with a hollow thud and he pulls me close. He has never been one to show such gestures, but in this moment, nothing else exists.

Ma catches a look at my companions.

"Come, come," she says, dabbing her eyes with her apron. "You all must be hungry. There's soup on the fire."

Aiden's face lights up at the promise of a hot meal. He leaps up the steps and pauses in front of Ma. "I'm Aiden," he says. She stretches up and kisses both his cheeks, the customary greeting of welcome.

"Geneva. It's very nice to meet you, Aiden." She purses her lips, noticing the wound on his shoulder. "Not to worry, I'll patch that right up."

As Leona approaches, her eyes are low, and her hands are clasped in front of her. She straightens up, removing the hesitation from her stature. "My name is—"

"Oh, I know who you are," Ma says, bowing her head. "You are the spitting image of your mother." She pulls Leona into a hug, holding her close. "Thank you for saving my son, Your Majesty."

Leona looks at me with unease. Her arms are stiff at her side until finally she relaxes them enough to return the gesture.

"So, if you're here, who's on the throne now?" Pa tears a chunk from the loaf and bites into it.

Leona rests her spoon inside of her bowl. "I'm not sure. It's likely either the Lord Commander or the War Master. Both seem to have the most to gain from the coup."

Ma wrinkles her nose and pauses from refilling our cups with ale. "Weren't you courting the Lord Commander?"

The dining room grinds to a halt. I lower my spoon from my mouth, mid-bite, and glance over at Leona. This is news to me. My time in the dungeons has kept me from staying on top of current relations—not that I subscribe to gossip, anyway.

All eyes are on her as we wait for her to respond. She sweeps a loose ribbon of hair behind her ear and darts her eyes to mine. A pang strikes in the pit of my stomach. Of course, she'd be courting someone of noble blood. I'd be a fool to think otherwise.

"I had no intention of pursuing a union with him. The courtship was pushed on me when I ascended," she says, her voice trailing off.

"Did he at least present an honorable proposal?"

"Ma…" My eyes widen at my mother's boldness.

Leona gives a tentative smile and stares at the soup in her bowl. "Actually, the Council called for a meeting, they told me I needed to marry Aerok, and I went along with it."

Aiden's mouth falls open. "That sounds… horrible."

"I always felt something wasn't right about it." Leona's foot bounces under the table. The vibrations travel the short distance to my feet as I sit next to her.

"I never liked that man." Pa pops another piece of bread into his mouth. "His fingernails are too clean. You can't trust a man who doesn't get his hands dirty."

Leona's lips tug into a smile. I appreciate that about Pa. Even after a long day when nothing seemed to go right, he could always make me forget my troubles with a few daring words.

"Would anyone like more?" Ma asks, walking over to the hearth. The hearty soup's aroma lingers in the air, even after most of our bowls are empty.

"No, thank you," Leona says. "It was very delicious, though."

Aiden chimes in agreement. Shamelessly, he already had a second helping and probably would've gone for a third if the waistline of his pants could handle it.

I cross my arms, my elbows resting over the table, and lean in toward Pa. "Has Kaleo returned?"

Pa dabs his mouth with a cloth napkin, balls it up in his hands, then tosses it into the empty bread basket.

"He's probably down at the shore. Why? What's going on?"

I look over to Leona. "We just have something we want to ask him."

He looks at me skeptically with an eyebrow raised. Ma returns to the table and stands behind him.

"We just got you back, Colton. Is everything all right?" she asks.

I open my mouth to explain the situation, but Leona beats me to it.

"I'm taking back my throne," she says decisively. "So, I'm going to ask for his and the others' help in doing so."

Pa leans back in his chair and crosses his arms over his chest. He scans Leona's face for a moment, as though he's gauging her resolve. Leona holds her own, her eyes never wavering from his. Impressive. My father is known to have very intimidating glares.

Finally, he smiles.

"Then, you, Your Majesty, will be a force to be reckoned with."

Leona

Chapter 15

"Are you nervous?" Colton grins as he leads me to the shores.

His hair swings in loose waves above his shoulder, still damp from the bath. He trimmed much of his beard down, so it lays closer to his jaw. Although my own skin and hair are clean, my shabby gown still hangs from my body.

"Nervous? Of course, not..." I try—and fail—to bite back my sarcasm. "I mean, it's not like the future of my kingdom is at stake here with a simple question."

It's anything but a simple question, however. I'll be asking these people to risk their freedom, their lives for me. And although I am their rightful queen, I am not all right demanding that of them without offering a choice.

"Who is it again I need to speak to?"

"His name is Kaleo," Colton says. "He's sort of our unofficial village leader."

"Wasn't he taken prisoner as well? Who took care of the village while he was away?"

"Probably his wife. They're alike in many ways."

As we near the shore, the hum of the villagers and the crash of the waves grow louder. Over the peak of a hill, the bright orange glow of a bonfire crackles. Many people dance and cheer to the sound of drums echoing in the night.

I look to Colton once more, and he smiles on confidently as though I have nothing to worry about. Oh, how I wish that were true. Part of me feels vulnerable. I'm an outsider. These people don't know me, and they probably hold the same opinion of me that Colton did.

The music and singing dies down when they notice us approaching. They stare at us with eyes full of fascination.

I wonder, for a moment, how recognizable I am. The last commissioned portrait of myself was done in my youth, and I've hardly made myself available enough for villagers to remember my face. Then again, Colton's mother knew who I was easily enough. Visiting the villages was one of Mother's favorite things to do. As massive as the castle is, it can feel quite cramped from lacking sincere human-contact.

I let Colton lead me to one of the large clusters of people sitting around the fire pit. We pause at a burly man with a piece of straw hanging from his mouth. He stands and removes the straw, flicking it aside.

"I see you finally made it back," he says to Colton. He holds out his arm and Colton grips his hand around Kaleo's forearm while he does the same.

"Yeah. Good to see you in one piece." Colton releases his grip.

Kaleo nods and drops his dark eyes to mine.

"This is—" Colton starts to say.

"Queen Leona," Kaleo finishes. "Of course. An honor to finally meet you. Though… you're a bit far from the castle, no? Can't imagine you'd travel all this way to try our pheasant." He bursts out in an exuberant laugh, one that resonates in his chest. "Where are my manners? I am Kaleo Doriar." He bows his head slightly.

"It's a pleasure to meet you as well. And… that's why I'm here. I've come to ask you—well, all of you—for help."

"Help with?"

"Taking back the castle."

Kaleo shifts his stance and crosses his arms over his chest. He tilts his head. A blotch of raised skin on his neck catches in the firelight, surely a reminder of darker days as a gladiator. His eyes level with mine and he studies me.

"You lost it?" he asks. "As in, was overthrown?"

I'm quiet and maintain his gaze. He takes my silence as confirmation and exhales deeply.

"Forgive me for interrupting your celebration." I glance at the other men surrounding Kaleo. "I know that many of you have been away from your family for far too long and all you want is a night of peace." My focus lands back on Kaleo. "But, with your permission, I'd like to speak to them all, pose the question, and give them a choice in the matter."

The orange glow of the fire reflects in Kaleo's eyes and for a moment, he doesn't blink. The sharp angles of his jaw are obscured by the shagginess of his graying facial hair. He rubs his fingertips against the scruff on his chin.

"You really think you can take back the throne?" he finally says.

"With all of your help, yes."

His eyes linger on mine for another moment. Then, he turns to the other villagers and whistles, calling them all to attention.

"Gather 'round, everybody."

A tingly sensation radiates in my hands. I find my fingers interlocked in front of me, the blood circulation at the tips in jeopardy. I relax my hands and force them at my sides.

People move across the sands and form a huddle around us. Murmurs of confusion bounce from all edges of the crowd. When the stirring settles, Kaleo says, "Have at it, Your Majesty."

I straighten my spine and lift my chin. A strong breeze passes over the water and whips strands of loose hair across my face. The fire beyond rises for a second, licking the air in kind.

"I'm guessing most of you already know who I am." I pause and glance around at the nodding heads. "Yesterday, I made the decision to end the prisoner fights and free those who were detained. But in doing so, I lost my throne to the same people who swore their allegiance to me. I've come to you to ask for your help in getting it back."

Hushed voices spread in the crowd. The people exchange looks with one another. Their jaws clench and worry creases their foreheads.

I hold up a hand to calm the muttering. "Now, let me make it very clear that none of you should feel forced into this. This is your decision and your decision alone. I won't press you to stand with me, but should you choose to, please understand the risk that will come along with it." Their eyes remain attentive to my words. "I've only recently learned of the transgressions of my court. I hope you can forgive me for placing my faith in a system I regarded as having the country's best interests in mind. I want to do better—be better than the previous rulers and their dynasties, but I can't do that while my reign remains in the hands of those who don't deserve it."

I take a step back from the center of the circle and stand next to Colton. The murmurs resume, much louder now.

"Nicely done," Colton says.

I bite my lip and nod, not quite convinced that my words were enough.

Kaleo moves to face me and folds his hands in front of him. "Give us a moment to talk it over, yes?"

"Of course." I turn and walk up the shore, stopping once the crowd's voices turn to a muted buzz. Colton follows.

I look past the villagers as they deliberate and aim my attention to the ocean. The moon reflects against the water, a channel of light flanked by darkness.

"They're not going to agree. There was reluctance on their faces." I peer at them, the glow of the fire casting a golden hue on their backs.

Colton shakes his head. "It was a lot to take in. We've never had a civil war before. You just have to give them time to process it."

I turn away from him and drop my gaze to the ground. Pearlescent seashells litter the sand, each one sparkling under the moonlight. "It's an insane idea that could possibly get more people killed." A cold shudder finds my body once more. I wrap my arms around my stomach, desperate to calm the uneasiness.

"Ne reka mora rediti sum kumu—"

"Jos vi rekan ni mor ir kezdet." I spin around, my hair slapping against the wind. My eyebrow raises. "That's a Daolic proverb. Where did you learn it from?"

He opens his mouth to speak then shuts it. His eyes shift subtly. "Just something I picked up," he finally says. "My point is, all great things start somewhere. This will be your start. You might not be able to fix all the past wrongs of the kingdom, but you can make sure our future is better than it would've been."

"If this doesn't work out, it's not too late for me to run away to Braer."

He laughs. "And what would you do over there?"

I look skyward at the moon hanging heavily in the distance. "I don't know. Become a barmaid? Have a normal person job with normal people problems?"

I drop my chin and regard Colton. A smile inches along his lips.

"And how do you plan on getting there with thousands of miles of water between us?"

I shrug. "How hard is it to stowaway on a boat?"

He tilts his head and leans backward. "What makes you think I would know?"

A giggle loosens my nerves. "Well, your Daolic accent was too perfect for it to be *just something you picked up—*"

"Excuse me, Your Majesty," Kaleo says as he approaches. "We've discussed it."

The joy on my face quickly fades into apprehension. This is it.

Kaleo's face displays no emotion. "Many of them have fears about the magnitude of the situation. The stakes here will be greater than anything we've encountered in the past." My hands go limp at my sides, but he continues. "You did right by us, so we'll do right by you. Have you got a plan?"

My jaw drops and I glance at Colton, then back to Kaleo. A flurry of emotions hover in my mind. I clear my throat in hopes of finding clarity, but it doesn't work. "Honestly, I hadn't thought that far ahead. I wasn't expecting you all to agree."

Kaleo laughs his hearty laugh. "Lucky for you, Your Majesty, you've got a couple of strategists on your side now. Come. Let's talk further."

We hash out the details in a large meeting cabin next to the church. Some of the men's suggestions are impressive, and I think how my council could've been enhanced if I had their wits under my advisement. An hour later, we smooth out a jagged-edged plan into something that bears resemblance to a certain victory. Still, it's easier said than done.

There are seven other villages in the kingdom. If they all choose to support me as Maburh has, I'll have the numbers to go against the guards in Demesne.

Back at the beach, I find a bare seat near the bonfire and sit with my eyes closed. The heat from the flames tickles my face. The blended scents of smoldering wood and oceanic breeze swirl around me. I breathe it in deeply, trying to somehow harness the moment, freeze the feeling of being here on this beach with people who celebrate life. I keep my eyes shut and listen. The laughter of children carries on the waves, sprinkling an airiness to the deep bellows of the drums. Conversations, each tinted in joy, come from every which way as loved ones catch each other up on the time lost.

"Mind if I sit?"

I open my eyes to find Aiden standing in front of me. I scoot over to make room for him on the bench. "Where have you been?"

"I just had some things to take care of."

"Is everything all right?"

"Yes, all good." His lip twitches as he gazes blankly at the fire.

I lean over to him. "You're very secretive, do you know that?"

Aiden grins but stays silent. As we sit at the fire, I notice a group, four women, looking at me from across the shore. I hold their gaze for a moment before breaking it and turning my attention back to the quiet man beside me.

"Did you hear? The plan's in motion to rally the villages. Colton's with Kaleo to send falcons to them right now."

He smiles. "I passed him on the way here. One step closer to getting you back on the throne, yeah?"

I catch the women looking at me again. "I know the men are on-board with this, but I'm starting to think the wives aren't."

"What do you mean?"

I nod toward the group. "They keep staring at me."

Aiden looks in their direction as well. "Have they said anything?"

"Not yet, but if looks could kill…"

"Why don't you just go talk to them?"

I shoot him an irritated glance, but he doesn't see it. "I feel out of my element here, like I'm trespassing on a tight-knit community."

"But this is your community as well. You're the queen, so—"

"I know, I know—It's just hard to explain." I grow quiet and take a moment to think. "I haven't been conditioned for life outside the castle walls. I was never taught what is means to work hard and acquire your own success. Everything I had was provided for me. So, to see these women and men contribute so much to their families, to know that every hard day's work means something, that's a strength not even the finest tutors could've taught me."

Aiden nods silently and reaches down between his feet to pick up a twig. He absentmindedly rolls it between his fingers. "What was it like—growing up royal?"

I look at him, hoping to find the simplest answer in his eyes. "It was… lonely."

"Why weren't there any siblings?"

My mind drifts to many years earlier when Mother was pregnant with my brother. She and Father had been so excited to bring a son into this world. Although I was older, that wouldn't have tarnished the fact that Father would've finally had a male heir to his throne. I'm sure he would've found some way of bypassing my claim onto little brother's.

All that hope, that joy, came crashing down when little brother was born sleeping. No heartbeat. No first breath. A young prince's life ended before it began. For a time, Father hated Mother, despised her for failing to produce anymore heirs. He had me, but I wasn't enough, for I was not male. It was strange, a reigning king and queen with only one surviving heir.

"I'm sure you've heard the rumors…?" I answer, looking sidelong at him. For a while, the kingdom was abuzz with malicious words of my mother. Stories spun of fact and fiction woven through the streets, although no one would ever dare to say them to her face.

He bites his lip, probably now unsure of the direction of the conversation.

"It's all right," I say, reassuring him. "She's no longer here and it's no longer relevant."

A long pause between us is filled with intermittent bouts of cheers as the celebration continues. A blanket of twinkling lights covers the sky, their brightness paling in comparison to the moon. Aiden and I continue to sit in silence for a moment longer.

"I'm an only child, too," he says, his voice startling me. "My mother died during childbirth with me."

I glance at him. His eyes are straight ahead. There's no emotion behind his words.

"I'm sorry. But your father is still alive and well?"

He hesitates. I fear he will retreat behind the wall he has so clearly guarded himself with. He takes a breath to calculate his thoughts.

"I wouldn't know. My father refuses to acknowledge me. I've been told that I resemble my mother and that frustrates him."

I shake my head. "What an awful man." I know firsthand how it feels to be a disappointment to a father. "To be born with a burden — we have that in common, you and I."

Aiden's lips turn up into a slight smile, but he says nothing more.

Children, two little boys and a girl dash around us, chasing each other under the stars. The girl's light-colored ringlets bounce with each step. As she runs, a tattered doll flies out of her hands and lands at my feet. In the boys' pursuit, she doesn't realize she's lost her companion and continues running. I pick the doll up and brush sand from its body. The children run across the beach straight toward the group of women who were looking at me earlier.

"I'll be right back," I murmur to Aiden.

The women grow quiet and bow their heads gingerly when I approach. The little girl with the ringlets hides behind one of the women's legs and peeks to see her doll in my hands.

"I believe she dropped this." I hold the doll out to whom I assume is the girl's mother. The woman is tall, with a slender neck that makes her stature all the more graceful.

"Thank you, Your Majesty."

I offer a kind smile and nod, then turn to walk back to the other side of the beach.

"Um, Your Majesty?"

I glance back toward the woman. The doll in her arms is now replaced with a garment.

"We wanted to offer you a clean dress to wear, but we weren't sure if the quality would be to your liking." She says the words cautiously as though I may take offense.

I smile and point at the clothes in her hands. She nods.

I lift and hold it against my body. The indigo dress cascades in front of me and sweeps over the tops of my feet. Great care had been taken in the detailed stitch work. I smile, probably more than the women expected. "It's lovely. You're all very kind. Thank you."

For the first time in a long while, I've felt courtesy with no ulterior motives attached. It makes me resent ever being born a D'Auron in the first place. There's another world out here that isn't stitched together with false truths and deceptions. Their adage whispers in my mind. *My brother is my shield, and I am his armor.* When I look at these people, I see not only my subjects, but also people that I'm sworn to protect.

And I *will* protect them.

Colton

Chapter 16

When the last of the falcons have been sent out, Kaleo and I return to the shore, the liveliness dying down as night creeps onward. Mothers escort their young ones home. Sleep weighs heavily on their eyelids, and through deep yawns from tiny mouths, they beg their mothers for more time at festivities.

Kaleo nods once at his wife, Maera, as she passes. Curly hair drapes over her shoulder as she carries their drowsy daughter, a doll clutched tightly under the small girl's arm.

They exchange a tender glance, and for a moment, I am in awe of their love for each other. It seems easy, almost effortless, to give love and receive it back. I used to think it was possible for me. Now, there's a dark stain on my life that keeps me from forming the bonds necessary for love to blossom. Despite the illusions I portray of a happy man, there's something dark inside me. I lost a part of myself in the arena—a piece of me that got dragged down to the underworld when the arena grounds cracked open and shadowed phantoms clawed at my soul.

I turn to face Kaleo beside me on the bench. "How do you do it?"

"Do what?"

"How do you not let what happened in the arena affect you?"

His eyes soften and he takes a moment to study my face. He rubs his knuckles against his jaw. "What makes you think it doesn't affect me?"

I look toward his wife, who has almost disappeared from view. I meet his eyes again. "You just seem calm and still sure of yourself."

He chuckles, mainly to himself. My face warms, a bit embarrassed of my question.

"Truth is, it has affected me. But in my position around here, I don't have the luxury of running around like a hen with my head cut off."

"No, no—yeah, I get that…" I glance down at the sand in front of me, and he touches my shoulder.

"How are you doing?" There's an immense concern in his voice.

I lift my chin and hold his gaze. Part of me wants to unload my pain onto him, but to do so would be selfish of me. So, I keep my mouth—and my emotions—shut, and elect to change the subject instead.

"Have you spoken to Phylix's widow yet?"

He sighs, accepting that I won't be disclosing my own personal problems. "I sat down with her earlier. She mentioned that she'd already come to terms with the fact that he probably wouldn't make it out of the arena. But to be told for certain that he wouldn't be coming home, she took the news as hard as can be expected. She's been in the church ever since."

I nod silently. Phylix was such a kind man, never one to raise his voice even during times of stress. He worked twice as hard to support his wife and four children, even sometimes skipped a meal to make sure his family didn't go to sleep hungry. My heart aches for his widow, at the hole his death will leave behind.

I look out across the water and watch as the waves crash against one another before calming into a gentle blanket. The moon's pull on the ocean brings it up the shore, and people laugh as the cool water covers their feet, their soles sinking deeper into the sand. I find myself grinning at their happiness.

The people seated with me begin to stir and I look back to see the fuss.

"Your Majesty," they all greet in unison and bow their heads.

My eyes land on Leona's, and I quickly drop my head into a bow as well, caught off guard by her sudden appearance.

She smiles and nods once, maintaining her gaze on me. "Could I speak with you?" She keeps a casual tone.

Kaleo shoots me a look of deviousness as he pulls his mug of ale to his mouth and takes a sip. I rise and follow

Leona toward the water, away from the men I'd been sitting with. She slows her pace to allow me to catch up. A different dress covers her body. The bottom hem of it glides over the sand behind her.

"New dress?" I ask, taking in her appearance from head to toe. She eyes me with a gentle grin, and my gaze darts away, suddenly ashamed to be looking her over so thoroughly.

She nods. "Yes. Some of the women were kind enough to give me a new one. My other gown was torn to shreds, though I'm sure you've noticed?"

My face turns warm again. I'm grateful she can't see me blushing in the darkness. I wondered when she'd mention our previous interaction near the stream. Still, she doesn't seem offended.

I clear my throat, hoping to squash any embarrassment from my voice. "Well, this new one looks nice on you," I manage to say.

She pauses and turns to face me. The moon captures her light eyes, making them seem even brighter in the night. There's a seriousness to them as she holds my gaze with urgency. I'm unsure why she's brought me down here, so I wait for her to speak.

"I wanted to say thank you for all you've done to help me thus far."

I release a breath, a breath that I'd been holding onto for the past few seconds. Air inflates my lungs in a rush of energy.

"I know we didn't start off on the right foot, but I do appreciate that you have my back."

I nod, the only thing I can do in this moment of humility. I search my throat for words. "You're welcome."

She smiles, then her softened eyes harden. "I do have a favor to ask you, though."

I bite the inside of my cheek. "What is it?"

"Teach me how to fight."

I take a step backward and survey her face. Her stone expression doesn't change. She's serious.

"Teach you how to fight?" I repeat back to her, somehow hoping I'd heard her wrong. She nods her head in agreement.

I blow out a sharp breath and cross my arms over my chest. The way I fight is borderline savagery. No mercy. No restraints. Practice or not, I could hurt her.

"Are you sure you don't want Aiden to teach you?"

"I'm asking you." There's a finality to her response.

I look back toward the people further up the shore, their voices a hum in the air at this distance. My eyes return to hers. "Why do you want to learn? You have a whole cast of able men—and there'll be even more once the messages reach the other villages."

There's a fierceness in her eyes tonight, laced with something sad. She stands before me, her head held high, her stance regal, and for the first time, I see her as the queen she is. She draws her strength from the support of those around her. A queen without a kingdom is just a girl with a shiny headpiece.

Her eyes stay concentrated on mine. "I don't want to be defenseless anymore."

A cool breeze wraps around us, bringing with it the light scent in her hair. She shudders.

"Okay." I drop my arms and fold my hands behind my back. A smirk rises in her lips, but vanishes just as quickly as it comes. "I'll show you basic moves. Do you still have your dagger?"

She reaches down to the thin belt around her waist and pulls out the blade. Her fingers wrap around it with care. I shift the knife in her hand until it is pointed downward, and her fingers are choking the handle. She watches, curiously, until I'm happy with her grip.

I circle around so I'm standing behind her. My hand moves to close around hers, but then I pause. "May I?" She nods, her head inches away from my face.

I step forward and dismiss the remaining distance between us. The heat from her back warms my chest, calming the raging storms building in my mind. My hand covers hers and I guide the dagger in a fluid motion up and across her body. She staggers, and without thinking, my free hand flies to her waist, stabilizing her body. In doing so, I pull her closer to me and our bodies press together. I release her immediately. "Sorry," I mutter.

She turns to face me with neutral eyes. She doesn't seem bothered by my slip-up. Her fingers flex over the handle. "Let's try again." She turns back around.

I take my spot behind her once more, this time careful of my movements, of my hand placements on her body. I feel a strange pull toward her, a feeling that I haven't felt even before my arrest. Maybe it's genetics and the emotions swirling around in my head aren't there. But for sure, I know this isn't the time nor place to dwell on such urges.

We continue to practice with the dagger until she's comfortable with holding and using it. Unassisted, she now knows how to wound a man with a sharp stab to the throat. Her form is perfect in theory, but I hope the day never comes when she'll need to put her dagger to use.

The moon drifts across the sky, casting long shadows against the sands. Much of the celebration has died down. A few people dot the shores as they revel in each other's company. In a quiet corner of the beach, with the forest at our backs, I continue to train Leona. This time, in hand to hand combat.

"Keep your hands up," I remind her. I lunge forward with muted speed and extend a fist toward her head. As expected, she dips to the side and quickly recovers into an assailing posture. "Good. Quicker now, and watch your angles."

She nods and her eyes focus on my entire body as she uses all sides of her vision to her advantage. She's picked up the moves with ease, and for a moment, I forget she's a noble girl.

I swing my foot out so that it swipes under her. She jumps and lands shakily onto the uneven sandy ground. Her lips turn upward into a smile that reaches her eyes, but she keeps her focus. I throw punches at her, one after the other, keeping my movements random. I take great care not to lose control and strike too fast. For months, I've used these motions to hurt—to kill—so to simply be sparring, it's confusing my muscle memory.

Her face is slick with sweat. Stray hairs stick to her forehead, jeopardizing her view. She pushes the hair away with the back of her hand and drops back into a defensive stance, ready for more.

I lunge at her again. Her fist reaches out too far and makes contact with my jaw. I stumble backward. She gasps and her eyes widen.

"I'm sorry!" she says, rushing to my side. "Are you all right?"

I open and shut my mouth, easing the slight throbbing in my jaw. My hand reaches up to the spot where she punched me. The level of worry on her face encourages me to massage my jawline tenderly and twist my face into one in pain.

"Oww...." I groan.

Even in the dim lighting, the color drains from her face.

"Let me see." She lifts her hand and removes mine from my jaw, giving her a clear look at her damage.

When there's no wound to be found, she looks into my eyes, confused. I try to stifle a laugh, but it squeezes through and fills the air. She lightly shoves me in my chest, then finds herself laughing as well.

"So, you're okay?" she asks when the laughter settles.

I grin. "You have the speed, yes, but you're not quite there on your strength yet."

She beams, no doubt proud of her improvement in agility. She's worked hard over this past hour or so, soaking in all I've taught her. She's a good student, and I know she'll be a good queen.

Something catches my eye in the treeline behind us. A light winks as though the moon is reflecting off of something metallic. I narrow my eyes and make out a shadow moving between the trees.

Leona lifts her damp hair from the back of her neck and lets the cool breeze reach her shoulder blades. "Do you want to keep pract—"

"Down!" I grab her shoulders and force her to the sand. The top of my arm burns. My heart pounds against Leona's as we lay chest to chest, my body covering hers like a blanket. I jerk my eyes back toward the forest.

Someone's attacking.

Leona

Chapter 17

My mind is racing, running closely behind the pace of my heartbeat. The moment is a blur. One second, I'm standing, and the next, I'm lying against the sands under Colton's body. My hands still clutch his shirt from the fall.

"Are you okay?" he breathes.

I nod frantically, unsure of what just happened. His eyes leave mine and gaze beyond us. I shift my head to see what he's looking at.

"Shit…" he growls.

He holds onto my body as he rolls us sideways over the sand, five, six times, until we near a large boulder. When we stop, I look back to our starting point as arrows rain down, stabbing the earth where our bodies once lied.

Behind the boulder, sharp pinging sounds ring out from what I can only assume are more arrows hitting the rock. Colton and I stay crouched down on the other side. He's breathing fast, his head turning as he looks for any other attackers. I keep my eyes on him, afraid to look elsewhere. There's a gash on his arm. Blood flows in a thin river down his skin.

"Your arm," I whisper. "You're bleeding."

He pulls his view from the survey and drops it to his shoulder, pulling his arm toward his center for a better look. "Just a graze." His eyes meet mine when arrows no longer hit the rock. "Stay here and stay down, okay? I'll be right back."

Before I have a chance to argue, he turns toward the village and lets out a call that echoes in the night. I flinch. In a chorus, other people respond by mimicking the sound.

"North woods! North woods!" Colton calls out as the others, maybe seven or eight men, run toward us. A gust of wind blows my hair off my shoulder, leaving my bare skin exposed. I look and Colton is no longer by my side. Recalling his words, I keep low and peek around the edge of the boulder. At the head of the group, Colton's outline dashes past the treeline. Their yelling becomes distant as they venture further into the woods.

When I no longer see them, the reality of my lonesomeness sets in. I shudder and press my back against the rock. Remembering my dagger, I pull it from my belt and clutch it tightly.

I look back and forth within my scope of vision. If there's anyone else out there, I'm going to be ready for them this time. At least, I hope. Colton has taught me well, thus far, but with only one lesson under my belt, I'm nowhere near ready to down a man.

The minutes drag on. I focus on my breathing and look out into the ocean. The moon reflects on the water, along with the countless stars that dot the sky. The water is a dark blanket that stretches as far as my eyes can see. I've never been this close to the ocean before. Of all the luxuries that was afforded to me during my life, spending time on the shore was never one of them. How amazing, it must have been, for Colton to grow up in a place where the sea breeze wakes him up every morning.

My cheeks warm at the thought of him. He was impressive tonight. I can still feel his hands on me as he pressed against my body, shielding me from danger. It felt… intimate. Though, I could be imagining things. Perhaps he was only protecting his queen.

I've seen the way he looks at me, caught him when his gaze lingers a moment too long. I don't bring attention to it, despite my deepest desires. I'm an ousted queen on the journey to reclaiming my throne. Romance will be a distraction.

I shake my head, pushing the thoughts from my mind. My eyes close and I exhale slowly. When something touches my shoulder, I gasp. My eyes snap open, and reflexively, I swing the dagger in the direction of the intruder. My wrist is caught in mid-air. I follow the hand gripping me up its arm until my eyes land on Colton's. He's crouched at my side.

I exhale again and shoot him an annoyed glare. "I could've killed you."

He releases my wrist, grinning. "Maybe you could've if I was blindfolded with bound hands while drunk and already on the verge of death."

I roll my eyes and put my dagger away. He rises and extends a hand to help me up. I quickly look him over. No additional injuries.

"So," I say, "is it safe?"

He crosses his arms in front of him and sighs. "We've caught the attacker." He nods toward the village. "Come."

I follow him up the beach. An uneasiness burrows a pit in my stomach as he leads me to the unknown.

"Who was it?"

He looks down at me as we walk, our footsteps in sync with one another. "A man. No one recognizes him and he's refusing to answer any questions."

"Was he alone?"

"As far as we know, yes. We have people keeping an eye on the woods just in case he has any friends still out there."

I nod. The uneasiness fades gradually but is still ever present. We're quiet for the moment. A nagging feeling pulls at my thoughts with words begging to be said. "Thank you," I say, simply.

He flinches his head back slightly. "For what?"

"I would've been dead if it weren't for you."

He stops walking and I stop with him. He looks at me, his light eyes appearing darker in the night. "Rule one of village life—you never have to thank me for protecting you."

I gaze up at him, trying to find any underlying humor on his face. There's none. My appreciation of him grows deeper.

"But," he says, resuming his walk, "you're welcome." He winks at me. I smile and hurry alongside him.

He leads us to the village square. Torches now surround the area, their cadenced flicker making the moment even more ominous. A crowd has gathered. Those in their homes must have come out at the sound of the chaos. They all look at Colton and I as we approach. The crowd splits to let us through.

In the middle, a man sits on his knees. His wrists and ankles are bound with rope. In the torchlight, his tawny hair is a reddish hue. I come from behind and slowly circle around to face him. Splotches of blood cover his forehead and cheek. When we lock eyes, he spits a mouthful of blood at the ground before me, then drops his head down.

The crowd is quiet and curious as they watch me inspect this man. He seems familiar, but it isn't until I notice the gleaming gold buckle on his belt that I realize I know who he is. The buckle is unique, foreign white crystals embedded in the metal, and there's only one man I've known to have it. The belt buckle at his waist was a gift from Aerok. Aerok, a man whose true joy comes from the things that glitter in the sunlight, uses such things as payment for services. Part of me knows the answer to my question. Yet, I can't bring myself to accept it. I may not have been in love with Aerok, and surely, he wasn't in love with me, but I would've never put assassination as a key element in our relationship. Uneasy, I step forward.

"Did Aerok send you?"

Kaleo steps forward as well, joining me next to the man.

"Do you know him?" he asks.

"Yes." I keep my eyes locked on the top of the traitor's balding head. "He's a bounty hunter from Heraeda." I turn to Kaleo. "The Lord Commander often employed him to capture debtors." I turn my eyes back to the hunter. "Your name's Crary, is it not?"

The man remains silent, his eyes focused on the ground.

"We haven't got much out of him, so far." Kaleo bends down and grabs a fistful of the man's remaining hair. He yanks until the man is forced to look at me. The man growls, dried blood covering his face like a mask.

"Who sent you?" I move closer to him. There's emptiness in his eyes, a pool of black surrounded by the whites. He doesn't blink. I stoop down so at I'm at eye level with my attacker. He reeks of destruction, but I keep my calm. "If Aerok wanted me dead," I whisper so that only Kaleo and Crary can hear, "he should've chosen someone more skilled than a failed bounty hunter-turned-assassin."

My words finally draw a reaction from him. "Bitch," he mutters. He growls again through gritted teeth. He tries to get at me, but his head jerks violently as Kaleo keeps a firm grip on his hair.

I rise and take a step backward. "You will stand trial for treason and be stripped of any titles and lands you hold."

His eyes soften, but his gaze is still cold and distant. Cracked lips turn upward into a sinister grin. "Trial?"—he chuckles—"You'll never see the throne again." His haunting laugh echoes throughout the square. The crowd murmurs.

Kaleo releases the man's hair and steps toward me. He pulls his sword from the scabbard, the torchlight beaming off of the blade. "There's only one way this encounter can end, Your Majesty." He extends the sword to me and juts his chin to the man. "You may have the honor."

I hesitate before taking it with both hands, the weight of the sword sagging my shoulders. Kaleo walks away, leaving me alone in the center of the crowd with Crary. His eyes are still down, blood falling in thick drops onto his legs. A surge of energy flows through my body as I watch him bleed. I'm finished bending to the will of others. Court has been ruthless to me—so maybe it's time I returned the favor.

I should kill this man. I should run the sword through him and smile as his blood soaks in through the dirt. My parents' deaths require penance, and he could be the down payment.

In the crowd, no one says a word. They watch me with anger in their fists and hope in their eyes—hope that I'll end Crary's life as he tried to end mine. My stomach twists into knots, and I loosen my grip on the hilt. It almost slips from my fingers, but I grasp it tighter, my knuckles turning white.

I want to kill him, but the sword gets heavier every second I leave Crary breathing. A tingling envelops my toes and paralyzes my feet, keeping them planted firmly in place. My eyes bounce from Crary to the blade and back again. My fingers produce another tremble that won't stop. I *can't* kill him.

A warm hand slides around mine, around the hilt.

"Let me do it," Colton says against my ear.

I nod, and Colton takes the sword from my hands, relieving the weight from my shoulders. He flexes his wrist as he approaches Crary, and in a swift motion, he drives the blade into the man's chest. The sound of metal on bone chills my spine as he retracts the sword from Crary's body. The bounty hunter crumples to the ground. Colton pivots and looks back at me, his mouth downturned. I drop my eyes to the pool of blood expanding near his feet.

From behind me, Kaleo whistles and calls two men over from the crowd.

"Get rid of him, yeah?" he commands the men. "I don't want the children to see it in the morning."

The men grab each end of the body and haul it away. Blood pours onto the ground as they move, leaving a trail of the disposal. I close my eyes and try to breathe through the thick air that threatens to crush me where I stand. When I open them again, Colton is by my side.

He leans in close. "Are you okay?" His eyes watch me carefully as though I might shatter.

Although my cheeks burn, I muster the strength to pull my mouth into a smile. "I'm fine."

He raises a brow and shifts his lips to speak, but I walk away, and hope, for my sake, that he doesn't follow.

Leona

Chapter 18

The muted chatter of the villagers drifts through the night as I bask in the privacy of the stable. Though their expressions had lacked disappointment from my failed attempt to kill Crary, my thoughts contain enough defeat for all of us. I should've been able to kill him. But instead, the idea of taking a life magnified my reluctance until Colton took the burden from me.

I lean against the stall and reach my hand through the slats. The white and chocolate-spotted horse swishes his tail and let out a snicker at my touch. I stroke my fingers between his large brown eyes, just as I'd done eight years ago. My shoulders slump as I release a sigh. So much has changed in eight years. The horse snorts then nudges his nose against my hand.

"Looks like Maxim remembers you."

My back goes rigid, but I don't turn to face the voice. I can't. If I do, I'll just be met with the affirmation that I'm who Colton always said I was—a noble girl—someone who's never had to take vengeance into her own hands when a perfectly capable guard was standing by. I run my fingers over the horse's snout until he shakes his head and steps to the strung bundle of hay in the corner.

"I'm glad you didn't kill him." Colton's voice is a murmur.

I pull myself from off the stall and turn around. Colton leans back against the planked wall, his hands stuffed in his pockets. He regards me with brows pulled in, the lantern next to him reflecting in his eyes.

"It should've been me who did it." I rake my fingers through my hair and sweep it to one side of my shoulder. "Everyone was expecting it to be me."

Colton lower his eyes to the floor and shakes his head slowly. "Kaleo shouldn't have put that responsibility on you. I think sometimes he forgets it's not easy to take someone's life." He pulls a hand out of his pocket and drags it across his jaw. I study his face and the grave expression it makes when he speaks. "When you do, it takes something from you as well."

I've seen him kill three men in the past couple of days, not to mention the countless others who died by his hand in the arena. If each death comes at a price, how much of himself has he lost?

"Does it get easier?"

The lantern's light casts half of his face in shadows. He stirs against the wall, his mouth opening and closing in failed attempts at speech. After another moment, he walks over to me and drapes his arm over the stall's wooden railing. Maxim glances at him. When Colton doesn't move to open the gate, the horse flicks his tail and returns to his meal.

Colton's chest rises and falls in an uneven rhythm as he fixates on a warped section of a slat. His eyes dart over the wood, but he says nothing. The stable shrinks in size from the silence between us and the air gets warmer. Finally, he looks at me.

"It does get easier." He taps his finger against the wood. "But that's not always a good thing."

I nod, keeping my eyes on his. The pale green contrasts against the red in his iris. Dark lashes rim the lids. Slices of moonlight streak through gaps in the wall's planks, leaving stripes of glowing blue along his collarbone. Colton's mouth twitches and he clears his throat.

"So, I lied to you," he says, turning his view toward Maxim.

My breath catches and my body stiffens. I shift away from him. "Lied about what?"

"I wouldn't have figured out how to calm him if you hadn't come along." He glances at me, his mouth pulling up into a grin. "I remember I'd been struggling for most of the afternoon because I refused to ask anyone for help."

My mouth falls open. The tension in my chest releases like the end of a coil being freed. The memory of that day comes rushing back to my mind in a flood of images. Though Maxim was much smaller then, the growing foal still towered over his poorly-trained handler. I click my tongue and cross my arms over the slats. "I *knew* you didn't know what you were doing." A lightness starts in my stomach and rises until it frees itself as a chuckle. "You were so arrogant back then. Not much has changed, I see."

Colton flinches and presses an open hand to his chest. "I prefer the terms *expertly unqualified*, thank you."

There's a brief pause as I stare at him, wide-grinned, until we both burst with laughter. Maxim startles and lets out a whinny at our pandemonium. No one has been able to make me laugh quite like Colton has. He gives me a different sort of adrenaline and a warmth that radiates within my entire body.

Through our mirth, a bell clangs in the distance. Colton's face sharpens as he snatches his attention toward it. What was once a bright smile, dims into a frown. His brows squeeze together again.

A quiver dances in my chest. "What is that?"

"A summoning."

I follow Colton and the rest of the villagers to the meeting hall. The largest building in the village, even bigger than the church, the meeting hall displays no decorations, only torches evenly spaced along the walls. A grand table fills the center of the room. Everyone gathers around it, and I find a spot at the head of the table near Colton and Kaleo. On the walk over, Colton explained that the bell is only used when there's an urgent need for the village to gather. He also mentioned that the last time they'd used it was after men began getting stolen away in the night for crimes they didn't commit.

Parchment messages lay neatly on the tabletop. I bite my lip and stare at them, the thoughts of doubt swirling in my head like a summer fog. The villages have already been through so much—lost so much. They've suffered while I was wistfully unaware. If they've chosen to refuse to help me, it'd be of no fault but my own. A few more people stroll into the hall, their mouths stretched long with yawns. When everyone's movements settle, Kaleo begins.

"We've received word from sister villages." His voice bellows in the hall. He glances down at me before turning his eyes to the group. "They're eager to join us on our mission."

I close my eyes for a moment and exhale a breath. Colton nudges my arm with a grin that can't be contained. Others in the room voice their satisfaction.

"However," he continues, and they fall silent, "our neighbors in the north, in Apsyn and Oerdin, have written to inform us that guards have begun recollecting men and boys in those villages for the arena."

The crowd's murmurs grow louder. At the other end of the table, my eyes find Aiden as he reaches up and rubs the back of his neck.

"So, they're coming for us again?" someone asks.

"I ain't going back!"

Angered voices fill the air. Kaleo raises his hands to calm the group. "My brothers, please." The men quiet down to let him finish. "Yes, there's a good chance that guards will be coming for us. In light of that," he looks at me, "I'm proposing we seek shelter elsewhere."

"Where?" I ask.

"Mount Grae."

He says the words, but I don't truly comprehend them. "You want to hide on the mountain?"

He smiles, bringing a gentleness to his roughened face. "No, Your Majesty, not on the mountain—in it."

I've never heard of the inside of Mount Grae being accessible, so his answer only confuses me further. Regardless, I nod my head and hope that my ignorance goes unnoticed. "Will the others meet us there?"

The room is quiet as the group awaits his answer. The glow of the torches highlights the shadows under many of the men's eyes.

"Yes. We'll leave at first light. Guards usually don't patrol during the night, and even on horseback, it'd take them half a day to get here if they left at dawn as well."

My shoulders feel lighter at this news. We're hours away from putting our plan into action. "So, first light then."

"First light," he echoes.

Colton

Chapter 19

The wind turns cooler as the night goes on. The village has gentled. Most people are at home getting much needed rest before our journey in a few hours. Aiden and I are awake keeping watch. Since Crary, we haven't seen any sign of guards or other assassins, but Kaleo insists that we remain vigilant. I agree. The shift in the country's dynamics is too extreme to leave our village further exposed. Luckily, our hour-long shift is almost over.

We sit on empty wooden barrels near the entrance of Maburh. Aiden's legs swing absentmindedly over the edge as he looks up into the stars. They stare back at him, blinking sporadically, as they study each other.

"What's wrong?" I ask.

He takes a moment then responds. "Huh?"

I grin. "I said, what's wrong? You're looking awfully hard at the sky."

He rubs his hands over his face. Puffy bags have formed under his eyes. "Sorry. Just thinking."

"Well, don't think too hard. You might hurt yourself."

With a smile, he picks up a stray chunk of wood from the barrel and tosses it at me. It bounces off my leg and tumbles to the ground.

"I was remembering something someone had told me long ago." Aiden turns his gaze back to the stars.

I look up as well. "Could you be any more cryptic?"

Aiden shuffles and I look over as he digs something out of his pocket. A small parchment message. He lobs it to me.

My eyebrow raises. "What's this?" I unroll the message.

To Mister Aiden Hastings,

I hope this message finds you well. I'm writing to inform you of Mister Bandyn Chagell's passing. He succumbed to his terminal illness nearly a week ago. As his most loyal friend, I also want to inform you of his wish to pass the shop down to you. I know the moment is bittersweet, but when you're ready, please come see me.

Mister Garret Lenore

I hold the parchment back out to him. "Who's Bandyn Chagell?"

"He's the closest thing to a father I've ever had."

There's pain in his eyes that lets me know this man meant a great deal to him. "I'm sorry."

He nods once and slips the message back into his pocket. He finds another chunk of wood and begins toying with it between his fingers. He's shutting down again. Most of what I've learned about Aiden has come from observing what he isn't saying. There's silence between us, and for once, I'm content to let him have a moment.

"Soon after we arrived here," Aiden says, pursuing the conversation on his own, "I sent him a falcon to let him know that I was alive. I guess Garret has been tending to the manor." Aiden slides off the barrel.

I slide off mine as well. "What terminal illness was he talking about?"

"His lungs. There was something wrong with them." Aiden looks skyward as though he's recalling past moments. "He was always out of breath, coughing up blood." He looks me in my eyes. "It was bad."

"I'm sorry to hear that." And I am. Whoever that man was, Aiden no longer has him in his life. From what he said about his father, it doesn't sound like he has anyone left. "So, what was the thing you were remembering from long ago? Clearly, it was something that Mister Chagell had said."

Aiden's eyes lift, revealing a lightness he's trying to suppress. "I had never put much stock into the old man's philosophical ramblings until now. He once told me to 'love the light, for it shows me the way, and to endure the darkness, for it shows me the stars.'"

"Smart man."

Aiden sighs. "He was."

"And now he's left you his shop? What—a bakery shop or something?"

Aiden laughs. It's the first time in a long while that I've seen him relaxed enough to do such a gesture. "No, not a bakery." He crosses his arms over his chest. "Bladesmith."

"Really?" I think back to the time earlier when we both dealt with the two guards. I didn't get a good look at Aiden's fighting form, but he did hold his own.

"Yeah," he says, catching on to my face of disbelief. "Though, I enjoy designing blades more than I like fighting with them."

I snap my fingers. "I knew it."

He jerks his head back and grins. "Knew what?"

"I had a feeling you were a craftsman or something. You're way too smart to be anything but." I lightly nudge his arm. "You've been holding out on us, sir."

He grins and it's a nice sight to see him opening up more to me. I look over his shoulder as two men approach, their feet shuffling over the ground. Their eyes are sharp and ready for their shift.

"It's time," one of the men says.

Inside, the house is quiet. Aiden finds a spot on the floor of the sitting room to lie down. Soft snores fill the room soon after he tucks his head against his arms. He makes sleeping look so effortless.

My footsteps become rhythmic as I pace in the kitchen. I should be resting, too, but my anxiety keeps me up most nights. I thought being back in my home would calm my tangled nerves. Instead, it just puts me further on edge.

I walk through the house and pass my parents' room. I hover in their doorway and watch for a moment as they hold each other close in their peaceful slumber. This is the same way they've slept for as long as I can remember. Regardless of if they'd gotten into a spat just after dinner, none of that mattered when bedtime came. Maybe that's the key to having a fulfilling life—to understand that life is too precious to neglect the bonds you form with others. I leave them to their dreams and go farther down the hall toward my bedroom.

In my bed, a wool blanket covers Leona. It folds into the curves of her body, peaking at her hips. Her black hair falls in waves over the small pillow. My steps are slow as I enter, taking care to not disturb her with creaky floorboards.

I pull out a chair from the small wooden table near the foot of the bed. Once I sit, the achiness of my feet rushes forward, my toes numbing in my boots. I prop my feet on the three-legged stool close to me. One foot lands with a dull thud. She stirs and shifts position, causing the blanket to reveal more of her skin. The top of her shoulders flows into a creamy complexion of tan. It runs the length of her arm until it disappears under the wool.

I've underestimated her. She's not the hare-brained royal I thought she was. She's the exception to the unwritten rule of monarchy. There's good in her that will heal this kingdom.

A single candle burns on the windowsill. It flickers with a mind of its own, mimicking the stars outside. *Love the light, for it shows you the way. Endure the darkness, for it shows you the stars.* I need a little light in my life to balance against the darkness within. I stare at the flame, the bright yellow at the tip and blue rim at the base. It dances against the drafts of the walls. I yawn and my eyelids become heavy until they're too hefty to stay open.

A constant drip of water lands on my forehead and forces me to open my eyes. I'm lying on the ground in the dark, cramped cell under the arena. Something's different. I'm alone and the cell gate is open. I pull myself to my feet, my knees wobbling. I reach out to the wall to steady myself. When I draw my hand back, it's wet—slick with blood that is still slightly warm. I wipe the blood onto my pants and make my way toward the gate. My hands grip the cell bars as I look up and down the corridor for the others.

"Aiden?" I call out. My voice echoes. I wait a moment for it to stop resonating.

No answer.

I put one foot out the cell, then the other. I could turn right and leave the dungeons or go left toward the arena. I glance both ways. A gust of wind tunnels through the corridor in the direction of the arena. My hair whips as my balance stumbles. The fighting grounds call me. They're a whisper in my ears, a hiss in my mind. Their words flutter like bats until they morph into a solid figure, its slotted eyes bright and focused. The rattle on its tail shakes and grows in volume as its body coils in the space between my ears.

The wind blows once more. *Come find me.* I obey and walk toward the voice. One step after the other, I rise from the underground dungeon into the bright sun of the day. I lift my hands to shield my eyes, but they're heavy, already occupied with holding two swords. My gaze runs along the blades, admiring the beauty in their sharpened edges. I see my reflection in them—a darker version of myself, the version that no one will understand.

I bring my attention back toward the arena. The stands are empty. No crowds to appease today. Good. One day, I'll make it up there to slit all their throats. Let them cheer while blood spills from their necks, ruining the pristine quality of their high-fashion. Let them heckle with their tongues missing from their mouths.

The wind becomes more aggressive. It swirls down into the arena and picks up sand, causing a sandstorm. I squint to keep my vision safe. I plant my feet on the ground and try to avoid being taken up by the current. Finally, the sand settles and my visibility is no longer hindered.

Someone else stands on the grounds with me. He approaches, a single sword in hand. I don't recognize him. Shaggy brown hair covers his head, a shaggy beard to match. When he comes closer, I take note of his eyes. Green eyes with a spot of red on one of the irises. Like me. Except, he can't be me. I shake my head, hoping to rid my mind of the illusion. The tail's rattle grows fiercer.

He takes advantage of my distraction and rushes at full speed. His sword lifts above his head then comes crashing down toward me. I cross my own blades to catch his, and for a moment, we're both suspended in time in a gridlock. His free hand whirls around and strikes my jaw. I stumble backward, releasing my hold on his sword. He flexes his wrist and the sword rotates in a circle, leaving a trail of smoke in its wake.

I drop back and watch him to learn his moves. He looks so much like me, but so different in the same breath. He even moves like me—quick and calculated.

He charges again with the same move as before. This time, I'm ready for him. I dodge to the side so that he misses, and as he does, my sword draws across his side. His shirt quickly stains red. He doesn't hesitate at the wound, though. He recovers and lunges at me again.

His sword thrusts at me in swift succession. I dodge each attack, my own swords clanging against his in the empty arena. The sound replicates against the stone pillars surrounding us. The tip of my blade slices the skin at his chest. He doesn't slow down. So, I speed up.

My arms move with fluidity as my swords cross over my body and drive him back. He growls. I knock his sword out of his hand, and it lands far enough away that he can't get to it without leaving himself even more defenseless. I toss both of my weapons aside as well. He smirks.

We clash. Our bodies wrestle on the ground, agitating the sand below so it kicks up and rains down on us. I shake my head to remove the debris from my eyelashes. He pins me, and it takes all my strength to force him off. With one roll, I press him to the ground and wrap my hands around his throat. He thrashes and gnarls, but it comes out as more of a whimper as I block his airway. I gaze down into his eyes, the ones that look so much like mine.

"You're not me," I whisper.

His thrashing slows and he stops fighting back. Instead, his hands grab helplessly at my wrists.

"Colt! Wake up!" Aiden's voice sounds so distant.

A hard shove to my side flings me from the bed to the floor. I press my hands against my eyes and rub the drowsiness away. When my vision adjusts, Aiden and my parents stand before me, along with Leona, who's sitting up in the bed looking...terrified. She clutches her throat and breathes heavily.

Color drains from my face. Our eyes lock for a split moment before she turns away from me. My legs are numb—along with my soul—but I try to stand and move near her. I need her to know it was an accident.

"Come on," Aiden says, grabbing my arms and pulling me away from her and toward the door. I try to resist, but all my energy is spent. I grab at the door frame to pause and look back at her.

She keeps her eyes averted from me as Ma sits nearby and inspects the thick roped bruises around her neck. She winces at each touch.

"I'm sorry. I didn't mean to," I say, but she doesn't look up at my words.

So, I let Aiden remove me from the room, away from the destruction I've caused.

Leona

Chapter 20

The morning sun peeks over the mountains, an orange glow that makes the ridges look like they're on fire. The sky is a mix of purples and blues as the night attempts to hang on just awhile longer.

Geneva follows me out the front door and stands with me on the porch. She ruffles her apron's hem in her hands as she watches her son. His back is turned toward us while he helps the others load tools and weapons onto a wooden cart. Though her eyes are downturned, the blue irises they withhold have the same vibrancy as the shifting skies.

"He *does* have a kind soul," she says, nodding.

My shoulders tense. I lower my eyes to the planks under my feet. My throat is still sore. I haven't yet tested my voice, but I manage a sound that resembles skepticism.

A faint chuckle fills the space beside me. I wish I could agree with her, and before last night, perhaps I would've. I keep my vision focused on the tiger lilies in the ceramic pot on the porch. Hairline fractures cover the surface, the apparent result of it being mended multiple times.

"When Colton was younger," she starts, "he shied away from other children his age." I raise my head to look at her. Soft wrinkles settle into the corner of her eyes as her thin lips stretch into a smile. "No matter how often I sent him down to the shore to make friends, he never quite felt he belonged here."

From the past couple of days that I've known Colton, *timid* wouldn't be a trait I'd use to describe him. He's been abrasive, disrespectful, and—yes—kind, at times. The different layers of his personality are rooted in elements beyond my understanding. I open my mouth to ask what she meant by *not belonging here*, but she continues.

"It wasn't until he saw a boy struggling to fish, that he finally came out of his shell. Fishing was something Colton excelled at, and it gave him a sense of purpose to teach Henrik everything he knew. They would spend hours at the water." She laughs a sound that fits her petite stature perfectly. Colton looks over his shoulder at his mother's laughter and flinches when he sees me standing with her. We lock eyes for a moment before he darts his attention away. "He wouldn't give up until Henrik caught at least one fish—even if that meant they were out there until dusk."

She turns to me and rests her hand against my cheek. A sad smile pulls at her lips.

"Give him time, Your Majesty." Her eyes drift to Colton once more. She drops her palm from my cheek and reaches for my hands. She squeezes them lightly then leans in as though she's about to disclose a well-kept secret. "The past year has changed him. I can tell by the way he now carries himself. His mind is fractured, and his heart is damaged, but both will heal with time." Her hands pull me into an embrace, a gesture that must come naturally for mothers. My eyes close, and for a moment, it *is* Mother who is hugging me. "Take care of each other, yes?"

I nod against her. I'm sure she means well, but I'm not yet ready to dismiss what Colton did. I can still feel his hands around my throat, his fingers gripping tighter and tighter with ease. My eyes burn at the thought and I quickly blink back the tears so she doesn't see.

"Thank you for your hospitality." I break away from her and offer a weak smile. "I hope for us to meet again under better circumstances."

Geneva's face lights up with contentment. She makes living seem effortless—everyone here does. Their lives are filled with only a fraction of the stress I've grown used to. Here, each morning breathes life into new possibilities.

I walk toward the village square alone. Clusters of families gather as wives and children say goodbye to their husbands and fathers. Parents bid their sons safe travels with pride beaming across their faces.

My heart shifts in weight and sinks lower into the pit of my stomach. There's a good chance some of these men won't be returning home. Regardless of how much faith I have in them, I know casualties in war are inevitable.

Certainly, they must know it as well.

Kaleo stands tall with his wife, the woman who gave me fresh clothing. He takes her face gently in his hands and kisses each of her cheeks. He drops his head down so their foreheads are touching, then speaks softly of which I can only assume are parting words. A single tear falls from her eye before she smiles. Such a happy expression masking her pain. I'm all too familiar with the chore. One night with her husband was all she got before he's off risking his life again.

He stoops down to his knees in front of the curly-haired girl. She's shining with youthful innocence. Her small arms stretch around her father's shoulders as best as she can manage. She holds him tightly and presses her head against his chest.

I turn away from their sentimental moment. I've never experienced this type of connection with my own father. He was a hard man. He had his moments of tenderness from time to time, but they never lasted long. Being affectionate wasn't exactly his most notable quality.

"Are you doing all right?"

I jump at the voice behind me. Aiden.

We stand shoulder-to-shoulder and watch as the rest of the supplies get loaded onto other carts.

"I'm fine." In the corner of my vision, I can see him looking at me, searching my face for the truth. I keep my eyes forward and avoid his gaze.

He sighs and faces forward as well. A bit of irony. Most times it has been him who has difficulty opening up to people. It is both strange and appreciated for him to check on me.

I turn to him. "Tell me, honestly, what are your thoughts about our odds of success?"

He takes a moment and stares hard at the men and supplies gathered. A lot of the volunteers were imprisoned with him and have survived the arena on multiple occasions.

He looks at me, flecks of gold dotting the brown of his eyes. "Honestly?"

I nod.

"I believe you'll have the manpower, especially once we meet up with the other villages."

"But?"

His eyes shift. "But...instead of the brute force approach Kaleo suggested, perhaps we could use a more clever strategy. It could reduce the threat of casualties on our side."

My lips pull downward. "Why didn't you suggest this at the meeting?"

His hands rake through his hair. He tilts his head back so that he looks up into the fading starlight. "I felt it wasn't my place. Kaleo and his strategists were pretty keen on getting it done their way."

I shake my head and hold up a hand. "Aiden, your advice holds just as much weight to me as a hundred war experts. Many of these men seek to strike using their instincts." My eyes float to Colton as he approaches, but I snatch them away. "You? You're different. You're very logical, which is something that is invaluable. So, please, if you have a better plan, I would like to hear it."

His mouth moves into a grin. "All right, so I was thinking—"

"Your Majesty?" Kaleo's voice booms in the square, startling me.

I look over. He and the other men are ready and waiting. Colton stands with them, avoiding my eye contact. I reach out and touch Aiden's arm. "Tell me on the way there?"

He smiles, slightly disappointed. There's a gentleness to him that makes me feel sorry he's found himself here. With the rising sun at our backs, we join the others and begin our journey to Mount Grae.

Colton

Chapter 21

It's midday when we reach the mountains. The sun hangs high above our heads, casting shallow shadows in front of us. We arrive without incident, which is a relief because I'm still mentally exhausted from last night.

I haven't been able to look Leona in her eyes since then. Every time I try, I'm met with the mental picture of seeing her frightened, her body shaking as she tries to regain a full breath. I did that. I caused her undue pain. I hurt her in a way I could've never imagined.

But it wasn't her, not really. I remember the dream—nightmare—vividly. My mind tricked me, giving me the illusion of an enemy that wasn't possible. Only, dream and reality clashed together when I woke up to my hands around Leona's throat. If I could take it back, I would, but I'm sure she'll never forgive me. She walks ahead of me with Kaleo and Aiden at her side. She's still close enough that I can smell the sweetness of her hair, see the softness of her skin under the sun's light. I drift back and let others pass me to increase the distance.

As we approach Mount Grae, all heads turn upward to the tops of the peaks. They extend endlessly into the sky, their ridges disappearing into the clouds. Though the ground is covered in fine-bladed grasses, the mountain erupts in jagged stone, bare of any possibility for greenery to grow.

We walk along the foot of the mountain until we find the opening to the cavern. To someone not familiar, the small gap might get overlooked under the cover of shrubbery pushing against it.

The narrow tunnel gradually opens wider and branches off into different directions. Our lanterns show our shadows walking alongside us. Stalactites hang from the ceiling like spears waiting to be released. The hair at my temples dampens from the humidity as we stay in the main tunnel. It zigzags until we reach the hollow space of the mountain.

I watch ahead of me as Leona takes in the vast cavern. She spins around slowly, smiling, her eyes scanning the tallest edges of the ceiling. When she drops her head and her eyes land on mine, the smile fades. In its place, her lips press together into a frown. We hold each other's stare for a second before she turns around and rejoins Aiden.

I swallow a hard gulp. If she would just let me explain…

There's a loud disturbance up ahead. My body tenses and my eyes are on high alert. I lift my foot to take off into a sprint, but pause when the commotion splits into laughter. My hand clutches the hilt of my sword as I jog toward the sounds.

Waiting on the far side of the cavern is another group. I squint and can make out the faces of men I'd shared the dungeon with. The tension releases from my shoulders, though not completely.

"It's an honor to meet you, Your Majesty." Nicolai reaches for Leona's hand and bends to kiss her knuckles. A few years older than me, he's the youngest leader Toveen has ever had. He was chosen by his neighbors because of his ability to handle the challenges Toveen endured when they lost the entirety of their crops to disease. I admired him for that, but now, a surge of jealousy flows through my veins.

"The honor is all mine," Leona says. Her cheeks push up as she smiles. "I'm grateful that you and your village have decided to join us."

"Of course. When we received Kaleo's message, we jumped at the chance to put an end to this madness." He tucks his thumbs into the belt at his waist and tilts his head, his eyes falling on the bruises around her neck. "Are you well?"

Her answer to his question will crush me. She could either lie and minimize the damage, or she could tell him exactly what happened. Either option makes my head throb. I pull at my shirt, the collar suddenly feeling too snug. Maybe she should announce my faults. I deserve for everyone to know what I've already come to terms with myself. I can't be trusted—not truly.

I turn and trudge past the men who'd arrived hours before we did. They shake hands and hug, happy to see one another. Under different conditions, I'm sure I'd feel the same way, but when I see them, I'm only reminded of our past. No matter how much I try to push the thoughts from my mind, they are always there, whispering demonic words into my ears.

There's something wrong with me. My breathing quickens and my head pounds. With a start, I look toward the path we traveled through and close my eyes. I listen to the whistle of the wind as it courses through the tunnels. It's telling me something different now.

I don't belong here.

Leona

Chapter 22

By the time Kaleo's finished introducing me to the leaders of the villages, many of the men have arrived. There's still one village that has yet to make it—Apsyn. The northern community has already been revisited by the guards. They sent word that they still had men available to fight, but that many of their strongest fighters were whisked away in the middle of the night and returned to the dungeons.

The cavern has calmed with excitement while the men rest from their long journeys. I take in the sight. At least three hundred men, all here because they believe in my right to the throne. I continue to scan the space. A pale blue glow reflected on a far wall strikes my interest. I stand from the rock I'd been sitting on and walk toward it. A few heads look in my direction, but no one follows me.

The glow builds brighter the further I travel down the tunnel. The passageway opens to a short cliff. Below is a pond, the water reflecting its blue ripples on the walls. I look down into the pool, past the surface, to see the bottom. The water is transparent—no debris, no obstructions, just liquid glass. At the bottom, the ground sparkles, almost as though crushed metals were embedded in the dirt. My focus shifts when I notice another person's reflection beside me in the water. I gasp and snap my head behind me.

Colton stands with his hands up in front of him. His eyes are narrow with wariness. The luminosity of the water makes the red patch in his iris more prominent. I try to relax my tense body, but my anxiety refuses to fade.

"Yes?" I ask, my voice unsteady.

He lowers his hands. My eyes follow them to his sides. I would hate if they'd found themselves around my throat again.

"I need to talk to you."

I take a step away from him, toward the wall behind us. "Go ahead." I already know where this conversation is heading. His face has said the words long before his tongue has had the chance.

He tries to maintain eye contact, but his sight drifts to and from the water. "I wanted you to know how very sorry I am for what I did." He glances at my bruises before quickly shifting away again. "It was an accident."

I scoff, heat rising in my chest. "How do you accidentally strangle someone?" I look down at his hands and they're shaking. He closes them into fists to hide it.

"It was a dream—or nightmare, I guess. But it felt so real…" His voice gets quieter.

My eyebrow raises. "You thought you were only choking me in your dreams?"

He shakes his head. "No, no, not you. It was"—he pauses—"someone else."

I watch him, patiently, as he stares at the ground and wrestles with the thoughts in his mind. The silence between us makes the lapping of the water sound louder.

"Tell me." My eyes are trained on him.

He looks up, puzzled. "Tell you what?"

"About the dream." If it had gotten to the point where he was left trying to kill a man, I'm curious to know what the dream was about.

He hesitates, then recalls what he can from his memories. He speaks of the dungeon, the arena, the man he was fighting who shared his eyes. His face twists up as he relives the torture. For once, I don't press him for details. There's silence between us as the diluted images of his nightmare swirl around in my mind.

'*Give him time,*' his mother said. Surely her love for her son has clouded her judgment on the situation. My own thoughts begin to torment my opinion as I consider her words. Before me, stands a man torn between his past and present. I've not forgotten of his time in the arena, nor of what he told me the first night in the woods, or in the stable. After everything that has happened, he's not to blame for his actions.

"I'll gather my things and leave," he says. His eyes hold defeat.

My jaw falls to my ankles. "So, that's it? You're just going to go?" My voice rises with a flourish of annoyance.

"Seems like the best thing to do." This time, he takes a step away. His eyes are now steady, indifferent.

Another flash of heat starts in my soles and travels up my veins, branching off until my entire body is lit. "What about what you told me in the forest—about channeling my anger and using it? You should heed your own advice. I took you for a lot of things, but being a coward wasn't one of them."

He cringes. "How am I a coward?"

"You're running away."

"I'm not running."

"Well, what would you call it then?"

He presses a palm to his forehead as though his hand might go through his skull. "I call it removing myself from a dangerous situation. It'll be better for everyone if I'm not here." He pivots on his heel.

I grab his arm and tug it back. "Don't walk away from me."

His eyes overflow with fury. "You should be wanting me to *run* away from you." He pulls the hair at his nape, a vein bulging in his forehead. "I could've killed you. Don't you understand that?"

"I understand that part perfectly." I glance away and then back again. "What I don't understand is why you're behaving like a brute."

He growls under his breath like a threatened wild dog, then turns and steps toward me, forcing me backward until my spine slams against the wall. "Oh? First I'm a coward, and now I'm a brute?" The warmth of his breath scorches my forehead.

"You say one thing, and then do the opposite." My hands tighten into fists. "You preach about protecting each other, yet you're readily willing to abandon us—abandon me."

He drops his head and stares at the ground between us. Slow breaths release from his chest. "I almost killed you," he says again, placing emphasis on each word. "Who's to say it won't happen again?"

I shake my head. "I don't think it will."

He raises his eyes to meet mine. A smirk pulls at his lips. "Are you willing to bet your life on that? Maybe next time, there'll be no one around to stop me."

My body recoils from the hint of a threat in his tone. I should be afraid. I should wonder if he'll finish the task he started last night. He's more than capable of carrying it out. I sink my fingernails into my palms until it hurts, then squeeze a little harder.

"Do it." My voice is unsteady. I swallow hard to reclaim my composure. "If you're so sure you'll hurt me again, then just get it over with and do it."

He lets out a sharp laugh and turns away from me. The darkness under his eyes announce that his sleepless nights have caught up with him. "Don't be silly. You know I'm not going to do that—not like this."

I throw my hands up. "All right, then. Like I said, stop acting like a brute." He turns back toward me, his brows raised. I jab my finger against his chest and hold it there. "You're not the only one going through something."

He reaches up and grabs my wrist firmly. It's not tight enough to hurt me, though I know he could if he wanted to. "You don't know what I've gone through." He leans in close. His face hovers near mine and we hold each other's eyes hostage, neither of us wanting to blink first. His glare scans my face, lingering at my lips, before bringing it back to my eyes. His breathing shudders. He looks down at me through long lashes. "You don't know anything... noble girl."

"Coward," I hiss.

Seconds get stretched past their breaking point. His face blurs as he drops his head down and presses his lips to mine. Fast and hard. He pulls away with the same swiftness. I'm caught off-guard and lost for words. Heat radiates from my cheeks and the fire simmering in my core is enough to burn down a forest. His eyes narrow, slightly crazed, daring me to say something.

Taunting me for a reaction.

My brain is still processing what just happened, and I forget that my wrist is still in his hand, against his chest. His heart pounds violently against my fingers, reminding me of my own heart and how I've been holding my breath for far too long. I force my lungs to fill and bite my lip.

He brings his mouth to mine once more with the same urgency. This time, he prolongs the contact. Carefully. Methodically. I don't pull away. Instead, I melt into the kiss, into his touch.

I free my wrist from his grip and bring my hands up to his face. My palms graze against the soft facial hair on his jaw. I pull him closer until there's no distance left between us. The stone wall is smooth against my back. He presses me against it, and I let him.

We shouldn't be doing this, but I don't want to stop. The taste of his kiss is overwhelming, and my body begs for more. It's like I'm at sea and while a violent storm thrashes my ship around, I can still find the beauty in the raindrops as they splash on my cheeks.

His lips leave mine and he softly plants them below my ear, down my neck. I wince when he reaches the bruises. He stops and pulls away, regarding me with caution. My fingers grasp his shirt and I pull him back. He's hesitant, but he comes. I push up on my toes and murmur *It's all right* against his cheek. Strong hands circle my hips, claiming me as his. And for the moment, I am. His lips find mine once more, this time, with a hunger desperate to be fed.

The heat between us builds. I'm out of my mind, but I don't care. My brain can take as long of a respite as it needs. I shift so that he's against the wall now. His lip twitches in surprise at my tenacity. My hands go to his waist. I take hold of the hem of his shirt and raise it. He pulls it over his head and tosses it haphazardly aside.

My eyes catch the glint of a pendant hanging around his neck. The water casts its reflection on his bare torso and his olive skin takes on a bluish glow. There are several scars, long and short ones, scattered over his chest. He looks at me, eyes dark, as I study the raised marks. Each one holds a story of its origin. Each one adds to the complexity of his past. He says nothing of them. Neither do I. Instead, I kiss each blemish, and as I do, he softly groans.

He stoops down and slides his hands under my dress. He hooks them around the back of my thighs and lifts me as he stands upright. My legs wrap around his hips, my ankles locked behind him. We're incredibly close, and I can't stop. We turn so that I'm against the wall again. He buries his head into my chest. I'm sure he can hear the hammering of my heart. My lungs struggle to keep up with my breath.

I put my hand under his chin and gently lift his face so I can see him. There's an emotion behind his eyes I can't quite name, though, it seems so familiar. We stay like this for a moment, savoring each other's presence, burning through each other's souls.

"Don't leave," I say, although it probably came out as more of a plea.

A small smile plays on his lips. "I won't," he whispers.

I smile, too, and leave a trail of kisses down his face until I meet his mouth again—a reunion that already feels long overdue. My hands caress him as he keeps my body firmly pressed against his. All the apprehension of him I had before vanishes. The negative thoughts dive into the water without so much as a splash to mark their departure. The calmness of the mountain pool contrasts against our ragged breaths.

The way I feel in this moment is a sensation I haven't felt before. Never have I given myself so freely to someone, to let another's hands roam my body so intimately. I know better than this. This isn't what queens do. And yet, rationality deserted me the moment his lips touched mine.

Someone clears their throat.

Colton and I both turn our heads in the direction of the sound. Standing at the mouth of the tunnel, Aiden stands awkwardly with a hand in his pocket and the other at the scruff of his neck.

"Sorry," Aiden says, "but you're needed in there, Leona."

I force out a steady exhale. Colton gently lowers me to the ground, and I flatten my dress back into place. We exchange a glance, one that speaks louder than the words unspoken. I walk away, leaving Colton shirtless and breathless, and join Aiden in the passageway.

"Did *not* see that coming," Aiden says once we're out of earshot. He grins.

My face flushes with heat. "Neither did I."

We continue down the tunnel in silence, our footsteps echoing in unison. I'm grateful he doesn't draw more attention to what he interrupted. When we return to the main cavern, the men have gathered into a sea of standing bodies.

"Did Apsyn arrive?" I ask Aiden as we approach.

He shakes his head. "No, not Apsyn. A girl."

"A girl? Who?"

"We don't know. No one's ever seen her before, and you know how that worked out last time. She wants to speak to you specifically."

We're getting closer now to the crowd. The men split to allow Aiden and I through. Their faces are all fixed on mine, searching for a response from me. I bite my lip and my breaths come quicker.

When we reach the front of the crowd, many of the men have their weapons drawn. A girl with golden hair stands with her back to me.

"Hello," I say, stopping a safe distance away from her.

She turns to face me, her green eyes narrowed on mine. The shape of her face, the structure of her cheekbones—she seems familiar.

"What's your name?"

The girl glances around at the faces surrounding her, at the tips of the swords pointed in her direction. Her fingers clutch the string of the bow stretched across her body. She shifts her weight between her feet, and finally, she answers.

"Merethe Tarva," she says. I flinch at the sound of her surname. "And I'm looking for my mother."

Leona

Chapter 23

I examine the girl's face as I search for the truth in her features. I circle her, all while my men's swords are aimed at her. She watches me carefully, rotating so her eyes are always on mine. The fact that she's heavily surrounded by armed men doesn't seem to faze her.

I nod at Nicolai, who signals to the men to lower their weapons. The girl lets out a subtle breath of relief as the men begin to disperse to other areas of the cavern. A few stay nearby, still not entirely comfortable with the stranger in our midst. We can't afford to have another assassin sneak by, but when I look at this girl, I see desperation, not malice.

"Have a seat." I drop down to the ground to sit and gesture for her to do the same. She pulls her bow over her head and lays it down beside her. "So, you're saying Gracen Tarva is your mother?" A tinge of guilt pulls at my heart.

Merethe looks me squarely in my eyes. "She *is* my mother." I must admit, she does share a lot of Gracen's features. "She's your handmaiden, right? Where is she? Did she follow you when you fled the castle?"

I glance at the ground between us for a moment before answering. If she really is Gracen's daughter, then she deserves to know the truth, no matter how ugly it is. I take a deep breath and pinch the fabric at my knees.

"I'm sorry," I start, "but the night of the revolt, she was killed by the guards at the castle."

As soon as I say the words, I regret their truthfulness. Merethe drops her head and stares into her lap. When she raises it again, her eyes turn glossy in the lantern-lit cavern. She breathes in sharply.

I take another deep breath to keep myself from tearing up as well. There is silence between us as I allow Merethe to process my news. She's come here in search for her mother, only to be told that she'll never see her again. Her head bows once more, and I watch as teardrops splash against the ground below.

A cold chill runs down my spine. I've been where she is. I remember vividly the moment when I was told of my mother's death. No matter the age, it always stings the same.

I look Merethe over and she seems a couple of years younger than me. There's still a softness to her face that hasn't yet disappeared with age. She sniffles then looks up at me, wiping the tears from her eyes.

"She was a kind person," I say quietly. "She saved me." Merethe's lips turn up into a brief smile before fading. "I never knew she had a daughter."

"We were separated right after she had me. She delivered me at her sister's home, but returned to the castle without me."

I frown. "Why's that?"

She shrugs. "My aunt Lizette always said it was safer that way."

"Where are you from? None of the men from the villages recognize you."

Merethe hesitates and toys with the frayed edge of her bodice. "That's because I'm not from any of the villages. I'm from Heraeda."

No wonder why no one here knew who she was. Heraeda is home to those with a higher station than the lower social status of a villager. Placed at the center of the country, the city is Erenen's largest marketplace.

"Heraeda isn't that far from Demesne. When was the last time you saw her?"

She drops her head down again. "Never," she says simply.

I tilt my head. "Never?"

Her eyes meet mine again. "The last time I saw her was when I was born. The only way we kept in contact was through falcons. I don't even know what she looked like."

My heart breaks a little at this. Now that I know Merethe's identity, I see so much of Gracen in her. Their mother-daughter bond was limited to words drafted on parchment.

"We had a routine," she says. "Once a week, we'd send falcons to one another. In the last message she sent me, she said there was trouble at the castle. Then, when she missed sending a falcon a couple of days ago, I knew something had to be wrong."

A bitter taste fills my mouth. Gracen knew something terrible was coming. I wish she would've confided in me sooner. I press my fingers to my temples, easing the ill thoughts out of my mind. What should've happened no longer matters. All that matters now is the present and the future.

"And what of your father? Where is he?"

She shrugs again. "Your guess is as good as mine. All I know is that he's a very powerful man who didn't want me." Venom laces her words.

I don't blame her. Fathers can be the worst. Maybe she was better off never knowing him. Her head drops down causing her wavy strands to fall forward. She pushes the hair away with her fingers. A small mark on the back of her hand catches my attention. Planted at the base of her thumb, an irregular teardrop-shaped discoloration contrasts against her caramel skin. My father had an identical mark.

Memories from my past come rushing to the surface. There was a brief time in my early years when all I could remember was the heated words between Mother and Father. They always thought I couldn't hear them—but I did. Their conversations were too complex for my young mind to comprehend, but I always could tell when they were upset with each other.

Their nightly shouting matches carried down the corridors, my father's booming voice shaking the walls. Many nights I'd lie awake in bed, listening to his roar against Mother's soft cries. Eventually, the arguing stopped—but not because their marriage was getting better. Soon, they couldn't stand to sleep in the same bedchamber together or sit at the same table for supper.

I recall not seeing Father for days at a time. I knew he was still in the castle, but for whatever reason, he kept his distance from Mother and I. For weeks, Mother kept her distance from me as well, though, not in the same way as Father. Mother's never-ending sadness took a toll on her, causing her to spend day and night in her bedchamber. Gracen was her handmaiden at the time, tasked with ensuring Mother at least ate a proper meal each day.

Gracen took a greater role in tending to me, too. We'd take walks in the courtyard, through the lilac gardens. Occasionally during our strolls, Father would pass us—on his way to some important meeting, I'm sure. And for once, his eyes would soften as he looked at us. No, maybe not at us. At her. Gracen's posture would shift each time we paused to let him pass.

Months later, as Gracen's presence dwindled, Mother and Father were eating at the same table, then eventually sleeping in the same bedchamber again. The arguing stopped, and we were happy. At least for a little while.

I press my lips together and hold Merethe's true lineage close. I glance around and realize that the men who'd been keeping a close eye on her have drifted elsewhere in the cavern. We continue to sit with silence between us for another moment.

"So, how did you find us?"

She clears her throat and looks at me. She took after Father's green eyes. "When word about what happened reached Heraeda, I left. I was going to go look for my mother at the castle, but that suddenly seemed like a bad idea, considering." She smiles slightly.

I raise an eyebrow. "So, you found us, how…?"

"Pure luck."

I narrow my eyes. The entrance to the cavern is well-covered. We nearly missed it when we arrived during the day, yet Merethe was able to find it when the sun had already set. My lips pull to the side.

"Is there any food here?" she asks. "I'm starving."

I nod behind her to the supply cart. "There's dried meat and bread. Help yourself."

She smiles widely and stands, throwing her bow across her body. Her steps are hurried as she walks to the other side of the cavern. Her hair swishes over her back, suspicions highlighting each strand.

Colton

Chapter 24

A new swell of energy courses through my veins. The weight on my shoulders feels a little bit lighter after my moment with Leona. My skin is still tingling. Her words, her touch was exactly what I needed to manage a side alley of my dark path.

I search the cavern for Rhyn Clarrick. According to Kaleo, he's a physician who arrived with those from Kaeshul. I spot him leaning against a tall rock column that reaches to the ceiling. As I approach, the thin man straightens his posture and puts the cap back on his canteen. I catch the scent of ale, revealing his drink of choice.

"Is your name Rhyn?"

He slips the canteen into a burlap bag at his feet. "That's what people call me." His lips curl upward. "What can I do for you?" His shirt hangs loose from his shoulders in a way that suggests he used to be able to fill it out more.

"I was told you're a physician. Thought maybe I could get your advice on something."

He slumps against the column again. I wonder for a moment whether he needs the rock for stability. Perhaps seeking advice from him is a mistake.

"You've come to the right person," he says, somehow answering my thoughts. "What's going on?"

I shift my stance. With a look over my shoulder, I check to see if anyone else is standing near. "Ever since the arena, I don't sleep much anymore. And when I do, nightmares haunt me." Rhyn watches me carefully. "How do I make it stop?"

He crosses his arms. They look like fragile sticks against his body. "Well, before I answer that, let me ask you this. How many people have you killed?"

My body tenses at his bluntness. I scratch at the hair on my jaw. "I—I don't know…"

"Yes, you do. How many?"

Anger builds in my core. He stands before me, his mouth pressing up into a sneer, his yellowed eyes scanning me over, his arms still crossed. "I don't know," I repeat, more firmly.

He snaps his fingers. "You're lying to me, and you're lying to yourself. Now, how many people did you kill?"

I ball my hands into fists, my fingernails digging into my palms. This is the only way I can keep myself from striking this so-called doctor. "Nevermind," I say, turning to leave. "Forget it."

"Until you can admit to yourself what you did," he says behind me, "you'll never be able to move past it."

I whirl around with heat in my eyes. "Forty-seven!" My voice echoes in the cavern and everyone stops to look at me. I ignore them. "Okay? Forty-seven."

Rhyn clicks his tongue and smiles. I still want to punch him, but I resist the urge. "There you go... See? That wasn't so hard. First step is done."

My face is stuck in a scowl, but I walk back over to him. "Why does it matter?"

He folds his frail hands in front of him. "It matters because you know how many. Obviously, their deaths affected you enough that you remember each one."

The tension in my forehead relaxes. This is true. I haven't let my mind dwell on it much, but I can recall the face of every life I've ended. And each one haunts my thoughts. I remember how each one was killed and exactly how I felt each time the light drained from their eyes.

"What'd you say your name was?" he asks.

I release my fists and let the anger fade. "Colton Rybolt."

"Well, Colton Rybolt," he says with a smile, "I'm going to tell you what I tell all the other survivors—because you *are* survivors. Stop blaming yourself for things outside of your control."

I roll my eyes. "Easier said than done."

"True. It is. But that's where it becomes your responsibility to be greater than your inner demons. Don't let them rise to the surface. If you keep holding onto the guilt, it's going to consume you." He tilts his head and gives me a sidelong look. "If it hasn't already."

I glance toward the other side of the cavern. Past the crowds, I find Leona sitting with Aiden. She's smiling, her hair contained into a single braid that drapes over her shoulder. I look back at Rhyn.

"So, I accept what I've done, I stop running from it, and then what?" I hadn't noticed, but the canteen is back in his hands. He holds it out to me, offering it. I shake my head.

"Then," he says and takes another sip, "you grieve their loss and move on. And make each day a little bit better than the last. Rinse and repeat."

I pull my lips to the side. "That's it?"

"Yep. Not what you were expecting?"

I run a hand through my hair, pushing it away from my eyes, and shrug. "I guess I didn't know what to expect."

His thin frame sways beside the column. He rolls his head, his neck popping in the movement. He stoops down to put away the canteen and retrieves a small parchment notebook. "You familiar with herbs?" His hand digs around in the bag until he pulls out a quill and bottle of ink.

I peer over the top edge of the notebook as he scribbles some words. "Some."

Noticing my rubbernecking, he steps closer to me. "Skullcap"—he draws a rough sketch of the herb on the parchment—"has lots of tiny purple petals stacked on top of each other. It's good for insomnia." He catches me squinting at the drawing, then laughs. "I never claimed to be an artist, mind you. Now, valerian, it looks like a cloud. Use it for sleep as well." His hand flies across the parchment, noting down the herbs. "And last, but not least, there's wort. It's got five yellow petals—not to be confused with a primrose, though."

"What's it used for?"

He tears the parchment free from the book and hands it to me. "Mood booster."

I glance down at the notes, at the physician's sloppy handwriting and crude sketches. I remember seeing wort growing near the foot of the mountain.

"Thank you," I say, tucking the note in my pocket.

He gives me a kind smile, one that reaches his eyes. The thin skin of his face wrinkles. I turn to walk away, breathing a little easier at the promise of my herb checklist.

The Apsyn fighters have arrived, bringing our total to about three-hundred and thirty men. The cavern is getting cramped, but we make it work. I stand with Leona, Aiden, and the self-appointed village leaders as the other men kneel around us in a half-circle.

"Now that we're all here," Leona says—her voice echoes throughout the cavern so that even the furthest man can hear her—"we should go over the plan of action." She glances at Aiden before returning her gaze to the crowd. "We'll likely only have one chance at this, so we need to be smart. I refuse to allow any more lives to be taken at the hands of the uprising." The crowd murmurs their approval. "So, instead of the previous plan we came up with in Maburh," she nods to Kaleo, whose eyebrows have raised in dislike, "we have another alternative, one that I believe will increase the chances of all of us surviving this."

The crowd mutters again, this time a layer of doubt hanging in the air like fog. I glance around at the diverse faces. The distinctions in the villages are shown in each person's skin tone, the hue of their clothing, the style of their weapon. We're all so different, yet we're more alike than we realize.

My eyes catch the face of someone who stands out the most from us. Her wavy hair hangs low past her shoulders. The fire of a nearby lantern reflects its flicker in her eyes. She stands off to the side with a longbow cradled in her hand. I don't recognize her. She didn't travel here with us. Maybe she came with Apsyn? No, wait—

"Are you all right?" Leona whispers. I glance at her and try to hide the bewilderment in my eyes. At some point during my survey, Aiden began speaking about his plan. He continues with the men's eyes trained on him. They absorb every word. Heads nod in acknowledgment, even Kaleo's.

"Who's that girl?" I ask, glancing in the direction of the stranger.

Leona exhales sharply. "Long story."

"What's the short one?" Maybe I should give the girl the benefit of the doubt, but there's something about the way she was watching that stirs my cautious side. I step backward away from the leaders and Leona follows.

Her eyes are grave. "She's the daughter of my handmaiden."

"The one who died?"

She nods, her eyes heavy. Then, she wraps her arms around her stomach and slowly brings her eyes up to meet mine. "She's also my sister."

She says the words so softly that for a moment, I think I've heard her wrong.

"What do you mean?" I search her face for the humor I'm certainly missing, but her face remains serious.

She swallows and lifts her hands, one by one. "My handmaiden. My father. She doesn't even know we're related."

I can't help the smile that glides across my face. Not that it's funny, but that it's unexpected. My smile must be contagious because Leona's lips shift upward as well.

"Pretty odd time for a reunion."

"Pretty odd girl," Leona says, the humor on her face fading. "She claims she found us by *pure luck*."

My jaw tightens. There are no coincidences when it comes to war.

Behind us, the hooting and clapping of the men startles Leona. I glance down and her hand is on my arm. It softens my heart to know that she once again reaches for me for security.

She clears her throat and removes her hand, then flashes a quick grin before turning toward Aiden. I turn my attention back to the girl, but she's no longer standing where I last saw her. My eyes dart around the cavern, over the tops of heads, until I spot her silhouette scurrying toward the main tunnel. No one else notices. They're all still wrapped up in discussing Aiden's airtight plan. I drift away from them, my steps light and quick, to keep up with the girl. I stay close to the wall as I trail her and keep out of sight. Occasionally, she glances over her shoulder, her hair whipping at the motion.

The tunnel begins to fork, but I'm familiar with the one that leads out of the mountain. Lanterns are spaced infrequently along the walls. I hurry forward but stop in my tracks when I don't see her ahead.

"Stop following me," a voice says behind me.

I spin around and my jaw clenches again. The girl stands with an arrow drawn, its tip aimed at my chest. I narrow my eyes. "Who are you?"

She smirks. "Not your concern."

"Well, if I'm going to die, I'd at least like to know the name of the person who kills me." I really have no intention on dying tonight, but it's worth a shot.

She shifts her stance, but the arrow remains locked on its target. "I'm just a girl doing what I have to do to protect my family."

She releases the arrow but instead of it impaling my chest, she shifts so it takes out our only source of light in this section of the tunnel. The lantern ruptures at the contact of the arrowhead and crashes to the ground. In the darkness, she pushes past me. I stumble on a cluster of stalagmites and catch my balance on the wall.

As much as I want to chase after her, I need to let Leona know of her alleged sister. I take off into a sprint back toward the cavern.

"What happened?" Leona asks, her brows furrowed.

"That girl—she's not who she says she is." My voice is loud enough that those around can hear me.

Leona waves her hands. "What do you mean?"

"She just drew an arrow on me."

Her face firms and she raises an eyebrow. "Where is she now?"

I glance back toward the tunnels. "She took off."

Leona goes quiet while the leaders argue their theories. She and I pass a look that lets me know we're thinking the same thing. That girl is bad news. And now she knows where we are and what we're planning.

Colton

Chapter 25

Tension is high overnight and into the next day as everyone moves uneasily around the cavern. The laughter has stopped. In its place are hushed murmurs of what is to come. I don't know what that girl was up to, but it was seven different kinds of trouble.

There are over three-hundred men here—far too many for us to uproot and seek safe haven elsewhere. So instead, sentries are posted at all the tunnels leading into Mt. Grae. They're alert, focused on searching out the first sign of danger. It's coming, and we all know it.

The afternoon hours drag. Each minute that passes is another minute the men fight to contain their angst. We're not due to leave for Demesne until the sun sets. With a group this large, the cover of night and the empty roads are key to getting us to the capital.

Leona and I make the most of our downtime by training in a quiet corner of the cavern. She's getting better, even managed to draw blood from me a few times. I put in enough effort to give her a challenge, but not so much that I'll hurt her.

Again.

I refuse to let that happen again.

My nerves go haywire whenever we practice close combat. The intoxication that comes with being in her air space is muddled with her persistence of keeping me as her sparring partner. I guess I shouldn't complain. Each time we wrestle, and she pins me to the ground, her position lingers longer than necessary for a simple sparring match.

She pulls herself to her feet and extends a hand to help me up. Her smile lights up my darkness. "You're not letting me win, are you?"

"No," I say, grinning. "Of course not."

She wrinkles her nose.

"Okay…" I confess. "Just a little—"

The warning howl of a sentry cuts through the cavern. All heads jolt up and toward the offended tunnel—the main one. No one in our area makes a sound as the warnings from the tunnels feed off one another into a chorus. Then, the howling stops.

"Arm yourselves!" one of the village leaders calls out.

All the fighters grab their weapons of choice. I stoop down to pick up my sword, the hilt like a magnet in my hand. Leona's eyes are locked on the tunnel. She's without fear. Her fingers grip her dagger as though it's an extension of her arm.

"Stay behind me, okay?"

She opens her mouth like she's going to argue, but then simply nods.

Guards file into the cavern, one after the other, with swords drawn. Our men waste no time in meeting their challenge. The sound of metal clashing echoes within the space.

I glance around. The cavern is steadily being filled with more guards. For every guard who is downed, two more enter and take his place.

Kaleo rushes over to where I stand with Leona. The battle axe in his hand is already wet with blood. "We need to get you out of here, Your Majesty. We're outnumbered."

She nods, her eyes darting around the cavern. "Where?"

"This way," Aiden calls from behind us. Blood drips from his sword as he stands near the glowing blue wall.

Without hesitation, I take Leona's hand and we run over to him. Kaleo follows. We race down the passageway, unsure of where we're running to. We've never needed to leave the mountains by any other means than the tunnels. Loud footsteps come up behind us. I glance over my shoulder and find Rhyn and another man, Skylar, hot on our trail.

We reach the pond, the pond where Leona and I—no, stop it. Not the time.

Aiden's pace slows as his eyes glaze over the water. "Hold on, hold on."

"What?" Rhyn says.

He points to the far side of the pool. "See that? The rest of the water is calm, but there's a ripple there. The water must come in from somewhere. *That's* our way out."

We all look at him with undeniable uncertainty. He rolls his eyes at our skepticism.

"Look, we can either keep running through the tunnels and hope not to run into more guards, or you guys can trust me."

Rhyn shuffles backward away from the edge of the cliff. "I can't go through there." He clinches the strap of his bag, his bony knuckles turning white. The shimmer of the water reflects in his eyes as he stares into it.

Skylar leans over the pond, then looks back at Rhyn. "Why not?"

"I'm more of a…land mammal."

The yelling from the cavern gets louder, the battle sounds echoing along the tunnel that leads to us. The fight is making its way in our direction.

"We're running out of time." Kaleo's jaw flexes as he glares toward the screams.

Leona steps over to Rhyn. She loosens his fingers from the bag and takes them into her own hands. A slow breath escapes her mouth. "We can't stay here. So, we—*all* of us—are going to jump into the water and pray to the gods that Aiden isn't wrong about what's under there."

"Hey…" Aiden chimes in behind her.

The corner of Rhyn's mouth lifts and he juts his chin toward me. "You won't let me drown like this one would, will you?"

My mouth falls open. Rhyn dashes his eyes to me and grins.

Leona chuckles as she pats his hand. "I won't let you drown."

Rhyn reaches into his bag and pulls out his canteen. Shaky fingers unscrew the cap. He takes another swig before putting it away, then nods. "Ready."

We sheathe our weapons and dive head first into the water. It's warm as though hot coals line the bottom. I open my eyes under the surface and search for Leona. I find her an arm's length away. We follow Aiden as he tracks the strange blue glow of the water. We swim deeper and deeper, my lungs burning with each passing second, until he leads us to a small passage under a rock wall.

Luckily, the hole is big enough for us to pass through. Once on the other side, my feet paddle with pressing need to reach the surface. My lungs are on fire, robbed of its much-needed air. We each explode out of the lake with a splash. I wipe the water and wet hair from my eyes. My arms wade as I glance around to account for everyone. Rhyn—we're missing Rhyn. Then, he breaks through the surface, coughing and spitting out water from his lungs. Ale and swimming don't mix. I know this from experience.

"Over there." Skylar points to the wall of trees alongside the bank.

We swim until the water becomes shallow and we're able to stand. There's a chill that slaps against the mountain and bullies my drenched clothing. As we stand on the edge of the water and recover, the cries of dying men from inside the mountain drift in the air. I shudder, not because of the breeze hitting my wet skin, but because I don't know if those cries are from the guards or our fighters.

Leona

Chapter 26

The evening's crisp air rolls in with the setting sun. Streaks of reds and purples coat the clouds. This should've been our moment to strike against the castle. Instead, our clothes cling to our bodies as we trek southbound from the mountains. My teeth chatter, more bumps rise on my arms than I can count, and my toes are numb. Still, I press on with only a minute fraction of my company with me.

We blend into the shadows of the darkening forest. Evergreens shoot from the ground like large blades of grass, their tips wagging from the wind passing overhead. Down below, the forest buzzes with crickets playing their nightly song. The wall of trees breaks off into a small clearing.

"It'll be dark soon," Skylar says. His voice is gruff and full of misguided anger. The tiny metal rod pierced through his eyebrow catches the emerging moonlight. "We should make camp, yeah?"

"Yes," I reply. I look to the others. Kaleo struggles to maintain an unfazed demeanor despite the slight limp in his walk and the hunch in his shoulders. With his husky size, getting through the pool's passageway had been the toughest for him. He'd ignored Rhyn's recommendations for the discomfort. Hopefully, rest will do him some good.

Skylar nods, then directs his attention to the ground, in search of firewood. Rhyn helps him.

"Where are we?" Colton keeps his head on a swivel, never letting himself venture too far from my side.

Kaleo peers in our direction of travel as far as his vision will allow. "I believe we're near the outskirts of Atmoor."

Aiden squints in the direction as well. "Yeah. The city should be just past the edge of the forest."

My body involuntarily cowers. Most of Atmoor's inhabitants are the same people who filled the stands in the arena. Though it is the smallest of the three marketplace cities, its moderate size doesn't hinder the traffic it receives. People from all over the country still travel to it to purchase fine wares.

A thought conjures in my mind. I stare toward the city. "We need supplies."

"You can't expect to just waltz in there and buy provisions," Rhyn says as he tosses kindling into a pile.

I shrug. "No, not buy."

Skylar stops his pursuit of firewood and walks toward me, revealing a crooked smile. "My, my, my. Now, you're speaking my language. Who would've thought our queen had a dark side."

Somehow, his words unnerve me. I tug at the damp fabric of my dress.

"So, you want to steal?" Colton raises an eyebrow. He looks at me with eyes that aren't quite judging but are considering my suggestion.

I hook my hands around the back of my neck. "We lost what we had at the mountain and we need to regroup for what comes next. It'll be hard to do that if we're wasting time hunting down food." I shift my eyes to Aiden's, as though somehow, I am letting him down. He doesn't look disappointed, however, and nods his agreement.

Skylar laughs, causing the crickets to silence for a moment. "Guess it's a good thing you've got a renowned thief with you. Haven't met a lock I couldn't pick." He steps past us and leads the way to Atmoor.

We creep toward a manor set just within the city limits. Red bricks line the path leading to the doors, twin arched slabs of cherry oak with iron knobs. The curtains are drawn back on the front windows, the rooms illuminated with lit chandeliers, revealing all the lavish items inside. I'd grown up with many of the same gaudy decorations, but after spending time in the humbleness of Colton's home, the flashy components that tend to represent social standing now seem to be excessive.

I sneak around to the rear of the manor and remove a cloak hanging on a clothesline. Guilt courses through my veins as I slip it on, but I will away the tightening in my chest. My theft will be for the greater good. Even though the sun is nearly set, the extra security of hiding myself while navigating the city is welcoming. We shouldn't encounter any guards here, but if one of the nobles recognizes me—

"Ready?" Colton whispers behind me.

I nod, pulling the hood over my head. With a creak, a side door opens at the manor, a streak of light pouring out into the surrounding darkness. Colton jerks his head toward the door.

A woman's voice disrupts the muted dusk. "The next time I have to tell you about leaving my garments outdoors, I'll send you back to that miserable village you came from."

"Yes, ma'am." A younger woman's tone quivers. "It won't happen again."

I bite my lip. When the girl's mistress discovers the absent cloak in the morning, she will pay the price for it. Judging by the tone the woman used with her, I doubt the household will allow for any exemptions.

The servant's boots click against the brick steps before falling onto the lush grass of the lawn. Colton brings a single finger to his mouth then nods toward the front of the property. We drift into the shadows, my hand in his, and we dash to where the others are waiting.

We venture further into the city and blend in with other passersby. No one casts a look in our direction, their attention fixed on the recent events of the kingdom. Malicious gossip spews from their mouths. My skin crawls as though a thousand fire ants have taken residence under my clothes.

Skylar hurries ahead of us, looting from the various crowds of people still out spending their coin. So, this is how he'd found himself in the dungeons. I'd heard of him before, though in the whispers of the streets, he usually went by the name *Coyote*. He slinks into the grocer's shop. Seconds later, he reemerges onto the stone-paved streets tucking a loaf of bread in his jacket with an apple hanging between his teeth.

I make sure to keep my face hidden behind the hood of the cloak. Lanterns line the pathways, casting an ambiance that encourages people to resist retiring to their homes. The days run longer in the cities. Bells ring at the opening and closing of shop doors. Consumers in elaborate evening clothes display wide smiles as they nestle their purchases in their arms. The tang of roasted salmon mingles with the fruity scent of the honeysuckle swathed around the signposts. In different circumstances, I'd be able to appreciate the beauty of this city. In different circumstances, I wouldn't be stealing from it.

My eyes catch the loose curls of a woman nearby. The light from the lanterns plays off her golden strands. My nostrils flare. Although I only see the back of her head, it's all I need to see to know who it likely is—a snake. She stares into the storefront window of a cobbler's shop. Her body turns slightly, and her eyes find mine in the crowd. She walks away.

I break off from the group. For once, Colton doesn't notice. Keeping my distance, I trail her down a dark alley, away from the throng of the marketplace. She slows her pace. So, do I. The alley leads nowhere and everywhere at the same time. Endless possibilities for this encounter. Different options for her death. I hesitated once, but I won't make that mistake again.

"Merethe," I growl, closing the distance between us.

She stops and turns. Her green eyes gleam in the sliver of the moon's light. My dagger is already drawn, cradled in my now capable hand. I put the point to her neck and force her against a brick wall.

Her eyes remain calm, but her pulse throbs against my blade.

"Why did you betray me?"

She keeps her gaze locked on me until Colton, Aiden, and Kaleo show up behind us. Rhyn and Skylar wait at the alley's entrance. She lets her eyes linger on Colton for a moment before speaking.

"I need your help."

I press the dagger against her dancing vein. My skin is on fire, hot with rage. I'm not in the mood for her games.

"Why did you betray me?" I hiss each word with conviction.

"Aerok has my aunt. He's holding her hostage in exchange for my obedience." She swallows. "He said that if I told him where you were, he'd release her, but he lied."

"How did you find us at the mountain?" The question comes from Aiden. He stands with squared shoulders and pinched brows.

"I'm good at tracking, believe it or not." She offers a nervous smile that none of us return. "I came across one of the groups and followed them. Turns out, a girl can be stealthier than a guard."

Kaleo walks closer. His face is pulled tight into a snarl. "Don't trust her. Might as well just kill her and be done with it." He waves a dismissive hand in Merethe's direction.

I press the blade harder. My eyes light up as I draw blood.

"Wait, wait, wait," she says in a whisper. "I can tell you everything about what Aerok is doing. Everything that I know."

There's desperation in her eyes—as there should be. She cost us our advantage. Who knows how many of my men lost their lives due to her betrayal?

"You're only saying this because Aerok betrayed you, *after* you betrayed us." I twist my wrist, the point of the blade burrowing deeper under her skin. For the moment, I've forgotten that we share a bloodline.

She glances to Colton once more, no doubt looking for an ally. She won't find one in him. His fists are clenched. He probably wants to kill her himself—and I'd let him. She looks back to me.

"The enemy of my enemy is my friend, right?" She smiles weakly. "Why do you think I let you catch me? Plus, I heard your plans, remember? I can tell you how to use them against Aerok's security protocols."

I ease the pressure on her neck. The thought crosses my mind on how knowing Aerok's plans would be beneficial to us. Still, I'm not entirely convinced.

"How do we know you're not just going to deliver us on a silver platter to him?" Colton asks. "Again."

"As I told you in the tunnel, I'll do whatever is necessary to protect my family."

I exchange a glance with Colton. The irony in her statement makes me consider her words. After a moment longer, I withdraw the dagger from her throat. Kaleo grumbles his objection.

Merethe reaches up to touch her neck. When she removes her fingers, they're wet with blood. I glare at her, unapologetic for the wound. She shrinks back then clears her throat.

"Right then," she says. "My manor's not too far from here. You can rest there... unless you'd prefer to sleep in the woods tonight?"

"I thought you said you were from Heraeda?" A wave of anger rises in my chest.

Merethe eases away from me, out of my arm's reach, away from my dagger. She steps gingerly past the brooding eyes of Kaleo and the death stare of Colton and Aiden. "I lied."

Leona

Chapter 27

The empty rooms of the home say much about Merethe's upbringing. Hollow. Non-existent. The walls are bare. Outlines of the stripped decorations stain the plaster walls. I step pointedly around the house, the heel of my shoe striking against the hardwood planks. My head throbs as I put the quietness of the night into disarray.

Everyone's asleep, even Colton. Rhyn mixed him a tonic full of herbs, and for the first time in a long while, it seems, Colton's found much needed rest. I hover over him as he sleeps on the sofa and watch his chest rise and fall. I feel some sort of way about him. He challenges me and says what's on his mind without regard for my position. I should be offended he doesn't see me first and foremost as a queen. Though, the fact that he sees me for me is probably the reason I'm drawn toward him.

Moonlight sneaks past the window shutters in slices, bringing a paleness to his otherwise dark hair. I smile and extend a hand to touch his face. He stirs, and I stop just before making contact. Soft murmurs come from his mouth, but his eyes are still closed. I bend down and point my ear toward him, hoping to catch his words. What once sounded like mumbled ramblings becomes clear when I close my eyes and listen—*really* listen.

He's speaking Daolic. And not just another proverb. He's speaking it conversationally. His voice is too low and choppy, and I only catch a few strings of words.

…don't leave me…

…I'm scared, Mama. Why do I have to go…?

My brows pull together in confusion as I try to make sense of what he's saying. What's more troubling is that he speaks another language with proper pronunciation. It took me years to be able to speak Daolic fluently. The exhausting task of being multi-lingual is an attribute carried by all monarchs. I spent countless hours with tutors until Father was pleased with my foreign speech.

The East Sea separates Daol from Erenen. I learned Daolic by necessity. What's Colton's reason?

I wait a moment longer to hear more of his words, more of his hidden truths. He's grown quiet, slipping away from the surface of his consciousness and disappearing within his sleep. I nod to only myself, acknowledging his ability to find peace during his slumber.

Around the sitting room, bodies drape the furniture as my men rest their minds. Merethe sleeps as well. Her head is tucked against her arm as she sits at the dining table. She hasn't left my sight since we've been here. Who knows if she'll send word to Aerok of my whereabouts? I won't make the error of underestimating her again.

The corridor leading to the rest of the house is dimly lit with two ornate wall sconces. I'm mindful of my footsteps now, as to not wake the others. My fingers trail along the wooden trim of the wall. A portion of the molding has been replaced with trim that is similar but not an exact match.

My feet carry me to the first bedroom before the end of the corridor. The door is ajar. I put my palm up to it and push, the hinges groaning in response. I glance down the hallway and pause. No sounds. No movements. No one's awake. I'm the only conscious soul in the house of a traitor.

I step into the bedroom, not the least bit guilty about entering a place that is not my own. A four-poster bed takes up majority of the floorspace. A pair of chests with the same carved pattern as the bed flank a broad window. Like the rest of the house, the bedroom consists of the bare minimum. I move further inside. The glint of metal behind the door catches my attention. Several bows, some with metallic adornment, lean against the wall.

This must be Merethe's bedroom.

For whatever reason, this sharpens my attention. I narrow my eyes and search for anything that can give me insight into her life. If there's a vulnerability of hers I can expose, this is where I'll find it. The pale blue light of the moon guides my eyes to exactly what I didn't know I was looking for.

I walk toward a small wooden box that sits on the table. Blank parchments and quills are sprawled around it. I run my fingers over the surface of the box, my tips catching on every imperfection in the wood. A small clasp holds the lid shut. As I open it, letters brim the top from being pushed down into submission. I take out a handful and skim over their words. One message, dated almost eighteen years ago, is tattered at the edges, the ink faded from time. I turn so the moonlight catches the parchment.

Dearest sister,

I do hope you are doing well. I'm sorry to hear about the passing of your husband. I know he was a terrible man, so take solace in acquiring his wealth. You deserve it.

My pregnancy is nearly over. Kol is permitting me to return home so that I may give birth. Home is wherever you are, sister, so I'll be there within the next couple of weeks. It pains me that I won't be able to return to the castle with my child, but I know she'll be in safe hands with you.

Forever bound,

Gracen

A surge of jealousy rattles my spine. I scan through a few more messages in my hands. Gracen not only called my father by his first name, but also mentioned him in letters that could be discovered by anyone. Anyone like me. I release my hold on them and the parchments tumble to the tabletop into a greater mess. I grab another handful from the box. These letters are dated more recently.

My beautiful girl,

Your Aunt Lizette tells me you've been excelling in your archery. I'm glad you are enjoying it. One day, I'll be able to see your skill in person. But until then, mind your aunt, and know that I'll always love you, no matter how far away I am.

With love,

Mama

I look over a few more scrolls. Each one is an update between a mother and her daughter, or between sisters. When Merethe became old enough, I suppose she was able to keep in contact with Gracen herself.

"You shouldn't be in here."

I set the parchments on the table and turn around to face Merethe. She leans against the doorway with her arms crossed over her chest.

"You shouldn't be a liar, and yet, here we are." My words are cold, distant.

She approaches the table and begins collecting the small parchment scrolls strewn all over. She cups them gently and lets them fall from her hands and into the box. Her eyes flit everywhere except to my own.

"So, I take it the *letters* story was true," I say, watching her carefully. "Well, at least, some of it."

She still says nothing. Her attention is on the full wooden box as she tries to shut the lid.

I slam my hand on top of the box, forcing her to acknowledge me. "You knew you were my sister, didn't you?"

She huffs and slowly turns her gaze to me. "Excuse me?"

I roll my eyes and grab her hand, the one with the birthmark. I hold it up and shove it in front of her face. "You. Me. Sisters. Stop acting like you didn't know." I nod toward the box.

She snatches her hand back and brings the wooden box close to her chest. "The letters never said for certain who my father was, and *Kol* is a fairly common name, but I'm not an idiot. So, yeah. I figured it out."

She carries the box to her bed and shoves it under her pillow.

"Sister, or not," I keep my voice calm, trained, "if you betray me again, I will kill you."

I walk toward the door to let her re-examine her next move against me. My promise roars louder than the silence filling the bedroom, so loud, that I almost want her to test my patience.

Leona

Chapter 28

The next morning, bowls of fresh fruit and soft bread layer the table. We sit around it, picking at the contents, filling our bellies. Merethe sits across from me, her eyes low, careful to not let her gaze linger on any one person for too long. The others' silent hatred of her is an invisible fog that flows around the food. She sighs then pushes her plate away and rests her arms on the table.

"Just so you all know," she says, finally bringing her eyes up, "it wasn't anything personal. I'm sure you are all lovely peop—"

Kaleo's fist lands with a bang on the table. "Cut the shit. What happened to our men at the mountain?"

Merethe flinches. My eyes are fixed on hers as she handle's Kaleo's aggression. After a breath, she regains her tact. She relaxes her shoulders and leans forward. Golden waves frame a heart-shaped face. Youthful. Naive. Deceptive. "As far as I know, your men were taken back to the dungeons."

Kaleo's knuckles pop as he flexes them back into fists. "How many did they take?"

"No clue." Merethe crumbles a chunk of bread between her fingers. "I never saw them."

"Tell us what you know about Aerok, then," Colton says.

"Word around town is that he has set his sights on reopening the arena with people from other countries as well."

"How does he expect to do that?" Skylar pops a strawberry into his mouth. "Can't imagine people will be lining up to volunteer."

Aiden shifts in his seat and crosses his arms over his chest. "That didn't stop him from forcing us into it."

"Which kingdom is he targeting?" I drum my fingers on the table.

Merethe shrugs. "I don't know. I've heard rumors of Braer and Espela. It'll likely be Espela since it's closest to the military port."

Less than a week has passed, and my nation may be on the brink of war with another equally strong nation. Aerok doesn't know what he's doing. He's always been driven by impulse, the need to do whatever necessary to win. It was one of the reasons he came so highly recommended as my Lord Commander. He's traded his title for one that is beyond his scope of understanding. He wants to be a king but has no idea how to maintain a kingdom. First rule:

don't steal people from other nations.

I push my own plate away. "Espela has a fortified military. How does he plan to breach their walls and take their people without alerting ground forces?"

Merethe looks up at the chandelier hanging above our heads. She studies it for a second before returning my gaze. "When I was leaving the castle, I overheard some of the guards posted outside when they didn't think I was listening. They were talking about how Aerok had sent a group, maybe thirty to forty of his best men on a single ship. No war banners. Nothing on the ship that would announce the nation that is invading." Everyone's quiet, hanging onto her words. "I'm assuming he plans to have the guards sneak onshore, collect people during the night, and set sail before anyone notices the absences."

"When does he plan on doing this?" Kaleo asks, his voice hoarse.

"Now." Merethe blinks. "If the guards I overheard weren't lying, they should already be on their way."

"You mean, if *you're* not lying." Colton's jaw is set, his eyes ten different levels of suspicious. "How old are you, anyway? Twelve?"

All Merethe can do in response is scoff. She flips her hair over her shoulder. "Eighteen next month—so, three years older than the age your brain is stuck in. And, I'm telling you the truth. Whether or not you want to believe it, that's on you."

Colton opens his mouth to launch another comeback. Under the table, I reach a hand out to touch his leg. He looks at me reluctantly then settles.

"There are nearly four-hundred guards," I start, "best case scenario, forty of them are on a ship headed elsewhere, half are off-duty in the barracks, and fifty or so are patrolling the castle—"

Merethe shakes her head. "Actually, there were a lot less guards in the castle when I was there. A single guard was posted maybe every thirty feet on the castle walls, and if I wanted to, I could turn down a corridor inside and not see anyone."

Aerok has decreased his defense. The move may be cocky or reckless—I'm not sure which yet. Of course, why would he have anything to fear at the moment? He's gotten everything he's ever wanted—a heavy crown to fill the hollowness of his heart. His choices will be the death of him.

"So, then the castle is under-guarded, is that what you're saying?" Rhyn asks. He fidgets with his fingers as though he's trying to distract his mind from something. It doesn't seem to be working.

Merethe nods. "That's exactly what I'm saying." She presses a finger to the table, dragging it as she speaks. "If you want to get into the castle, now is your best chance to do it."

"And what do you get out of it?" Colton asks. Surprisingly, his voice is calm and level, probably luring Merethe into a false sense of security.

"My aunt," she says merely. "I want her out. You want to get in. Everyone wins."

The room goes quiet. A dozen eyes all look to me as I consider Merethe's words. It wouldn't be the first time she's misled us. Then again, if she is genuine in her family values, she wouldn't allow her aunt to remain a pawn in Aerok's game.

I nod. "For your sake, I hope you're not lying."

One of the things Merethe's aunt had acquired was a stable of horses. Dozens of them. Each one primed and healthy and available for use. Aiden pulls me aside while the others are preparing a few horses for travel.

"We're still going to stop by Durst, right?" he asks.

"Of course." I smile.

"Do you trust her?" He peers at Merethe as she slips the bridle over her horse's head.

My smile fades. "Not at all."

"Do the others know? Colton?"

The pressure in my temples build and my eyes are grim. I shake my head. "No. They'll know when it's time."

A crease sinks into Aiden's forehead. I look over his shoulder as the others approach with the horses.

"Can I count on you?" I whisper.

He nods solemnly then wipes his face clean of angst before Colton notices.

Colton guides a chocolate thoroughbred to me. Draped over its hindquarters are riding bags full of supplies Skylar pillaged from the city. He extends his hand to help me up. His palm is calloused and delicate all at once. My thoughts swirl back to what it felt like to have them on my body. I flush and quickly mount the horse, hoping he didn't see his effect on me. It pains me not being upfront with him, but it's better this way. In time, he'll see that I'm protecting him. Colton offers me a kind smile then mounts his own horse. Soon after, we're trotting out of Atmoor under the rising sun.

By mid-afternoon, we enter the small village of Durst. What it lacks in size, it makes up for in beauty, just as I remember it. Blossoming flowers of all colors line the pathway into the community. The homes are similar to the ones in Maburh, except here, most are two-story constructions.

We capture the attention of the few people littering the streets. I pull the hood of my cloak down to cover my face and tuck my dark hair back as well. *Hair so black it looks blue*, people described it as. They glance up from toiling away in front of their homes as we pass by on our horses. A young child tries to dash toward us, but his mother pulls him back and hides him behind her legs. Is this what life in my kingdom has come to? Instead of visitors being welcomed, people fear newcomers, fear the unknown?

Some people must recognize Aiden, though. He rides at the front of our group, guiding us to his destination. Eyes peer at him, then dart back to the rest of us, no doubt silently questioning his safety.

One set of eyes are set on him with utter disgust. Brows screwed up, eyes narrowed, lips fixed in a fragile line that they almost disappear. A man stands in the doorway of his home, staring at Aiden as he rides by. Aiden doesn't look straight at the man, but I can tell he's trying to steal a glance. The man grumbles something then retreats into the house, slamming the door shut. Aiden's shoulders relax and he sighs.

Colton shifts his horse forward, so he and Aiden are riding side-by-side.

"Are you okay?" he asks.

Aiden nods. He keeps his eyes focused ahead of him. "Garret's house is this way." He turns his horse onto a secondary path.

We stop in front of a two-story home, its structure like every other house in the village. Empty flower boxes hang outside each window with the ghost of floral decor that used to be. The home is offset from the others and with the straight trunks of the aspen trees that surround it, it almost looks as though the home itself is imprisoned.

Aiden enters the house alone while we wait outside. I look over as Merethe graciously rubs down her horse's neck and Skylar massages his thighs from the trip. I suppose the great *Coyote* isn't accustomed to traveling by horseback. A smile nearly wriggles along my lips, but vanishes when Colton comes to stand by me.

"How are you doing?" he asks. "You haven't said much on the way here." My heart aches a bit. Unintentional or not, my muteness hasn't gone unnoticed.

"I've just had a lot on my mind." I don't tell him that I've been tearing myself up about keeping things from him and the others. About lying. No, not lying. I'm omitting the truth—there's a difference. He nods and doesn't press me for further details.

"Can I ask you something?" I bite my lip and focus my eyes on the thin necklace strap peeking above his collar.

"Go for it," he says softly.

"You're not from Erenen, are you?" I keep my voice easy, non-threatening. Depending on the circumstances, I'm not sure how loaded this question is.

He's quiet for a moment as he searches my eyes. I reach up and pull the necklace out so the pendant lays over his shirt. The sun catches the metal disk and the blue-green gem inset in the center. Tourmaline, a native earth stone to Daol.

"I saw it when we were… in the cave." Heat flushes my cheeks. "I didn't think much of it until I heard you speaking Daolic again in your sleep last night."

He steps backward, allowing enough of the afternoon breeze to caress us separately. He looks to the ground and crosses his arms over his chest. His jaw tightens and he avoids my eyes. "What was I saying?"

"I couldn't tell," I lie. I don't wish to torment him with his subconscious thoughts. He has enough to deal with. "I guess whatever Rhyn had you drink worked a little too well." I laugh faintly, hoping to ease the tension building in his shoulders. He lifts his head and bears a semblance of a grin. I wait patiently to see if he'll speak. Seconds turn into minutes.

"I was six when I came here." He speaks low enough that I have to step forward to hear him. "My mother—the one you met in Maburh—found me drifting to shore in a dinghy. She saw the necklace, too, and said I had to have been on the water for at least five days if I came from Daol. I had nothing but dried meat and a canteen with me." He presses his eyes shut. "I remember sleeping most of the time. Keeping my eyes closed was better than looking out across the vast sea and not knowing where I was going or if I would end up dead." He squeezes his arms tighter against his chest.

The hairs lift on the back of my neck. "Who sent you in the boat?"

He shrugs and drops his arms. "I… I don't know." He's avoiding my eyes again. He's lying. *I'm scared, Mama…why do I have to go?* He doesn't know that I know his truth.

"Oh," I manage to say. "We don't have to talk about it if you don't want to." He's offers a weak smile. I mirror his gesture and turn to walk away. "Excuse me," I say quietly.

He doesn't stop me. He doesn't say my name. He lets me go.

I walk over to where Rhyn sits against a tree. He clutches his canteen in his hand. I know it's not water inside, but he functions well with the ale, so I don't mind. I brush away pebbles from the dirt and sit beside him.

"How's our boy doing?" he whispers. Colton is far enough away that he wouldn't have been able to hear anyway at normal volume.

"He's…" I start to say. "Do you really think those herbs will help him?"

Rhyn tucks the canteen away in his bag. He pulls his legs in so they cross in front of him. He's limber for an older man.

"The herbs will help, so long as he lets them help." He clears his throat and rotates a silver band on his finger. "But it'll take time to break down the wall he's guarding himself with."

We both look across the lot at Colton. He leans a shoulder against a tree with his back turned to us. His head is down, his arms are bent at the elbows. I wonder if he's looking at the relic of his past.

I feel a tinge of guilt in my veins as I discuss him with a third party, but it seems Rhyn has a better understanding of Colton's anguish than I do. I sit up straight and pull my shoulders back. My hands are folded neatly in my lap. Correction: my hands grip one another to soothe my anxiety.

"But it's possible for him to recover from... this?"

Rhyn chuckles. His voice is smooth, relaxing. Exactly what you would expect from a physician. "It's possible," he says. He runs his fingers through the length of his beard, a sea of varying gray strands. "Now, I never experienced the arena myself, so I don't know exactly what he's experiencing. But I do know that the mind is stronger than most people give it credit for."

"How so?"

"I'll put it like this—you have power over your mind, not outside events. Once you realize that, you'll find strength. So, Colton needs to find a way to take back control of his mind."

I look down at my hands, open and close them, and hope to find the answer to all the world's problems in my palms. All I find are healed scrapes from my new reality.

"Do you care for him, Your Majesty?"

My head snaps up in Rhyn's direction. His eyes are soft, paternal. He's grinning like he already knows the answer. He's analyzing every nuance, every gesture of my face, anything that will support his theory.

"No."

He leans back and tilts his head. "No?"

"*No.*" The muscles in my arms twitch and my brows pull together. "At least, not in the way you're suggesting."

He catches my underlying tone and smiles. His arm reaches blindly for his bag, for his canteen. He finds it and brings it to his chest, then holds it out to me. My eyes dash from the canteen to his face. I force a smile and shake my head.

I didn't mean to snap at him, but his question crept under my skin and nestled around my veins. I've known Colton for less than a week. I can't deny that I'm attracted to him. And I like that I feel less burdened when it just the two of us. Regardless, there's still plenty that we don't know about each other, and those secrets keep me from give Rhyn the answer he expected.

"Back the hell up—"

I'm jarred from my thoughts at Merethe's voice. She and Colton are going toe to toe, yet again. His tall frame towers over her petite one, but his size doesn't seem to intimidate her. Kaleo stands at Colton's side, content at letting the two argue. I grumble and pull myself to my feet.

"You should leave, little girl, while you still have a chance."

"Is that a threat?"

"What"—I step between them—"is going on?" My eyes shift to each of their faces.

Colton speaks first. "She needs to go. There's no way we can trust her." His hand rests on the hilt of his sword.

Fingers flex around it like a cobra right before it intends to strike.

"Yeah, well, no one can trust a loose cannon like you," Merethe spits back.

My eyes shoot daggers at her. She catches my warning and changes her attitude. I look to Colton and soften my own demeanor. "Do you trust me?" I instantly regret the words as they pass over my tongue.

He stares at me, his tense forehead relaxing as he considers my question. I wish I could say his hesitation comes as a surprise to me. "Of course, I do."

I turn to him and block Merethe from his view. "Then, stop all this. Please. All of this will be for nothing if we keep fighting each other." He peers over my shoulder at her. She rolls her eyes and walks away. I hold a hand to his chest, directing his attention back toward me. "All right?"

He sighs and mumbles his acknowledgment.

I look away to find Aiden standing outside the door. He nods once, his ginger hair highlighted in the sun.

I lift my foot to walk toward him when Colton seizes my hand, clutches it firmly within his. I cock my head to the side. He leans down, his voice a whisper. "There's something not right about her. I know it." He holds my hand and my gaze for a slow second before releasing them both. His words aren't of spite, but of caution.

Colton

Chapter 29

We arrive in front of stone house with sharp corners at three edges and a cylindrical tower at the fourth. It's bigger than many of the other homes around here and has a smithshop attached to the ground floor.

Skylar whistles his amusement. "Damn," he says, taking in the structure. "This is pretty decent."

Aiden stops in his tracks and glares at Skylar. "Keep your hands to yourself." His words are curt. "Nothing better come up missing."

Skylar grins and holds his hands up. "Relax, relax... I hear ya." Still, his eyes dance around the concrete porch and land on a golden vase set in the corner. Though blue flowers cascade over the rim, it's not the perennials that has Skylar's interest.

We wait for Aiden to open the door with the set of keys Garret Lenore gave him. The door creaks open and we follow him in.

Sunlight shoots into the house, every which way, from the windows lining the walls. Cobwebs and dust litter the area. It doesn't look like the house has had much use in the past few weeks.

Aiden tries to hide the pain behind his eyes as he surveys the interior. He blows the dust off a couple of lanterns and wipes their glass clean with his sleeve. He lights them, offering a little more light into the rooms. The others might be buying into his indifference, but I read the unsaid words of his tense shoulders.

"So, this is all yours now?" Kaleo asks. He pulls a chair out from the table and sits down, not bothering to remove the dust first. His ankle rises and rests on the knee of his other leg.

Aiden shoves his hands into his pockets and half-smiles. "Yeah. I guess so."

Kaleo laces his fingers together and cradles them behind his head. "Not bad. Shall we get started, then?"

"Yeah." Aiden looks to the rest of us. "Um, make yourselves comfortable." He hurls Skylar another warning glance, then he and Kaleo disappear through a door leading to the shop.

Hours pass while Aiden and Kaleo forge a variety of weapons. Swords, arrows, knives, each brought to life using Aiden's designs for a more efficient weapon. For a while, I sit in the shop and watch them work. The room is hot, a sweltering dry heat, but it doesn't seem to bother them. Tools line the walls, each serving a different purpose in producing something out of nothing.

I can see why Aiden took to weapon-making. There's something mesmerizing in it. To take a piece of raw ore and forge it into a piece of art. It's intriguing.

Not after long, neither of them notices me in the room. They're both focused on creating as many weapons as they can for us. We're going to find the men that we lost, and when we do, they'll need to be armed.

I wander around the shop, careful to stay out of their way. On a far table, there's a small, whittled piece of wood. Earlier, Aiden had been hunched over it as he worked. I pick it up with both hands and it lays across my open palms.

An intricate scroll pattern is carved on one end. Meticulous detail went into making the wood appear to swirl around itself into a flawless flow. The other end tapers to a rounded point. I turn it over in my hands, appreciating the wood grain that runs the length of the tool.

I look over my shoulder at Aiden. His back is turned to me as he leans over the kiln. The flames rise and lick the air as he moves a red-hot piece of steel in the embers.

As I put the wood back onto the table, the scroll end shifts away from the other half. A knot forms in my stomach and I check Aiden's attention again. I know he hasn't killed much, but he'd probably kill me for breaking his thing, whatever this is. I bring it closer and squint, hoping I can fix it before he notices.

A difference in the material catches my eye. I pull the two halves further apart. Attached to the scroll end, there's a thin knife that fits securely into the rounded side. A dagger. He made a dagger. I remove it completely from the wooden sheath and inspect the blade. The thickest part of the steel is the width of my pinkie. I lay a finger on the blade and without applying any pressure, the metal bites into my skin. Droplets of blood squeeze through the cut. I pop my finger into my mouth and absorb the metallic taste on my tongue.

"You'll want to be careful with that."

Aiden carefully takes the dagger and inserts it back into the sheath. He lays it down on the table.

"Sorry, man. What's it for?"

Soot is settled into the thin lines of his face. His usual paleness is darkened from the time by the fire. He leans back against the table and folds his arms over his chest.

"It's for Leona."

I glance down at the tool again, then back at him. "It doesn't look like a normal dagger."

He picks it up and rotates it around the rounded point. "That's because it's not supposed to look like a normal one. She'll wear it in her hair while she's there." His eyes are weary, his voice is grim.

I cock my head to the side. "While she's where?"

"Huh?" He sets the dagger back down and wipes the sweat sitting on his forehead.

"You said, *while she's there*. Where's *there*?"

He shakes his head and pushes his damp hair from his eyes. "Sorry, must be the heat finally getting to me."

I pull my lips to the side. "You're a bad liar. Tell me what's going on."

His silence confirms my suspicions. There's something he's not telling me. "Aiden…" I wait for another moment.

"You should talk to her," he finally says, pushing himself from the table. Without saying another word, he turns to walk back toward the other end of the shop. He rejoins Kaleo and the strike of the hammer hitting the metal amplifies the questions in my mind.

Leona

Chapter 30

The air is hot tonight. Or maybe it's the heat from the smithshop spilling into the atmosphere. Regardless, I take advantage of it by lying under a tree in a secluded area of the property. The earth is soft, the grass providing extra cushion against my back.

Every now and then, Rhyn's head peeks over the stone wall to check on me. If he's trying to be stealthy, he's failing, but I don't mind the security of knowing my welfare is being watched.

We received word that many of our men escaped the mountains and took refuge in Oerdin. The guards have already scoured the village and isn't likely to make a return trip so soon. They also wrote about the ones who didn't survive. Six casualties, so far. Six souls that were unjustly released from their bodies.

Aerok hasn't given up on hunting me. In Oerdin, a home was reduced to ashes and a young girl perished in the flames. The message said she resembled me and made the mistake of running into the house to dodge the guards' pursuit. When the guards returned the next morning to verify my death, not so much as a hint of remorse passed their lips when they discovered the girl was not the queen.

My laced fingers rise and fall as they rest over my stomach. My eyes scan the skies above as hundreds of tiny stars blink back at me. Against the vast expanse of the sky, I'm so small in comparison. Suddenly, my issues don't seem so dire. The stars remind me that there's a whole world out there I haven't yet discovered.

I find a group of stars true to the old tale Mother once told me. *Ursidae Micro*, or *Little Bear*. Four points of the constellation form a box with three more stars extending from a corner. Mother said that in a sleuth, the strongest member will always be the youngest bear. The group's entire future rests on his success. Although he is small, and therefore underestimated, he will bring along a brighter tomorrow when all the seasoned bears have long passed. My heart sputters as I remember her calling me her little bear. There was so much adoration in her voice as she crooned the words.

"You're hiding something."

I bring my elbows behind and prop myself up. Colton stands before me, arms crossed, face stern. I groan and pull myself upright. No sense in keeping it from him any longer. I pat the ground beside me. He blows out his cheeks and releases the air, then reluctantly sits.

"Tell me what's going on." His face relaxes from anger to confusion, then to anxiety.

I take a deep breath and turn to face him. His eyes peer through mine, past the defensive walls I can't keep up. "I'm letting Merethe take me to Aerok."

He flinches. His jaw falls into his lap. He pinches the bridge of his nose between his eyes and forces a hard exhale. Every reaction I predicted from him rushes into existence. "What the hell are you thinking?"

I stiffen my spine and sit up a little taller. "I'm thinking that if there's a chance for me to end this, then I should take it."

"Is that what the hair thing is for? And *Merethe?*" He stabs a finger toward the house. "You're going to trust her to get you there?"

"She was going to betray us again—you and I both know this—but at least we can use it to our advantage."

"What advantage is there? You're surrendering to that piece of shit." His body is shaking from the anger building within. I reach out and lay a hand over his. His skin is hot as flames simmer in his veins, but his shuddering calms at my touch.

"Colton," I say delicately, "while I am there, the rest of you need to continue with the plan. Regroup with the rest of the men in Oerdin and find a way to take the castle."

"What about you?"

My smile reaches my eyes and I withdraw my hand. "Don't worry about me. I'll do what I can from the inside —hopefully that includes killing Aerok." He casts a sidelong glance and chews on his bottom lip. "I can *do* this," I say, trying to convince myself more than him.

"And what if he kills you on the spot?"

"He has no reason to kill me if he believes I'm no longer a threat. It would still be in his best interest to marry me."

He rubs his palms against his eyes. "You're insane. You know that, yeah?"

I laugh and it catches him off guard. He looks at me as though I have two heads and one is on fire.

"Why are you laughing? You're literally walking up to the devil's door."

I try to suppress my grin, but it breaks through the seams. "This is the most levelheaded I've felt in a long while. I can't keep letting others fight all my battles. Too many people have already died because of me, and it's time I extend the same risk."

He drags his hand down his face. A plume of smoke rises from the shop's chimney. We watch in silence as the smoke loosens its shape and scatters into the night.

"I don't want you to get hurt." Colton fixes his view onto the ground in front of him. He plucks a blade of grass from the soil and wraps it around his finger.

My mouth shifts into a smirk. "It almost seems like you care about me."

"And what if I do?" His face is firm, no humor visible. He blinks. Blinks again.

My smile wanes. "You can't... You don't even know me."

"I know how I feel when I'm around you." He flicks the grass away. "It's like I can finally breathe again, and my issues aren't weighing me down."

My heart freezes. I shake my head, my thoughts rattling. "I can't be your… escape from reality."

He runs his hand through his hair and sighs. "No, I know. I mean—I can't be the only one who feels something between us? The only one who felt something last time?"

I've made it a point to not think about what happened *last time*. I can't afford the distractions, not when we're so close to everything changing. Then again, not only would I be lying to him, but I'd be lying to myself by dismissing whatever feelings dredge up to the surface.

I wrap my arms around my torso and look up into the night sky. I search for an answer in the cosmic sea but its ruthless, watching as I drown, refusing to throw me a buoy. I can feel Colton watching me as well, awaiting my answer.

My eyes land back on his. I clear my throat and focus to steady my voice. "You're not the only one." A lightness fills my chest as I say the words.

He releases a slow exhale and smiles. It's contagious, and soon I'm smiling, too. He leans over. "Really?" His voice is a whisper, but I hear him perfectly. The warmth of his breath tickles my cheek and sends a chill down my spine.

I nod and his nose grazes my face. He's testing me. Again. He knows if I turn my head, we'll make contact.

So,

I close my eyes

and turn.

Our lips meet in a gentle way. I break the connection and shake my head. "You don't know me," I whisper against his mouth. His hand comes up behind me as his fingers suspend themselves in my hair. He cradles a palm against my cheek. His thumb brushes against my bottom lip.

"I'll get to know you," he replies. He presses his lips to mine again. I pull away.

"You have secrets." My fingers skim the length of his arm and I hold his hand against my face. I breathe in the scent of his skin.

"And one day," he says in between the kisses, "I hope to tell you of them." He deepens the kiss and any other excuse I had fades from my thoughts. He lowers me onto the ground and slides down beside me. His arms, muscular and rigid, wrap around my waist, pulling me close.

For a moment, I remember something else. My eyes shift to the stone wall. "What about Rhyn? He's been keeping an eye on me."

Colton looks back toward the wall. "He knows I'm out here with you, so he went back inside."

I nod my acknowledgment and let his lips continue to taste mine. I didn't realize how much I've missed this. I've missed the way I feel when his arms are around me—the way they envelop me with a sense of safety I've never known.

My hands explore his chest, the hills and valleys of his torso. His muscles tense as I pass over them. He shivers against me and his breathing quickens. I smile against his lips. He pulls back and looks at me.

"What?" He grins as his finger trails the side of my face.

"Nothing. It's just, I like that I can make you shake like this."

He pulls me closer. "Oh, is that right?" His lips find my neck. I angle my head to let him in. I choke back a gasp, but it doesn't keep my body from quaking. He lifts his head, smiling, pleased with himself. "You were saying?"

My hand slides under his shirt, along his rib cage. Even without seeing the scars, I know when I've touched them by the sudden change in texture. His eyes are bright in the dark. He sits up and takes off his shirt, then tosses it aside. I press a palm against the ground and push myself up as well. He wastes no time guiding my lips to his. He slips a hand down my back and follows the curve of my spine. It arches in response. I hook a hand behind his neck and throw my leg over his so I'm sitting in his lap. His breathing shallows.

Right now, there's nothing else in the world that matters. In this moment, it is me and him and the thousands of stars looking on in wonder. Part of me cares for him—and that's the part that scares me. I've never prepared for the recklessness that comes with being a young adult. And yet, I feel so ready.

I hitch up my dress and pull it over my head. His mouth parts and his eyes never leave my skin. They drink me in with an insatiable thirst. There's a sudden chill in the air that hits my back, but the warmth of his hands caressing me quickly resolves this.

He looks me over, his face betraying the anxiety his eyes try to hide. "You want to…?" His fingertips trail the curves of my waist.

I nod, biting my lip. I force away the urge to cover my unclothed body. "But I've never done… this." A fluttery feeling rolls in my stomach. I'm almost embarrassed to admit nineteen years have passed and I haven't executed such a basic human task. He doesn't react to the news in the way I feared.

Instead, he smiles and pulls me to him, our bare chests sparking a fire in the night. Smoke rises above, sending a signal that I don't need a buoy, after all. He kisses my forehead and nose before his mouth finds a home against mine. He's drawing me in, holding me close with the same hands that once threatened my life. It's peculiar how circumstance can change perception.

The sounds of nature play us a lullaby as our breathing quickens and he lays me down. His body hovers over mine while he showers me with kisses. His lips journey across my skin, touching old places, new places, all of which are good places. There's a gentleness to him, one he doesn't let exposed too often. My steel walls are down, and I completely surrender myself to him.

The moon drifts across the region and begins to abandon the night in lieu of the sun. There's still enough darkness that the morning birds haven't awoken yet. Carefully, I unwrap Colton's arm from my waist. He sleeps soundlessly. No nightmares. No sleep-talking. Just effortless rest. For a while, I watched him sleep. I committed the image of his face—this face, one without burden—to the safest vaults of my mind.

I pull my dress back on and quickly finger-comb my hair. Blades of grass tumble out of the strands. I walk back toward the house, pausing at the stone wall to catch a last glimpse of him. His body is silver in the moonlight.

Inside, the house is quiet. Aiden and Kaleo finally yielded to the night after working diligently on crafting weapons for use. The dagger Aiden made me sits on a table near the door. I inspect it, marveling at the beauty of such a deadly device. With one hand, I wind my hair into a thick rope and use the hairpin to secure a coil to the back of my head.

Floorboards creak in the distance. I look up.

"Ready?" Merethe asks. A bag is hoisted over her back. Her bow is securely cradled in her fingers.

I nod. "Let's go."

Merethe and I quickly put distance between us and the others left in Durst. Our horses charge forward, the sounds of hooves thundering against the ground. We limit our time on the main road to avoid unnecessary trouble.

A sense of acceptance washes down my back, flowing out as my cloak trails behind me in the breeze. I could turn back if I wanted to. I could tell Colton that he was right, that I *am* insane, and let his lips kiss my worries away. But I won't. I'm a queen, and this is the burden of my status.

I meant it when I told Colton I can't always let people fight my battles, even if their loyalty to me swears them to. I must've missed the lesson where I should cower behind a net of safety and let others bleed for me. Maybe I am insane. Maybe this is why I'll fail as a monarch. Or maybe, this is the type of response my reign requires for its success. I need to show my people—my traitors—that I won't be bullied or cast aside while my nation collapses. I live for my country. I will die for it, too.

We take occasional breaks to rest the horses, and by nightfall, we're over halfway there. Halfway home. Halfway to the point of no return.

We make camp in an area of a forest dense with trees. The small fire between us fills the silence of the night. The wood crackles as the flames consume everything it touches. The blaze is similar to my half-sister. Her eyes are down, focused on the bread she's been picking at for the past few minutes.

I clear my throat and her eyes dart up abruptly. The fire turns her face a deeper golden color. She looks so much like Gracen, with the complexion of my father. Our father.

"I find it ironic that your loyalty lies with your family, and yet you so easily are willing to betray me although we are bound by blood."

She sits up straight and holds the bread in her lap. "Didn't you threaten to kill me, dear sister?" She chuckles. "How's that for irony?"

"I'm protecting myself. I have no clue who you really are, and you've already proven that you can't be trusted."

"So why are you letting me take you back? Why have you let me know the other side of your plan?"

"Because," I say, keeping my eyes trained on hers, "you wouldn't have stopped trying to betray us until you got your aunt back. At least this way, after she's freed, you can crawl back to whatever shadow you stumbled out of, and my people can finish doing what they need to do.

She twists her mouth as though she tasted something sour. "And how do you know I won't just tell Aerok what you're really doing?" Her age is highlighted in her tone.

"I don't. But I'm hoping that if family means anything to you, you won't interfere."

She tears off a piece of bread and tosses it into her mouth. Her eyes stare into the flames.

"Besides," I continue, "in a way, Gracen was my family, too. I won't dishonor her by letting her sister's life hang by the thread of a madman."

Merethe smiles but it disappears as quickly as it comes. "Did she suffer?"

Images flash in my mind, one after the other, of a time filled with much more chaos than I've ever known. It has been nearly a week since Gracen died, but when I close my eyes, it's like I'm standing back in my bedchamber, watching helplessly as her blood stains the marble. I watched the moment when she knew she would not make it out alive. She died trying to warn me, and for that, I'll always be grateful.

I shake my head. "No. It was quick." Truth is, I don't know if she suffered at all. I don't know how many seconds lulled between the time the blade ran through her to the time she took her last breath. And I don't want to know. Neither should Merethe.

Thankfully, she doesn't press the topic further. We sit in silence and let the flames hold its own conversation. The moonless night is made darker by our pasts. Only the glow of the fire brings about a glimmer of a future.

"I wouldn't have pegged crazy as your type."

I cock my head. "Excuse me?"

She grins. "You and Pretty Boy."

Warmth finds my cheeks in an uncontrollable blush. I wrap my cloak tighter around my shoulders. "What are you talking about?"

"No need to be bashful." She laughs. "I saw you two. He's very attractive"—she connects her thumb and forefinger together in a circle, the other three fingers pointing skyward—"so good job on that. I'm just surprised you can see past his psycho-ness."

"He's not psychotic," I snap.

She throws her arms up defensively, making no effort to hide her display of amusement. "I was just joking. Lighten up."

I drag my bag closer to me and lay my head against it. My mental capacity to engage in an altercation with her has dwindled with the heat of the fire. I brush dirt over the remaining embers until they're snuffed out. Merethe scoffs then shuffles against the ground to make herself comfortable.

"Goodnight," she says in an animated tone.

I don't respond. Instead, I press my eyes closed and hope I don't end up killing her before morning comes.

Colton

Chapter 31

By morning, Aiden finishes up our new weapons. The humid air sticks to my face as I test my sword in front of the house. The grip of it feels extremely comfortable in my hand. I flex my wrist, shifting the blade with ease as though it were a weightless device. Aiden's talent will change weapon-making for years to come. He discovered a way to thin out the blade to reduce the weight, then also temper it so the thinness doesn't interfere with its durability. Bladesmith work certainly suits him.

Kaleo's weapon of choice, a warhammer, is beyond intimidating. On both sides of the hammer, four sharp points will do extensive damage should someone ever find themselves at the business end of it. Its weight is massive. I tried wielding it yesterday and nearly pulled a shoulder. Kaleo's tall and broad stature has no problem swinging it like it was made of clouds. A brutal weapon for a brutal man. Well, when he has to be.

He'd never openly admit it, but the distance away from his family is weighing on him again. At times, I've noticed him toying with the leather wrist cuff his wife made for him. He'd run his fingers over the tattered material, his eyes concentrated in deep thought. He never takes it off. He told me that once, while in the dungeons, one very foolish man tried to steal it from him while he slept. Needless to say, that man didn't have to wait until the arena to pay for his crimes.

My sword makes a clean *zing* when I sheathe it. I jog past Skylar as he lets out a yawn and enter the house to find Aiden.

"Are you almost ready to go?" Aiden glances over his shoulder as my footsteps approach. He's hunched over a wrought iron table in the sitting room, stuffing the last of his supplies into his bag.

"Yeah, and you might want to pat Skylar down before we leave." I plop into a chair at the table. "Pretty sure I saw something gold in his jacket."

Aiden groans. "He would steal the blue from the ocean if he thought it had value."

My mouth widens into a smile. That's probably true. Skylar, or *Coyote*, has made his living off other people's wealth. Although he fancies the nobles as targets, he wouldn't miss an opportunity if it came knocking in Durst.

Aiden lifts a leather-bound journal to put it in the bag and reveals a small wooden coin underneath. I pick it up from the tabletop and hold it between two fingers. The oblong edges are smooth, though it feels as if they'd been jagged at one point. One side of the coin has a sloppily carved *'AH,'* while the other has a *'BC'* etched with precision.

"What's this?"

Aiden holds his hand out and I drop the coin into his waiting palm. Color flushes his cheeks. "It's a good luck charm."

"Did you make it?"

He nods and slips the charm into his pocket. "It's the first thing he taught me how to make when I came here." His shoulders droop and his voice cracks at the mention of his mentor. Until now, I haven't seen him display any raw emotion over his loss, but I suppose we all grieve in different ways.

I nudge his arm. "Everyone else is waiting outside. You want a minute in here before we go?"

He looks at me, his eyes reddening around the edges. "I'll be out in a bit."

I stand and walk toward the door, leaving Aiden as he stares distantly across the room.

The sun is long gone by the time we reach the outskirts of Oerdin. A sack of weapons is slung across each of our backs, Aiden's designs making the load effortless. Despite Rhyn's objection, we decided to leave the horses behind. They would've been too much to maintain when we reach the village. There's a subtle shift in the terrain that lets us know we're getting close. Dry dirt patches replace the full greenery.

It's been two whole days since Leona left. She was gone before the sun rose, before any of us had a chance to protest. Though, I realize now Aiden had to have known her plans.

That night with her was nothing short of amazing. Her skin was so soft. Her body the perfect proportion to mine. We fit. When she kissed me, I felt a new freedom of something, and for that moment, she kept my demons at bay. Her lips, her hands, both left an imprint on my skin that I can still feel under the surface.

And now, she's gone. I have no idea whether she'll survive her stubborn idea. I should've stayed awake. I should've tried harder to talk her out of it. I should've made sure I went with her, to protect her from Aerok— and that *girl*. I drag my hand down my face and try to shake the thoughts from my mind.

I'm hyper aware of my surroundings. Every snap of a twig or whistle of the wind causes my head to jerk in all directions. The sensitivity comes and goes. The others look at me like I'm crazy. And maybe I am.

I can't dull my senses. I don't know how anymore. I've fought to survive for so long that to be surrounded by the darkness of a moonless night, my brain is over-reactive.

I grip my sword a little tighter and force away the urge to draw it. I don't want to make the others more nervous than they already are. Even Kaleo is finding himself uneasy around me. He goes to place a hand on my shoulder in an effort to calm me, but quickly thinks better of it. I don't blame him. I'm unhinged.

"You okay?" he asks.

I keep my eyes forward and try not to think about my shallow breaths. "Uh huh," I manage.

We surge onward in silence. Our footfalls are quiet which only makes my thoughts deafening. We need to make it to the village before I really lose control. I need to make more of that concoction Rhyn suggested. It worked well to calm my nerves last time, though not as well as her touch did.

Her touch.

For the life of me, I can't understand why I'm spiraling. My mind is getting the best of me, and I'm free-falling, being thrashed about in a storm of emptiness. I swallow a mouthful of nothing, nearly choking on it. My throat is dry, my forehead damp with anxiety.

We stop at the edge of a lake. They're looking at me. Kaleo. Aiden. Rhyn and Skylar. Eyes staring at me, watching as I lose grip with reality.

"Hey, are you all right?" I hear Aiden ask. His voice echoes and hits my ears from multiple directions.

They come closer, circling me. My breathing quickens and I squeeze my eyes shut. When I open them again, no longer do I see the faces of my traveling companions. Faceless creatures surround me, each identical to the next, each with dark sockets where the eyes should be. They tower over me, dozens of them, and I feel myself sinking into the earth.

I think that'd be nice, to let the earth consume me. Let my flesh rot away, and from my remains, let something better grow in my place.

I squeeze my eyes shut again, ready to let whatever happens next happen. I think I'm ready now. I hold onto her touch in my mind, and I'm ready to fade from the world.

Something presses against my arm. My eyes fly open and reflexes betray my subconscious. The impulse to survive takes over. My hands grab whatever has touched me, and with a shift of my weight, I lift a body up and drop it to the ground. In the same breath, I draw a knife from my ankle.

"Damn, Colton. It's me!"

I'm heaving, gasping for air. Red drains from my eyes until my vision clears. My knee is centered on Nicolai's chest. I hold his shoulder down with one hand while I press a knife to his throat with the other. I blink. Blink again, until his face fully comes into view.

"Dammit," he says. "Ease up!" His hands are freezing as they try to pry my grip from his shoulder.

The change in temperature is enough to force me back to sanity. I release him and backpedal away. He sits up and holds his chest as he collects his breath. I hadn't noticed it before, but a buzz of commotion filters in through my thoughts. I glance around as not only Aiden and Kaleo watch me in horror, but also the eyes of several other men. Our men.

Nicolai gets to his feet and walks over to me. He shoots me a look of irritation before bending down to offer me a hand up. I slide my knife back into my ankle holster and accept his help.

"Sorry, man," I start. "I—"

He waves my apology away. "Don't worry about it. A reunion isn't a reunion unless somebody's getting their ass kicked." He smiles a lopsided smile then wraps his arm over my shoulders, letting his hand dangle. "Nothing to see here, people," he says. "As you were." The crowd begins to disperse, the murmurs of my outburst still on their tongues.

When mostly everyone has walked away, only Nicolai and the group I arrived with remain.

"Damn, sir." Skylar's arms are crossed. He rests the elbow of one arm on the hand of the other. He cocks his head to the side. "You had the look of pure rage just now."

I sigh and massage my forehead with the heel of my hand. "I know… I'm working on it."

"Yeah, well, you might wanna work a little harder," Nicolai says, grinning. "Saw my life flash before my eyes."

I shrug his arm off. He laughs and says, "Follow me."

Upward of a hundred and fifty men sit around the bonfire. I recognize all of them from Mount Grae. Most of them look healthy after the attack.

"The guards had the main entrance to the mountain blocked," Nicolai says. "They killed the sentries that were posted out there."

"How many men did they collect?" Kaleo asks.

The men look at each other as though they are remembering the details of that night.

"About half of us." Nicolai's voice is grim.

Kaleo nods and drops his head for a moment longer in a silent prayer.

Nicolai digs his foot into the ground. "The rest of us escaped through a secondary passageway out of the tunnel. I suppose the spy wasn't aware of that exit." He tugs at the strap of the quiver across this chest. "Anyway, once we got out, we came up here."

Mount Grae's cavern was a well-kept secret until Merethe told the guards about it. My blood simmers just thinking of her name. Nobles never knew anything about the hiding spot because they had no reason to. To them, it was just a mountain. There was nothing appealing about it on the outside. The beauty of the inside was something that only villagers could appreciate. We didn't have much in this world, but the one thing that was ours, and ours alone, has been compromised.

Aiden runs his knuckles against his jaw. "And you're sure the guards won't circle back through here?"

"I almost hope they do," Kaleo says, smirking. "I've been itching to use my hammer."

Nicolai steps forward, eyeing the weapon strapped on Kaleo's back. His lips curl. "May I?"

Kaleo laughs and frees the warhammer. He hands it to Nicolai, who nearly stumbles over from the weight.

"Beautiful," someone among us says. "I can already picture all the noble heads that thing'll cave in."

Nicolai gives it back to Kaleo and clears his throat. "Speaking of nobles, where is the queen?"

I knew this question would get brought up. And I know they aren't going to like the answer. I glance at Aiden, who nods, then I rise to my feet.

"She's gone to Aerok."

Chaos erupts around the fire. The men's disapproval and anger choruses through the night. I hold my hands up, hoping to silence them long enough so I can explain.

"You, lot! Quiet, so he can talk." Kaleo's voice booms over theirs. I nod my appreciation.

They finally settle down and sit. Their eyes are locked on mine, ready to listen to what I have to say.

"I know this isn't what you wanted to hear. Yes, she went to him. No, she isn't surrendering." The men's audible tension relaxes. "She did it so we may have a better chance at seizing the castle."

I tell them of how she plans to kill Aerok at the first opportunity she gets. I explain how if he isn't sending guards out to search for her, then they'll be less likely to anticipate our movements. I explain her plan to the men the best way I know how, although I still don't entirely agree with it myself. By the end, what started as chaos changes into understanding. And I think the men appreciate her more for it. The same opinion is masked on each of our faces. She's counting on us, and we refuse to let her down.

Leona

Chapter 32

It's late.

After another long day of riding, Merethe and I have finally made it back to Demesne. The city streets are empty. Tonight, there isn't much activity after dark. There's a bitterness in my stomach as I ride past the homes of those who want me dead.

Our horses trot up to the castle gate. Under my hooded cloak, I glance up as archers draw their arrows at us.

"Identify yourself," one of the guards below barks.

"Merethe Tarva," she says. "King Aerok is expecting me."

The guards look her over, then turn their eyes toward me. I keep my face hidden under the fabric, sit up straight, and focus on my breathing. There's a chance these men may shoot an arrow through my heart on Aerok's instruction.

"I have a package for the king." Merethe nods to me.

I exhale sharply, then release the reins from my hands. Slowly, I reach up and reveal my face to the guards. A few of them draw a sharp breath in surprise. I'm sure to not show any emotion. No anxiety. Just procedure.

"As I said, I have a package for the king," Merethe repeats. "Do you really want to keep him waiting?" She tilts her head at the guard between us.

He calls out to a guard above who then opens the gate to the wall. Merethe and I exchange a glance and ride toward the castle by ourselves. We dismount our horses once we reach the doors. Another group of guards escort us to the throne room. They say that the *King* will be with us shortly. The guards' eyes linger on me, but I refuse to let them make me feel uneasy. I'm sure they're shocked that I've returned. My guards, men who swore to protect me, now gaze upon me like I'm prey.

The throne room is just as I remember it. Floor to ceiling windows line the walls. Exquisite candelabras hang from above, casting a romantic aura in such a powerful room. I used to think the room was overwhelmingly large. Now, it feels too confined.

Months ago, though it feels like years, a plush rug ran the length of the room, leading up to the throne. My coronation day. It was such a long walk as I passed rows and rows of people on either side of me. They watched silently, no doubt judging me on the day I was meant to ascend the throne.

My gown, my hair, my makeup—all pristine. Fit for a new queen. There were hushed whispers of my beauty among the crowd. But that's all I ever was to them— beautiful. Just a pretty face without anything substantial behind the mask. No one expected me to rule this country, only to serve as a pretty accessory to a man who would one day be my husband.

My nerves ricocheted in my gut. Each step I took past the spectators, each step that got me closer to my throne, doubt crept around my ankles, threatening to bring me to my knees before all who were present. Finally, I made it to the priest waiting for me at the front. Even he gave me a disapproving glance as he handed me the orb and scepter. I spoke my oath with conviction, hoping to convince all who stood before me that I was queen, and I was here to stay.

The throne room doors burst open. Aerok enters with two more guards flanking his side. As he approaches, a metal crown sparkles atop his head. I narrow my eyes to get a better look and lose the breath in my lungs. He's wearing my father's crown.

Aerok circles around Merethe and I, never letting his eyes stray from mine. I will myself to keep a neutral expression.

"Well done, love," he says to Merethe. "I knew you just needed the right type of motivation."

Merethe rolls her eyes. "I held up my end, now release my aunt." She forces her voice to calm. "Please," she adds.

Aerok glances at her, calculating her emotion. After a moment, he nods to a guard standing near the door, who then abruptly leaves. Minutes later, he returns with a woman. He shoves her into the room and she nearly loses her balance from the effort.

Merethe rushes to her aunt's side. My eyes widen at the woman's features. She looks exactly like Gracen, just with a little more graying hair. I never knew Gracen had a twin sister. I never knew a lot of things about her.

"Are you all right?" Merethe asks her aunt.

Lizette nods and pulls Merethe close in an embrace. Aerok makes an obnoxious sound that resembles a yawn. Merethe shoots him an irritated glance.

"Are we free to go now?"

"You've served your purpose. I have no further need of you."

Merethe and I pass a quick look before she and her aunt disappear into the corridor. Aerok turns his attention toward me. His eyes are colder than the warmth the brown should hold.

Breathe. Just breathe.

He comes closer and stands opposite me at my side. His mouth is close to my ear. I tense.

"That was a fun twist, wasn't it?" he asks. "You didn't even tell your sister goodbye."

My eyes dart to his. "How did you know she was my sister?" The revelation wasn't common knowledge. I quickly wonder about any other secrets of the castle he knows about.

He laughs. The sound echoes against the windows and sends a chill down my spine. "Funny you should ask that." He steps away and circles me again. My head turns to follow his movements. "I found it rather endearing that your handmaiden was so loyal to you she sacrificed her life to warn you of my attack. So, naturally, I looked to her for clues of your whereabouts." He chuckles. "I asked myself, 'who is the one person who spent more time with you than me?' Well, with me, the time spent was more like a chore."

I cringe at his words.

"I searched the servant's quarters, and do you know how pleased I was to find dozens of little messages written between her and her sister? Do you know how excited I was to discover the irony of the situation? That the one person left as your relative would be the same person who would destroy you? Of course, I hadn't expected this to drag on for as long as it did. Crary was supposed to kill you."

Aerok steps in front of me. He trails a finger down my cheek, and I resist the urge to pull away. I hold his glance, struggling to see his soul in his eyes.

"Why shouldn't I just finish the job and kill you myself?" His hand lingers along my jaw before clasping around my throat. I choke back a gasp. I don't struggle despite what my body craves.

"You could," I force out. He releases his grip just slightly. "You could kill me, but then your reign wouldn't be nearly as strong without the D'Auron bloodline."

"I don't need your bloodline," he hisses. His grip tightens. "I'll start my own."

"You… you'll need— an heir—" I reach up and try to pry his fingers away. "I can give you— that—"

He holds his grasp just a moment longer before releasing me. His lips twist up into a smile. He folds his hands together behind his back and looks upward as he considers my words. I tenderly touch my neck and push away the trembling of my fingers.

Seconds seem to turn into minutes as we stand in the throne room, surrounded by a dozen armed guards. Aerok's dark eyes land on mine. He grins in a way that is unholy and takes my arm, guiding me toward the door. The guards stand at attention when he approaches. As we spill out into the corridor, he leans over, his breath hot in my ear.

"I've been waiting a long time for this."

I'm in my bedchamber. And I'm not alone.

The thinnest silk material hangs from my body. The hem of it stops just above my knees. I've worn this sleeping gown many times before, but somehow, I feel so exposed in it now. My arms, my legs, much of my skin is bare.

I stand in front of the mirror, watching Aerok behind me in the reflection. His eyes are watching me, too, thrilled at the scene laid before himself. He's never seen me in so little clothing. He sits on the bed across the room. Only his pants are on. The other layers of gaudy accessories are removed from his body.

I look at myself, silently telling myself I can do this. The only way to get him alone, away from the watchful eyes of the guards, was to promise him me. The hairpin is still twisted in my locks, revealing a slender neck that encourages the ogling of a madman.

My bare feet pat against the floor as I stroll around the room and re-familiarize myself with the things I'd left behind. I pause once I reach the spot where Gracen's blood covered the floor. I close my eyes and can still see her lying there, the life in her eyes draining with each ounce of blood that poured from her wound. I open my eyes and force the image from my subconscious. The floor has been cleaned as though her death never happened.

I glance over my shoulder at Aerok. He's still watching me, watching how the silk glides over my skin as I walk. There's nothing but delusion in his eyes.

"You were right," I start.

He raises his eyebrows. "I usually am. But, about what?"

"The villagers are savages." A heaviness forms in my chest with each word. "They lie and steal. You were right to want to keep the arena open and I shouldn't have tried to change that."

He leans back on his arms and crosses his legs at the ankles. "So, where are they now? The fighters?"

"I don't know." I continue to walk around the room, my hand trailing over the furniture. "I left them after Mount Grae. It won't matter if you can't find them once you collect fighters from other nations, yes?"

He tilts his head and sits up. His lips press into a thin line.

I freeze. "I only mean to say that it's a good idea, if it's true, of course."

His face relaxes and he leans back again. "Enough talk of business. We can discuss it in the morning. Now, come here."

I shudder and focus on my breathing. My feet are weighed down by the possibility of tonight. I'm trying not to panic, but my stomach is a twisted mess of worry and uncertainty. When I get near the bed, he stands, his frame still towering over mine. He runs his hands down my arms, from my shoulders to my wrists. A needles sensation is left in his path.

Breathe.

He leans in close. He reeks of sandalwood and insanity. His lips are at my shoulder, dropping lower as they trail along my collarbone. He breathes in deeply against my neck. My hands are down at my sides, my fingernails digging into my thighs to remain calm.

His hands glide around my waist as he pulls me to him. He kisses me. I force myself to not bite him. My eyes are wide open, staring at a spot behind him on the wall. He doesn't understand the amount of loathing I have for him. As his hands grip my body, I focus on the one goal in mind.

Slowly, I bring a hand up and reach for the hairpin. I need to end this now before things go too far. One slice to his throat and this could all be over with. I could stand over his body and let his blood color my floor next.

My fingers are inches away from my freedom.

Aerok jerks me in a fit of one-sided passion. He spins me and I reach out to grip the edge of the bed. He's behind me now, leaving kisses between my shoulder blades, down my spine. A coldness suffocates me as my hair falls to my back. He has the hairpin in his hand and tosses it aside. I watch helplessly as it clashes to the floor. A bout of nausea grounds me to my present.

His hands are all over me, touching every part of my skin I've never wanted him to touch. His movements on me are rough, desperate, and I have nothing to guard against him. He pushes me to the bed. Silent tears roll down my cheeks as panic laughs in my face.

Leona

Chapter 33

I am disgusting. My skin is crawling with thousands of disappointments under the surface. I slip out of the bed, careful not to wake Aerok. His body is stretched out. Soft snores play his victory march.

I wipe semi-dried tears from my eyes with the heels of my hands. My fingers tremble and I press them against my lips to center myself. I've never been fond of crying. But today, at this moment, the urge to spill countless tears at my feet is overwhelming. I will not break, though. Not yet. I breathe in deeply and glance around for my gown. I find it halfway across the room, close to where I lost a good friend. I will not think of that, though. I will not break. Not yet.

I slip on the gown. My body is sore, tender from misuse. I wrap my arms around myself and hold me tight.

I hold until I'm ready to proceed. The snoring reminds me I am not alone in this room and I shake my head to focus.

I need to find that dagger.

I tiptoe around the room, my eyes glued to the floor, in search of the one tool I need to satisfy my goal. I find it peeking halfway underneath my desk. My heart jumps at the feat.

I hold it in my hand and pull the two halves apart. A quiet *zing* sounds when I remove it from the sheathe. Candlelight bounces off the metal giving the blade a golden hue. I lay the wooden husk on the table.

My fingers grip around the intricate design Aiden painstakingly carved out. The point of the dagger screams for blood, and I intend to fulfill its wish. Aerok's blood will spill today.

I creep toward him. Darkness turns my eyes black. I'm breathing fast. I don't know if it's from the adrenaline or because I'm frightened.

Why should I be afraid?

He's killed plenty of people who didn't deserve it. I could end his life tonight. I could end him just as he wanted to end me. Should it matter that he's unarmed? That he's resting comfortably, unaware, in the royal bed that he stole? He's tried to kill me multiple times. The only way to stop a maniac saturated with rabies is to

put

him

down.

I raise the dagger above my head and keep the spot over his heart in my sights. There. That's where I'll draw blood. I lean forward, the dagger still hovering above him. The muscles in my hands tighten and cause my palms to dampen. I need to do this. He's not a man, he's a monster, and the world will be better off without him. The dagger won't move from its suspension. I exhale sharply. Why can't I do this?

Aerok's eyes flutter open in a daze. A rush of heat burns away my hesitation. I drive the dagger down, caring less about my own safety, and more about completing my task. He sees the blade shining in the room and reacts quicker than I could've imagined.

He grabs ahold of my wrist. I'm pushing, pushing the dagger toward him while he counteracts my efforts. He's strong. He squeezes my wrist until I'm certain that my bones will crush within his grip. I lose my grasp of the dagger and it tumbles out of my hand and clangs against the floor.

"Bitch..."

He forces me away and shoves me to the floor. I scramble to pick up the dagger, but he's already on his feet, blocking the way. He's still naked, and I do the only thing I can think of in the moment. My hand closes in a tight fist. I pull it back and launch it forward, straight at his groin. He shouts unkind words before doubling over.

I try to dodge beside him, my heart still focused on retrieving my weapon. So close. My fingertips barely skim the handle when he grabs a fistful of my hair and pulls me backward. I cry out and my eyes instantly begin to water.

I'm fighting him, desperate to free my hair from his grip. He doesn't let go. Instead, he stands before me with his head cocked to the side, a demented smile on his lips. With his free arm, he reaches across his face before swiftly connecting the back of his hand with my cheek. My skin burns, lit with the fire of an exploding sun. My legs try to give out on me, but he doesn't let me fall. He keeps me suspended in time by my hair. His hand strikes me again and again, all while the dagger gleams in the darkness.

Sometime after the eighth strike, my body gives up and my eyes fall closed, heavy with the false hope of a future.

My head is the consequence of a failed plan. A throbbing starts at one temple, walks a tight line across my forehead, and ends at the other side. I welcome the cold stone pressing against my cheek. It's soothing. My eyelids are heavy, likely swollen, but I force them open anyway. I blink a few times to adjust my vision. The room is circular. A thin stream of daylight pours in through a small window. I'd almost forgotten about these cells. They stopped being of any use while the arena dungeons were active.

I try to shift into an upright position. My wrists are bulky. I peer closer at the metallic shackles embracing my skin. My eyes follow the chains from my wrists to the wall. The clinking echoes in the cell as I move to sit up. I don't have much leeway. I scoot back until my spine is hugging the wall. I'm no longer wearing the skimpy silk gown. They've put me back into the dress I arrived in. I brush my fingers over the bottom hem and feel for the metal tools Aiden added for me.

Images rush into my mind, one scene blurring into the next. My body shakes and I can't catch my breath. My skin no longer feels like my skin. My body is no longer my body. I rub my arms, desperate to cleanse myself of the horror I subjected myself to.

Aerok's hands were all over me. They felt me in a way that they never had before. It wasn't supposed to get that far. He was supposed to be dead before he ever laid a finger on me. But I failed.

I begged him to stop, but he dismissed the notion as though it never existed. I was nothing but a tool to him. My royal blood with the promise of a royal heir. I detest myself. I should've never suggested the bait.

Icy tears splash onto the back of my hands. I shudder a shaky breath and will myself to not break down. To not shatter into a million pieces on this dirty cell floor. I really want to though. I so want to.

I flinch when the door creaks open. Two guards file into the room, each holding a lantern. I wince, my eyes sensitive to the sudden brightness. They stand on either side of the door, chest out, backs straight. Then, Aerok enters. He's fully clothed in his usual immaculate fashion.

I do not cower. I keep my eyes trained on his as he walks forward to stand in front of me. He crouches so we are eye-level. His lips twist up into a smile as he notices the thin wet lines trailing from my eyes. He reaches a hand forward to wipe them away, but I jerk my head before he can touch me. He'll never touch me again.

He laughs. It's a cold, distant sound, empty of the joy usually found in laughter.

"Your first mistake," his voice is low, "was believing you'd ever be fit to rule Erenen."

My hands squeeze into fists. I press them against my thighs to keep from lashing out. "Better a woman reign than a fool. You'll destroy this country." Venom dwells in each word.

"No, love, I'll improve this country. I'll bring it back to its former glory."

"By stealing people from other nations? You're an idiot. You'll start a war!"

His smile fades. A crease creeps along his forehead. "I know war. I've commanded the Crownsguard, or have you forgotten? A battle won is just another Tuesday for me."

I can't keep myself from laughing. It's a sad, maniacal laugh, but I don't care. "You truly are a fool." I lean close so that only inches separate our faces. "You have no idea how to run a nation. It's not all about wealth. What good is coin when your guards are hungry and tired of fighting a war that serves no purpose?" I spit at the ground in front of him.

He stands. "Well, fortunately for you, Erenen is no longer your concern." His strides are long as he walks toward the door. "You were right about one thing, however. I'll need an heir from you." He pauses just inside the cell. "So, tonight, tomorrow night, and every night following, I'll be back until you give me what I want."

Aerok and the two guards leave the room, the door slamming shut behind them. Despair quickly keeps me company. I'm left with the realization that I've lost. I push the thoughts from my head and focus my attention. I can't let emotions overwhelm me. It's not over yet. I pick at the threads of my hem until it unravels, and two thin metal pieces roll to the ground.

Colton

Chapter 34

We travel along the shadows of the evening until we reach Demesne. Entering the city was no problem. Now, we're camped outside the castle walls, blending in with our surroundings, invisible to the guards posted at the gate.

Six guards. Three at the top, three at the bottom.

Six bodies we must drop simultaneously to keep them from alerting the other guards in the area. If we miss even one of them, he could set a fire signal mounted at the top of the lookout, which would cause a chain reaction to all other lookouts along the length of the wall. If we miss one, the guards will know we're here.

And we can't have that.

We need to maintain our invisibility for as long as possible. We're outnumbered, three-to-one, easily. Until Aiden and Skylar can make it to the arena dungeons and free our remaining men, we need to play it safe with our odds.

So, we're waiting.

Waiting on Kaleo to give the signal so our archers can put an arrow into the skulls of six unsuspecting bodies.

And he does.

Arrows fly like a whisper in the night, each meeting its target. The guards are dead before their bodies hit the ground. We wait and listen for any sign that the other guards have noticed their fallen men. It's quiet.

Our men move forward, one of which is holding a device that Aiden created. It has four metal claws attached to the end of a rope. A man, Petyr, swings the hook around at his side before letting go. It arcs in the air and lands with a muted clank on the top of the wall. Slowly, he pulls on the rope, making sure the claws are holding against the stone. He's swift as he climbs it, one hand over the other, until he's at the top.

Moments later, the gates open. Petyr stands over two more dead guards as we all file into the castle grounds. I nod to Aiden, who breaks off into a sprint with Skylar toward the arena.

My sword is out, ready to claim the lives of our enemies. There's chaos up ahead as guards charge toward us. The castle grounds are lit enough that it's impossible for us to enter without being seen. There's over a hundred men with me. We're a cloud of well-armed anger.

I catch the whites of a guard's eyes right before I plunge my sword into the unprotected area of his torso. They should really reconsider their uniforms. For months,

I've fantasized about killing the guards. I've memorized their uniforms, their formations, the way they move and speak. I've prepared for this moment, and I'm not alone.

One after the other, guards fall by our hands. Bodies litter the courtyard, both ally and enemy. I try not to focus on the faces of the men we're losing. There will come a time to grieve them, but now is not that time.

We surge forward as guards pour out of the castle doors. Swords clang and arrows fly in the chaos. I look over just as Kaleo's warhammer crashes into a guard's head. Well, it used to be a head.

In the anarchy, I sneak into the castle. Leona is here, and I need to find her. I'm met with two guards in the corridor. They lunge at me with their swords. I maneuver between them, my fist striking out against one's jaw. He stumbles backward and I shove his partner's arm so his sword impales the guard's chest. I pull the knife from my ankle and spin on the ball of my foot as my blade slashes the guard's neck. Their bodies crumple to the floor, their blood pooling together into a red blanket.

I catch my breath. My eyes dart around the entryway to the secondary corridors that branch from it. I've never been inside the castle before. I have no clue where to go or where I could possibly find Leona. I grumble and choose the path in front of me.

I dash down the corridor, only stopping when guards try to engage me. A breadcrumb of bodies is left behind. I find a stairwell and climb it, three steps at a time. My lungs are on fire, but I ignore it. The pain only drives me forward. The white-hot fury I've been afraid to embrace now has full control over me.

"Leona," I call out. My voice echoes against the high ceilings. My yelling brings about more guards and my sword slices the air and sinks into them.

My head jerks from side to side as I search the rooms lining the corridor. They look like meeting rooms—long tables lined with chairs.

"Leona!"

I reach a door at the end of the corridor and another flight of stairs—one leads up and one leads down. Guards emerge from both directions. I step back, gripping my sword like it's my lifeline. Before me stands a dozen guards, each with blades pointed at me. I swallow a painful gulp of anxiety. I could choose to take them on, and maybe disable four of them before the others run their swords through me. Or, I could turn back the way I came and possibly lose Leona in the process.

My eyes scan my enemies as I wrangle a solution, but one of them makes the decision for me. He rushes forward, his sword held high, intent on putting me down. I brace myself.

Before he reaches me, an arrow replaces where his eye once sat. I snap my head behind me. From the shadows, Merethe approaches, bow drawn, as she lets arrow after arrow fly toward the guards. They try to scatter and take cover, but she hits her mark. Every time.

Critically injured guards layer the floor. The ones who are still writhing, she shoots another arrow for good measure. She looks at me, her eyes abandoned of their natural animosity. There's no hesitation, no doubt on her face.

"Shall we continue?" she says.

I'm at a loss for words. All I can manage to do is nod. The girl who've I've been against from the beginning has just saved my ass. And she didn't even break a sweat to do it.

"I've already checked the main halls," she says as we step over the bodies. "There are cells through that door" — she nods to the end of the corridor — "so that's probably where she'll be."

"How do you know?"

"Call it a strong hunch." Her green eyes look hazel in the torchlight. She reaches for the door, pulling it open with a loud creak. I check behind us to make sure no other guards are coming. When I turn back around, she's already disappeared through the doorway. I follow her in, picking up my pace to catch up with her.

It's a short passageway that leads to another door. It's already open.

"Leona?" Merethe says softly, peeking her head inside.

We enter. The scent of mold and misery reminds me of my time in the dungeons. It also has the same shadows where hope tends to hide.

I cross the cell to the window. It doesn't offer much of a view, but under the oil lampposts' light, Skylar and our captured men race from the arena, eager to join the battle. I glance back. "So, where is she?"

Merethe shakes her head. "I don't know… We're too late."

I whirl around, panic tensing my shoulders. "What do you mean *too late*?"

She's crouched near the wall with her back toward me. I walk closer as she holds up small metal rods and an opened shackle that catch in the stream of moonlight. "She's already escaped."

Leona

Chapter 35

I wasn't a good child growing up. I was restless. Curious. Defiant. Most of my adolescent years were spent slipping away from my guards during the day and exploring the castle during the night. When everyone else was asleep, I was awake. When they said everything was fine, I searched for the secrets.

I used to be in awe when Father and his lieutenants would be huddled around the table discussing battle strategies. Like a quiet mouse, I would sneak into the room when their backs were turned. I was enamored with the passion Father had for warfare and keeps our lands safe. I thought if I learned how to be a proper defender like the Crownsguard, maybe he would finally notice my value. But eventually, the years went by, and my curiosity died as he molded me into the perfect submissive queen.

At the first sign of a disturbance outdoors, I freed myself and took to the hidden spaces of the corridors I'd occupied as a child. I've never picked a lock before, let alone, shackles. In Durst, Aiden explained the general components of the mechanism—how to use the picks to push the pins and engage the tumbler. It was overwhelming trying to soak in his instructions, but I absorbed enough to get the job done.

I pause in a recessed panel of the corridor and listen to the commotion rumbling outside. Although I can't see them, I trust my men are out there fighting for us. A sense of pride washes over me and lifts my chest at the comprehension that they made it within the walls. I just hope they can sustain the guards. My heart beats fast and slow like a tornado that is stagnant on the outside, but the eye holds momentum. It's a weird sensation to feel anxious yet empowered.

The corridors are quiet. Merethe was right. There isn't as many guards patrolling. I suspect they must have already been called away to the fuss outdoors. Still, I'm careful to keep hidden as I make my way through the castle. I have my own score to settle. I need to find Aerok. In a moment of hesitation, I failed to complete a task I had risked so much for.

I can't keep repeating my mistakes.

Aerok stole more than just my throne. He will die by my hand tonight—I refuse to allow anything less. My lips twist up into a grin as I scurry past the library, from one shadow to the next. The intrigue of claiming another's life renews in my mind. After the countless innocents Aerok has sacrificed, joy teases me at the thought of watching his blood seep from open wounds. I could free myself and the rest of the nation from his torment. All it would take is for me to cause his death. No longer does the sight of blood terrify me. It excites me.

My fingertips skim the walls as I get closer to the bedchambers. This wing of the castle is still secluded from the madness. I hope to find him here, preparing to come visit me in the cell as he'd promised. If the guards had alerted him to the activity in the courtyard, the castle would've been on high-alert by now. Merethe did mention Aerok's reduction of the castle's guard presence. Perhaps he also has left them to delegate problems without bothering him.

I stand in front of my bedchamber door and pause. No guards, no sounds, just the mild crackle of the lanterns hanging from the walls. I rest my palm against the door's smooth wood. After a deep, clarifying breath, I push the door open, inch by inch.

It opens silently, and I peek inside. My shoulders sag in disappointment when I don't see him. I push the door open wider, still taking care not to announce my presence.

A few candles illuminate the room in an amber glow. I enter, leaving the door open behind me. I squint toward the bed. Empty. The sheets show no evidence of someone who had slept there. The evidence of Aerok putting his hands all over my body are missing, too. I shudder and walk further inside.

On my vanity, I spot the dagger Aiden crafted for me. I creep toward it and let my hand hover over the wooden hilt before slipping it into my belt. After one last glance toward the bed, I cross the room to the door. My chest expands with readiness as I take a step into the corrid —

"Looking for me?"

Aerok's silhouette stretches and he grabs me by my throat. His merciless grip lifts me until my toes graze the floor. My mind flies to the dagger, but my hands fly to his fingers in a desperate need to free them.

"Well, aren't you a clever girl." He forces me back into the bedchamber, his eyes darkened with satisfaction. He laughs. The harshness of it pierces my skin, my hair raising on end. "You think you can take back a crown that doesn't fit you? You're just as naive as everyone thought you were."

His words are meant to hurt me, but they only fuel the embers that are simmering in my core, on the verge of igniting me into an all-consuming ball of fire. I reach for his fingers again, but they press harder around my neck. My pulse pounds in my ears until they drown out the stream of words tumbling from his mouth.

It's good to know that your fingernails can be used as a deadly weapon if it comes down to it.

I claw out at Aerok's face. My nails drag against his skin, collecting flesh as they pass. He jerks his head away and releases his hold on my throat. I crash to the floor. My breaths come in rapid waves, but I crawl backward and jump to my feet. Tingling fingers seize the dagger from my belt.

With the back of his hand, he wipes the blood from his face. His lips curl into a sick smile and he takes a step toward me. I take a step back.

I roll the dagger between my fingers. "I'll give you one chance, Aerok. One chance to surrender and I'll grant you mercy for your crimes." By mercy, I mean a quick death with minimal pain. I keep this clarification to myself, though.

He grins, steadily reducing the distance between us. My body tenses, but I stand my ground. His eyes glance at my dagger. "You are in no position to bargain. You must have forgotten that the guards are now at my command. While I admire your courage,"—he runs a hand through his hair and smooths it back into place—"unfortunately, you lack the resources to follow through with any threat. You are but one woman—a girl, playing in a man's world."

I bite the inside of my cheek to keep from lashing out. I can't let him charge my emotions. Instead, I clear my throat. "Do you hear that?" I pause and tilt my head. He turns his ear toward the door. The uproar that has finally drifted toward us. His brow raises, and I continue. "I have men outside who are taking the castle as we speak." Honestly, I don't know for sure, but I ride my wave of confidence. "It's only a matter of time before you lose all you've worked so hard to steal." I shoot him a grin. He grimaces. For the first time, his forehead creases with worry, but it fades, and his eyes harden.

He steps forward. "You know, you surprise me, Leona." I don't like the way he says my name. "I hadn't anticipated how good you'd feel in bed." He draws his bottom lip into his mouth, grinning.

"You disgust me." A rush of heat warms my cheeks, not from embarrassment, but rage. My skin starts to crawl at the thought of his hands on my body. If anything, he's just going to make me kill him right now for bringing it up.

He crosses the room toward me gradually, his hands up in front of him. The smile of a maniac is plastered on his face. "I'm just saying, maybe you've found your calling. Once I get a couple of heirs from you, perhaps we can secure a position for you at a brothel—"

"Fuck you."

His face splits into a smile. "Already did that, remember? Or, do you need a refresher?"

It's taking all my strength to not let loose and dig my dagger into his face. Then again, what am I waiting for? Aerok doesn't deserve the privilege of a trial. I already know he is guilty. So, what's stopping me from ending him now? Hesitation ruined me last time.

He's trying to get into my mind, and I'm letting him. I shake my head to rid myself of the poisonous thoughts.

His movements blur in front of my face and he knocks the dagger from my hand. It clashes to the floor and slides toward the bed. He tries to grab my arms, but I squeeze free from his grip, pivoting on my foot to get out of dodge. His feet pound the floor as he lurches toward me. My hands fly out in a panic and my fingertips find a metal candelabra. I swing it at his head, the flames blowing out from the action. He ducks backward but I manage to clip his jaw. He staggers, almost losing his balance, and bumps into the nearby table.

I take the reprieve and dive onto the floor toward the dagger. I will not stop until he is dead. This ends tonight.

My arms stretch, farther than physically possible, as I strain to reach the blade. Just as I have a hold on the handle, Aerok grabs my ankle, pulling me toward him. His fingernails dig into my skin. I kick frantically to free myself, but he has a strong hold. I twist and pull myself up then swing the dagger at him. The tip catches his cheek. He curses and releases my ankle, his hand shooting up to his face. More blood flows in ribbons down his cheek. A few inches below and it could've been his throat.

I get to my feet. My palms are sweaty, but I hold onto the dagger like it's my salvation. I lunge at him, my eyes focused on death. I aim the dagger at his head. He reaches up to stop me and catches the blade in his palm. A river of red streams down his forearm and drips to the floor from his elbow. His eyes are bleak and jaw is clenched. He doesn't scream out in pain even though I'm sure it hurts. His fist connects with my jaw. Air rushes out of my lungs, but I absorb the ache. Colton taught me how to channel pain and use it to fuel aggression. It's a mind game, I guess. Even though the punch sends me flying backward, I refuse to let go of the dagger again. So, it ends up ripping out of his hand from the impact.

I find my footing and charge at him. I'm a bull let loose and all I see is red. He takes a defensive stance, spreading his feet wide and sitting back on his heels. Right before I reach him, I drop to the ground and slide between his legs, letting the dagger cut into his calf as I travel. His legs wobble and he tries to turn around to face me. I explode from the floor and sink the blade into the softest part of his lower back. I drive it in three, four times. My adrenaline makes everything a haze.

His legs buckle and give out on him, but he refuses to give up. His hands are pressed against the floor, ten fingers splayed out, as he struggles to stand. One foot, then the other. A bloody hand print smears under the shuffle of his feet. I stand back, eyes wide, as he faces me. Blood seeps out of the corner of his mouth, but the anger in his eyes remain. His breathing is labored. He's always been a persistent son of a bitch.

I circle around him, breathing hard myself, as his clothes stain red. A surprising sight from his usual spotless style. He watches me. His mouth opens and closes, but his words are lost. So, I speak.

"I've never been keen to killing. You know this, yeah?" I twist the dagger in my hand. It's covered in his blood. "But thanks to you, I found the beauty in it. There's a freedom that comes with extinguishing a person who wants to cause you harm. Surely, you've experienced this feeling during warfare?" I pause. He doesn't answer. His body grows weaker with each second he fights the inevitable. "I'm going to kill you, Aerok. I've thought about making it as humane as possible. But then—" I laugh, mostly to myself. He just looks on in horror, the only thing he has the energy to do. "Why should I extend that courtesy to you? You're an animal—a flea-ridden, rabies-infected dog."

Aerok falls to his knees and holds at his stomach. In the candlelight, his eyes shift into an expression that looks unfamiliar on him. I squint as though it'd help me recognize it better. Is that fear? I smile, delighted at what I see before me. I'm not crazy. This is justice.

I crouch so we're at eye-level. He moves his lips to speak, but the words are incomprehensible. His language is drowned by the blood filling his mouth. I lean in.

"What was that?" I whisper.

Another string of gurgled speech. His breathing is getting shallower.

I purse my lips. "Oh, no… you're fading. We'll need to hurry this up, then." I press my palm against his chest and shove. He tries to lift his arms up, but they fall limp to his side. He topples backward and I straddle him. His body seizes underneath me. "Hold on," I tell him. "Just a few more minutes."

I grab at his shirt and use the dagger to cut it open. His bare skin is already losing the heat in his veins. There's still a slight rise and fall as he breathes, and that's all I require. I lean forward, staring as I touch the tip of the dagger to his chest. I press until I draw blood. He tries to scream, but it comes out as a muffled mess, like yelling under the sea. I drag the blade across his skin in a few straight lines.

Sometime during this, he stops thrashing and his body goes still. I even think I hear a gasp as his lungs exhale their last breath.

I stand and look over his dead body. His eyes are stuck on the chandelier above. His lower face is painted red. Crimson fingers hang from his open mouth.

My racing heart declines into an easy rhythm as my adrenaline finishes running its course. I'm left with only one thought circling my mind. I have never felt so alive.

Colton

Chapter 36

The castle has erupted into chaos. Man against man, each side fighting for the success of an opposing leader.

Merethe and I race through the castle, dodging the clusters of guards who have arrived from the barracks. When we near the throne room, two guards come out of it and block our path. Their swords are drawn. I take on one of the guards, our swords clashing together. The sound of metal pierces and echoes into the room. I glance over as the other guard deflects Merethe's arrow with his sword.

I sweep my leg at my guard's feet. His hand jets out and catches a tapestry hung on the wall. It loosens from the brackets and plummets to the floor with him. Once he's down, he tries to appeal to my sense of leniency. I have none. I run my sword through his chest, ignoring the cries from his disloyal mouth. After both guards are dealt with, Merethe and I continue.

We've been searching everywhere for Leona. I'm left to the mercy of Merethe's direction since she's far more accustomed to the castle's layout.

"This way." She points toward a darkened corridor.

"We've already checked that one." I groan and pull at the hair on my nape. "You're leading us in circles."

"No, I'm not." She cocks her head. "Look—see that portrait? I would've remembered seeing it before." She stands with her hip jutted out.

I look at the portrait. It displays some dark-haired man with too sharp of angles in his face. He doesn't look realistic. The colors are dull, and dust settles on the edge of the frame. We've already spent enough time scouring the halls in vain. No sense in wasting more time arguing.

I nod. "Fine. Let's go." I follow her down the corridor.

A sinking feeling nags at the back of my mind. What if we're too late? What if Leona failed and Aerok has already killed her? She seemed so confident, saying how it wouldn't be wise for him to harm her. Something about how she's worth more to him alive than dead. But still, she couldn't have guaranteed her safety. Anything could've happened. She's so stubborn and reckless.

We pass a balcony that overlooks the grand entryway. Bodies lay motionless, all of which are guards who have paid for choosing the wrong side.

"Come on," Merethe whispers over her shoulder. I pull myself from the banister and catch up with her.

We each take a side of the corridor, peeking our heads into the rooms lining the walls. No activity.

"By the way," I begin, "thanks for your help earlier."

She glances at me, a slow grin pulling at her lips. "Probably pained you to say that, huh?"

I roll my eyes and continue checking rooms. As much as I don't want to admit it, I'd likely be dead if she hadn't shown up. My eyes scan a room with floor to ceiling shelves of supplies. A pantry. "You know, most people would've just said *you're welcome*. Why'd you do it?"

She's quiet for a moment. I shut the pantry door and look across the corridor. She's gone. My body tenses and I grip my sword tighter. Just as I lift my foot, she pops out of the room she was checking.

"Sorry. Thought she was in there, but it was a few of the servants hiding until all the madness dies down." She shuts the door. "They did tell me that they heard screaming from the bedchambers, though."

She starts moving toward the end of the corridor, then pauses and flashes me a smile. "Oh, and I did it because even though I don't know Leona all that well, she's still my sister, and she likes you. So, I figured I should probably not let you die." She doesn't wait for a response from me before she's sprinting around the corner.

Her words drive me further to find Leona. I take off in a dash behind her. When we finally reach the corridors with the bedchambers, we don't hear anything. No screaming. No disturbance. It's almost as though the dark walls have absorbed the agony of whatever has happened down here. There's a strange prickling on the back of my neck. I rub it away and get to work checking each room. Eight rooms so far, and each one turns up empty. They don't even appear to have been used for quite some time. Perfect silk sheets pulled taut on smooth wooden bed frames. It must be nice to live in such luxury.

There's one more door at the end of the corridor. An outline of a person comes out of it. The dim lighting makes it hard to see anything other than a shadowy figure. I grip my sword tighter, intent on cutting him down. It's when they step forward out of the darkness that I see it is Leona.

I loosen my fingers and the sword falls to the floor with a clang. I quickly close the distance between us, pulling her to my chest. Tension eases away when her arms wrap around my waist. I lower my head and let my nose rest in the crown of her hair, savoring the familiar sweet scent.

I pull back, taking her head in my hands. Mottled patches of red and purple cover her face. Dried blood marks her cheek. Through the swelling, she is still beautiful. "Are you okay?" I whisper.

She smiles weakly. I gently touch a finger to her bruised lip. I lean down and kiss it, once, twice, just to make sure she's really here. My eyes fall on the blood covering her dress in red splotches.

"Where are you hurt?" I scan her body for wounds.

She shakes her head and struggles to find her voice. "I'm fine. This isn't my blood."

I tilt my head. "Whose is it, then?"

"I'm going to bet that it's his." Merethe's voice carries from the bedchamber Leona came out of. For a minute, I'd forgotten the golden-haired girl was even with me.

My hand slips into Leona's and I start toward the room. There's some resistance from her, but she follows me in.

I'm taken by surprise by the size of the bedroom. Much larger than any of the other rooms I've checked so far, my home in Maburh could fit inside of here twice over. My eyes shift from the tall ceilings to Merethe as she stands over Aerok's body. I'd never seen him up close like this. He's taller than I thought. The whites of his eyes are the color of dirty water. He gazes up into the air above him, his pupils no longer able to focus on anything in particular. A puddle of blood spreads out on the floor around him.

I glance at Leona. Her eyes fall to the floor in what looks like shame. I give her hand a brisk pump and pull her so she leans into me.

"Damn." Merethe draws a hand over Aerok's eyes, shutting them from the world. "So, since this asshole's dead, all of the mayhem should be over, right?" She and I both look to Leona for the answer.

Leona raises her head from my arm. She clears her throat and stands up straight. "I hope so. It seems like Aerok was calling all the shots, but the Council was in his pocket. I don't know if one of them will try to seize power once they find out Aerok is dead."

"Guess we better go seize it first, yeah?" Merethe turns to walk toward the door. "Let's go."

Before I turn to leave, I catch a symbol carved into Aerok's chest. It's covered in blood, but it reminds me of one of the constellations in the sky. Leona notices me staring.

"Come on," she urges, pulling at my hand.

I follow her out the door and toward the promise of a brighter tomorrow.

Leona

Chapter 37

Yellows and reds bleed into the night sky as dawn approaches. Inch by inch, the castle grounds stumble out of darkness, revealing the aftermath of our revolution. The grass is covered in a murky sheen of blood and dewdrops. There's a shift in the air.

I survey the area, stepping over loose limbs as I do. Two separate groups form the deceased. Those who stood against me now lie in layers on a cart to be hauled away. The bodies are a tangled mess of arms and legs. Empty faces peek out in random spots in the pile. Graying eyes and open mouths, the expression of death.

There's no order in the discarding. These men had a chance to support my rule and they chose wrong. My sympathy is lost on them. They'll get no burial. No funeral rites. Their families will receive no condolences for their loss. If it wasn't for Aiden, I'd have half a mind to rid my kingdom of them, as well. Insurgency stems from the home.

I've assigned Kaleo with the task of carting the dead guards away and setting fire to their bodies until all that remains is ash. He's more than happy to see this through.

Thirty of my men lost their lives tonight. They lie on the blood-stained ground, shoulder-to-shoulder, in two rows. Veils cover their eyes. I silence my footsteps as I walk between them, so I don't disturb their eternal slumber.

I can't express how much their sacrifice has meant to me. The best I can do is send a severance to the surviving relatives. Though, it will never be enough. I think back to how little boys and girls hugged their fathers tightly right before we departed Maburh. Now, they're left fatherless, their mothers left widows.

When the final casualty count was totaled, Colton reminded me that the men chose to fight for me and that I shouldn't feel guilty. But still, the guilt is a needle that constantly pokes at my conscience. Even though I've had guards who were sworn to protect me, to die for me, ever since I was a child, it's different now. These men chose to place their loyalty with me—and it won't go unnoticed.

My eyes scan over each cloaked face and stop once I reach Rhyn's. He's the last one in the row, his thin frame standing out among his neighbors. I stoop down beside him. The rising sun casts an orange glow on his paling skin. He looks at peace, no longer weighed down by the burdens of this world. I reach out and cup my hand to his cheek.

"I'm sorry," I whisper.

He was a good ally and an even better friend. I hate that we didn't get more time together. He seemed to know me better that I knew myself. Even with his canteen in his hand, he could read the emotions I tried in vain to suppress.

"You were right—about Colton, by the way." I laugh softly to myself and gently pat his cheek. It isn't until I withdraw my hand, I realize how cold his skin is.

He didn't speak much about his own life, always busy analyzing everyone else's, but he did mention that he has a daughter. Rowena, her name is. He said that after his wife died, he leaned on ale more than he should've while trying to raise Rowena. When she became of age, she left their home, breaking off any and all contact with Rhyn. More than twenty years have passed since he last saw her face, and now their relationship will never be mended. I owe it to him to track her down and inform her of her father's passing. I think he'd want me to. It'd bring him some semblance of reconciliation.

Hours later, the jagged edge of chaos has been smoothed out. In the plaza, there's a stillness to the air now as over a thousand spectators hold their breath in anticipation for what comes next. They watch as those deemed as traitors squirm in anxiety on the gallows. Sweat beads on their foreheads under the afternoon sun. Among those are the guards who refused to accept my rule even after I extended them a chance to repent. My former council stands at the gallows as well.

Davrit almost escaped his fate. My men found him near the docks trying to secure safe passage to Braer like the rat he is. No. He doesn't get off that easily. I had him beaten and dragged back here so he could join us today. After all, he's one of the many guests of honor for this gathering.

He looks paler than normal, even underneath the angry red bruises on his face and arms. It's almost as though he's already dead and what stands before us is the husk of a man who thought he'd get away with stealing power. No matter. He'll hang with the others.

Since by the end of the day I'll be out of a Council, I've decided to erupt a new system that will not only protect my reign but will also protect my citizens by giving them a voice. Each city and village is to select a representative who will meet monthly with me at the castle. We will discuss citizen welfare, kingdom funds, and work together to secure a successful future for all of us. Kaleo and Nicolai have been chosen by their respective neighbors. I have no doubt they'll be a great addition to my new Council.

Messages have been sent to all the other countries. The words speak of what happened here, and to warn the monarchs of a possible invasion. They have my blessing to kill the infiltrators on sight and toss their bodies into the sea.

A gentle wind whips around all of us, bringing with it a promise of a new beginning. But first, we must let go of the past.

A priest stands in front of each traitor, presses two fingertips to their foreheads, and speaks a grave prayer. The undertaker follows behind and covers their heads with a black canvas bag. Once the bags are on, I can see the anxiety building as their hands shake, their wrists rubbing raw from being bound behind them.

After the last man receives his prayer and covering, all eyes are on me. I stand at the end of the gallows with fingers laced in front of me. I look across the crowd below at the faces I've come to know over the past few days.

Merethe leans her head against Aiden's shoulder. Nicolai stands next to her with fervor drawn across his face. Colton, who watches patiently at the bottom of the gallows' steps. And innumerable faces of other villagers who made this possible.

This is for them as much as it's for me.

My eyes land back on the undertaker. I give a minute nod, and at once, he releases the trapdoor. The traitors fall through the false flooring, the ropes pulled taut as they tether to the overhead beam. The bodies thrash violently. Members of the audience gasp and cry out, horrified at the picture unfolding. There's ice in my veins that embraces me in this moment. My eyes are glued, and I don't look away.

A few more minutes pass until the last body relaxes into its hung state. My gaze shifts to the crowd, at the nobles who've allowed injustice to go on for so long during the years. Their eyes are still stuck in shock.

I step forward. "This is just one of the many outcomes for those who threaten my right to rule." My voice carries in the plaza. The hushed murmurs silence altogether. "I want Erenen to succeed and I won't stand by while its stability is shaken. I encourage all of you to lean onto me for strength, and in return, I will do the same."

Eyes drift from me to the dangling men, then back to me. I suppress a grin at the sickened faces of the nobles. I wonder if this is how I appeared to Colton when we first met. I walk down the steps of the gallows to where he waits. Once I'm at the bottom, a low buzz rolls across the crowd as the murmurs start again.

I brush against Colton and nod for him to follow me. Two guards flank behind us as we walk toward the castle.

"Are you okay?" he asks. Our pace is in sync and there's a shift in electrical current as our arms skim against one another.

I nod. "Yes. Why?" I glance up at him.

A crease forms in his forehead from where his eyebrows pull together. "Just meant the hanging—I'm sure it couldn't have been easy to watch."

The guards posted at the castle doors open them and bow their heads as they wait for us to pass. Inside the foyer, the air is cooler, somehow freer. A rainbow streak of light reflects on the floor as the sunlight catches the crystal chandelier above.

"I'm fine." I smile and glance at the guards who escorted us. "I'll be all right from here. Thank you."

The guards also drop their heads in a bow and leave back out the door. Such a strange feeling to have the Crownsguard back under my direction. It's even stranger to me that they give me the respect I deserve without any underlying resentment in their eyes.

It truly is a new day.

When the guards have left and the doors are closed behind them, Colton and I remain in the entryway. I take a step toward him, closing the distance between us. His lips twist up in a mischievous grin. My arms slide around his waist, my fingers interlocking at the small of his back.

He reaches up to smooth stray hairs from my face and chews on his bottom lip. I can tell there are words on his mind he hasn't yet figured out how to say.

"What is it?" I whisper.

He doesn't respond immediately. His hands cradle my face as his eyes search mine. Finally, the hardness of his face melts into a smile.

"Nothing," he says, and he kisses me.

His touch is enough to unravel me, to make me forget about the last couple of days. In his arms, I feel both stronger and more vulnerable than I've ever been. Here in this moment, I have more to lose than just a shiny crown. I'm putting my heart on the line, and by association, my sanity.

The hooves of my horse stomp against the ground, stirring awake the sleeping woodland animals. They squeak and dash under us. Crickets chirp and owls hoot in a chorus of nighttime song. The moon is bloated and hangs heavily in the sky.

I ride up north to the woods outside of Demesne. My guards have been given strict orders not to follow me. They obey with no resistance.

Colton has left for Maburh. By his choice, he stayed with me in the castle for several days until the dust of my revival settled. I insisted that he return home. His parents have missed him, and he, them.

The sound of waves crashing against the rocks gets louder. The northern woods lead to the cliffs, which lead to the docks. The scent of salt water fills my nose.

I slow my horse when I reach the abandoned cabin. I found the home by accident on one of my explorations as a child. I'm surprised it's still in stable condition after all this time. I slide off my horse, and he neighs as I tie him to a nearby tree.

The cabin's step creaks under my weight as I open the door. Inside, the air is stale, the result of poor circulation. It's dark and I feel my way to the table. With a flick of my wrist, I turn on a lantern. The single room illuminates in a golden glow. Muted moaning drawls behind me.

"I'm sorry it took so long." I pull a pouch from my cloak and set it on the table. My fingers undo the thin cord that keeps it tied shut and the pouch rolls open. "I had to wait until it was safe for me to come alone."

More mumbling.

"Ever since Gracen died, my punctuality has left something to be desired." I run my fingers over the metal tools. Each one lays perfectly straight, perfectly sharp. I asked Aiden to craft them for me, no questions asked. He's really good about minding his own business.

"Time is just something we never have enough of. Gracen sure didn't." I select a triangular blade from the pouch. With tool and lantern in hand, I walk toward the moaning in the far corner of the room.

I put the lantern on the floor beside us. His arms are raised above his head, drawn up by ropes attached to the beam. His legs must have grown tired—he slumps forward, placing his weight on his shoulders. Our shadows merge on the wall behind him.

I reach up to pull the canvas bag from over his thick head. His sweat-drenched hair is plastered to his face. His eyes shift from mine to the blade in my hand. With whatever energy he has reserved, he flails and tries to yell, but his mouth is still gagged.

I smile. "Hello, Regineau. Shall we get started?"

Thanks for reading!

If you enjoyed the story, please consider leaving an honest review on Amazon or Goodreads.

Visit Alex at
www.alexshobe.com
Twitter @alexshobe
Instagram @alexshobe

Join Alex's mailing list for updates on **DROPS OF HAVOC's** release and to stay informed of all other things to come. Subscribers are also automatically entered to win free copies of her books and merchandise.

Turn the page for an exclusive sneak peek at

Leona

Chapter 1

I've killed seventeen people so far.

Each time, a burst of adrenaline courses through my body and my nerve endings sizzle with an electric heat that gets my heart pumping. I savor each minute—every second—until what lies before me is a crumpled mess of flesh and bones. Each is a life that has been snuffed out for the good of humanity.

No one will miss them or mourn them. No one will say sentimental words at their funerals or lay flowers at their graves. I take great pleasure in reminding them of these facts as they stare into the face of the last person they'll ever see.

Mine.

A shiver of joy runs down my spine just thinking about it. I tighten my grip on the balcony's rail, pressing my fingertips against the metal.

"Can't sleep?"

Colton's arms come from behind and wrap around my waist. A surge of warmth comes with them, a warmth that fights the chill of the nighttime air. He drops his chin to my shoulder and lets his head nuzzle against mine. The scent of his skin has become familiar over the past few months. I lean back against him and layer my hands over his.

"I just have a lot on my mind."

"I'm supposed to be the one having nightmares, remember?" Colton plants a kiss on my neck and turns me in his arms. His hair sticks up in wild directions. I stifle a laugh and run my fingers though the strands in an attempt to tame them. I fail.

"I'm fine." I push up on my toes and press my lips to his. "Really. I'm fine." His eyebrow arches the way it does when he doesn't believe me. I offer a weak smile to reinforce the words. Again, I fail.

He takes my head in his hands, and his thumbs stroke my cheeks. "You know you can talk to me, yeah? You've been so good about listening to me while I vent about my problems." He kisses my forehead. "Let me be here for you, too."

I wish I could tell him the extent of my issues. I wish I could share with him the delight I feel each time I claim a life. He wouldn't understand, though. While he's learning to run away from death, I'm learning to run toward it. Each experience builds on the last, and my efficiency and tactics are something he'd be proud of.

If he could understand.

But he won't.

So, for now, I'll keep my problems to myself.

"You *are* here for me." I smile and glance over my shoulder. The sky is a swirl of blues and purples, the colors bleeding seamlessly into one another. "There's maybe another hour of night left. Do you want to go be here for me in bed?" I bite my lip and tug at his pants, another tactic I've learned when I need to redirect his thoughts.

The corner of his mouth turns up in a grin. I like this grin. This grin lets me know trouble is on its way—the kind of trouble I wouldn't mind getting into every night. He leaves a trail of kisses from my temple to my neck, letting his hands glide down my back. They rest at my hips with just the right balance of delicacy and firmness. I also like these hands. They know what they're doing.

He kisses me with a longing that could never be put into words. Luckily for him, though, I'm now fluent in his language of desire. My fingers tangle into his messy hair as I pull him closer, deepening the kiss and claiming his tongue as my own. My feet leave the ground as he lifts me to his body. Without missing a beat, my arms and legs wrap around him and he guides us to the bed.

His pants are off, so is my gown, and I reach for him.

I reach for him because his touch distracts me from the other urges that tend to consume my thoughts—the ones he wouldn't understand.

The summer sun struggles to break through the overcast sky. I don't mind, otherwise I'd be more drenched in sweat than I am. My feet dig into the courtyard's grasses and leave dents in the soil. I'm breathing hard. Colton's arms are wrapped around my neck, and he applies pressure as my chin sits on top of his elbow.

Breathe. Focus.

I pull my arms up and lace my fingers behind his

neck. My palms are clammy, but I secure a good grip. With as much strength as I can muster from my legs, I drive through my heels and flip him over me. He lands with a thud on the ground.

Colton blows out a sharp breath and pulls himself to his feet. "Good. Next time, though, don't hesitate. It doesn't take much to cut off air circulation at the neck." He flexes the arm he landed on.

"Are you all right?" I nod toward his arm.

He smiles and wipes the sweat from his eyes with his discarded shirt. "Yeah, I'm good. Let's go again."

Since that first night on the beach, we've continued with our training sessions. It has proved to be mutually beneficial. I learn the skills needed to protect myself, and he learns to tone down the rage he feels when he fights.

I break out of his choke holds three more times, and each time he lands on the same arm. I'm certain it's sore by now, but he refuses to let the pain be known until he's sure I've mastered the technique. We're just about to try again when a handmaiden crosses the courtyard grounds in our direction. I catch her eyes lingering on Colton before she stops in front of us and drops her head into a bow.

"Hello, Merys," I say with a grin.

She lifts her head and her eyes involuntarily shift back to Colton. While he's been staying here, he's captured the interest of the women around the castle. And now that sweat glistens off his bare chest, Merys can't stop herself from looking. I don't blame her.

"Merys." I break her from her trance.

Her face flushes with color and she struggles to swallow. "Sorry, Your Majesty. I, um—there's a message for you." She extends the parchment to me. I take it out of the girl's quivering fingers.

"Thank you."

She nods a few too many times. "Is there anything else I can do for you, Your Majesty?" She clasps her hands tightly in front of her.

"No, that'd be all."

She bows her head and steals one more glance at Colton before turning to scamper back toward the castle. When she's out of earshot, I turn to Colton and laugh. "Looks like I have some competition, yeah?"

He closes the distance between us and rests a hand on my waist. "You might have to start auditioning for time with me." He leans down and kisses me. When he tries to pull away, I draw him back for more. We both taste of salt, but that's easily ignored when I'm in his arms.

He releases me with a wink and turns to pick up his shirt from the ground. I bring my attention back to the message and flip it over in my hand. The golden foil seal reflects the sun as the clouds part. I look closer and gasp.

"What's wrong?" Colton asks, now fully clothed.

I hold up the parchment and show him the seal. "The message is from Daol."

Deep creases form in his forehead. "What does it say?"

I pry the message open and read it quickly to myself. Then, I hand it to him. "Royal wedding invitation. Prince Jax to some duchess."

Colton frowns and gives it back to me without reading it. "I'll pass."

"What?" I laugh. "This *has* to be a sign. We've been talking about taking you there to visit, and now we have a reason to go. Don't you still want to find your mother?" I cup his cheek with my hand.

"Yes, but—"

"Then, no buts. We're going, all right?" I kiss his cheek and level my eyes with his for a moment. We hold each other's stare.

He groans. "Fine," he says, smiling. He pulls my hand from his face and kisses my palm. "You're very bossy, you know that?"

"One of the perks of being queen." I scan over the message again. "We should see if Merethe and Aiden want to come. It's been awhile since we've seen them."

Colton threads his fingers through mine as he leads me back to the castle. "Yeah, Aiden probably needs a change of scenery from the shop. I can't say the same for Merethe, though." He gives my hand a light pump. "Fair warning, if you're going to stick us on the same boat, I can't guarantee her mouth won't make me push her overboard."

A smile pulls at my lips. "Be nice."

Even though Merethe and I constantly exchange messages, there's nothing quite like face-to-face interaction as we learn how to be sisters. We've grown close, and it almost makes me regret threatening to kill her. *Almost.*

As the day winds down, I take my weekly walk around Demesne. After I recovered the throne, one of my vows to the citizens was to make myself more visible. Regardless of the previous assassination attempts on my life, I want them to know that I won't hide behind the walls of the castle.

So, here I am, exposed, with a single guard by my side. Colton insisted I take half a dozen guards since I won't let him accompany me, but anything more than one could be seen as contrived. I want my walks to appear as casual as possible. Not only am I here in a semi-political fashion, but these walks also serve as my hunting ground for my next target.

And I think I've found him.

I slow my pace as I near the house. My guard's speed adjusts accordingly. In front of the chateau, a burly man raises his voice at his wife. I could hear him before I even approached the home.

"Goddammit, Lynda!" He shakes a finger at her. "How many times do I have to tell you not to leave my boots outside?"

His wife, drastically shorter than him, seems to get smaller as she cowers. "Forgive me." Her voice is weak, barely audible. "It's just that the mud on them dries faster when they're left out."

"That doesn't help with the birds' shit in them now, does it?"

The woman says nothing, only stares at the ground and twists her fingers in her hands. Along her arms, purple bruises disturb her pale complexion.

The man sucks in air to deliver another barrage of abuse until our eyes meet. There's fire in his eyes, which is matched with the embers simmering under my skin. I arch an eyebrow.

His eyes cut from me to Lynda. He points to the door. "Get in the house. Now."

She wastes no time collecting his muddy boots and hurrying into the oppressiveness of her family home. It's no wonder they've decided to live outside the heart of the city. His bellowing would be sure to keep all his neighbors awake. The man eyes me once more before mumbling something and follows his wife inside. He emphasizes my obtrusion by slamming the door behind him. My mouth shifts into a grin.

Don't worry, Lynda. The pain will be over soon.

Printed in Poland
by Amazon Fulfillment
Poland Sp. z o.o., Wrocław

53743210R00195